Never Kiss an Outlaw

Deadly Pistols MC Romance

Nicole Snow

Description

ONE KISS CAN RUIN A GIRL, OR MAKE HER WHOLE AGAIN…

CORA

Never kiss an outlaw, they said. Easy advice, until the day my father's dirty secrets made me property of the Deadly Pistols Motorcycle Club.

Easy, until I came face-to-face with the beautiful bastard who makes me burn with every glance. Firefly.

I tried to fight it. Threw every insult in the world his way, hoping to hide how bad my lips were begging to be kissed.

Now, I'm losing the battle. Completely.

I turned his life upside down. His cocky, unbelievable promises are flipping mine right-side up.

He says he's going to make me his. I'm going to love it. And he isn't taking no for an answer.

I should slap him upside the head. Instead, I'm becoming a believer in his caveman promises because I can't keep my hands off him…

FIREFLY

No more games. I cut Cora a hundred kinds of slack when she landed in my world, one that's too twisted for a sheltered spitfire.

I laughed at the sass and smears coming out of her mouth 'til the day the Prez made me her bodyguard. Then I put an end to her crap.

I protected her. I laid down the law.

One raging kiss shut her up for good. Never expected what came next, this urge to rip off her clothes, throw her on my bike, and own her.

The monsters coming after her, they're already dead. It's the future that counts, and there's only one I'll live.

Cora, she'll get my ink on her skin. She'll wear my ring. She'll have my kid.

I'm taking what's mine, taking her night after night, and she's gonna get used to my lips on hers forever.

The Outlaw Love books are stand alone romance novels featuring unique lovers and happy endings. No cliffhangers! This is Firefly and Cora's story in the Deadly Pistols MC series.

I: Fireball (Firefly)

My dick never quit.

I had my second fuck of the day under me, squirming like a cat in heat, just the way I liked them. Blonde, curvy, a tramp stamp on her ass.

Her green eyes flashed as they rolled back in her head, begging me to slam her harder.

Fuck yes, I obliged.

"Shit, baby, open those legs wider. All for me. It'll feel better when you start getting the shakes." I shifted, grabbed her heels, and threw her legs over my shoulders.

She screamed when I plunged deeper. *One-two-three.*

She moaned in perfect sync to my balls slapping loud on her ass. Rhythmic, wild, and hot as fuckin' lava.

My cock owned every inch of her soft wetness, stretching her a little more each time I dug in to the hilt. I always left my mark on a woman, one way or another. Inside and out. Once they'd taken my dick, they'd never be fit for anything less.

One-two-three. Her overpainted lips popped open, making her moans louder. Bitch thrashed, clawing at the

1

sheets around her.

One-two-three, one-two-three, one-two-fucking-three.

"Fireball!" Slut practically screamed it as I felt her heat gush wetter around me.

She couldn't remember my name. Fuck if I cared. When I was this deep in pussy, bringing us both off like a champ, a girl could've called me Santa Claus.

That shit went both ways. I'd stopped remembering their names the second we had enough small talk to get her hand on the bulge in my jeans. This one…fuck, I couldn't even remember the first syllable of her name.

I growled, pushed her over the edge, and brought her home.

The bed shook like it was about to break. My balls clapping her ass must've set off something wild inside her. She went ballistic, raked her nails down my back, thrashing like she'd lost her mind.

I let go with a roar. The rubber wrapped around me swelled something fierce. My load shot hot and deep, saved from pouring in her womb only by the sheath. I ground my pubic bone *hard* into her clit, making her sputter the mangled name over and over again like a damned chorus.

Always counted on those fucking things holding. The last thing I needed was to end up like my old man – knocking up a biker bitch too blasted out of her mind to deal with a hellspawn like me.

Fireball! Fireball! Fireball!

My balls throbbed, ached, and spat more fire. Shakes were an understatement when this girl's legs started twitching. They shook like I'd reached down and sent a damned current through her.

That pussy clenched me tight, and I smiled through my release, loving the lightning I'd created.

She came for what felt like five minutes, only stopping when I had to pull out to discard the shit holding my seed.

"Holly hell. Jesus. Wow. Just…wow!" Blondie twisted underneath me, reached up, and smiled.

Gave her a playful pat on the cheek before I turned around, tied up the condom, and threw it into the beat up can across my room.

Mission accomplished. Thirty-four years on this earth, and I'd satisfied the greedy bastard below the belt one more time.

I stood up, hearing her coo when she caught a view of my ass. She already wanted more.

Hell, they always did. Too bad a man could only fuck so many times in a day when he had the patch calling him.

Her little whimper quickly turned to disappointment when I found my boxers and started rolling 'em on.

"Aw, already? Don't tell me you have to work today?"

"Club business, doll. You know that shit never stops. Go shower and get dressed. I need you outta here."

I gave her a sharp look as I rolled on my shirt. She wrinkled her nose, thinking about razzing me, but the girl had enough sense not to talk back.

Good. That instinct would serve her well if she ever wanted my dick inside her again.

Obviously, she did. They always came begging for more. *Always.*

I was still rejecting bitches who came from Georgia and the Carolinas every so often for another piece of me. Women I'd fucked years ago.

Just an endless, nameless train lined up like Cinderellas hoping I'd hand 'em their damned slipper, head over heels for a chance to be that special gal I'd slap my brand.

Sometimes, they got another fuck outta me. But they all walked away empty handed because the girl worth wearing my name on her ass real official didn't exist. Especially not in this world of easy pussy.

"Oh!" I spun around to see why she looked so surprised when she stood up naked, desperately tearing the sheet off the bed to hide her body.

My eyes followed her to the tall silhouette standing in the doorway. "Shit."

How fucking long had the Cap'n been standing there watching?

Dust's salt and pepper stubble twitched on his chin as he reached up and pulled the smoke out of his mouth. "Get your ass together. Need you clean and on your bike in the next five minutes, Firefly. We've got work to do."

"How long you been there, Prez?" I said, rolling my cut on over my shoulders.

"Long enough to wonder why the fuck you can find something better to do in your free time." He gestured at the blonde bitch sneaking into the bathroom.

The door slammed shut, but not before the whore gave him a scorned look.

"What goes down in my time off's none of your damned

business, Cap'n," I growled, smoothing out the wrinkles in my vest. My fingers tingled when they brushed the skulls and pistols I'd earned over the years.

Every single stitch of this death meant something, born in blood, sweat, and tears.

"No, it ain't," he said with a nod, stubbing out his smoke on the wall. "You being sober enough to ride when I tell you to is. Pussy makes you suck the bottle like a fucking pacifier, brother."

I clenched my teeth, but didn't say shit. The bastard was all too right. Drinking and fucking went together like peanut butter and jelly.

"Five minutes." He held up his hand – as if I was so bombed out I needed a visual. "Tell the slut to get out, then lock up the garages. We're stretched too thin today to have any thieving skanks in the clubhouse, siphoning our booze."

"Yeah."

Prez turned around without another word, and I watched the club patch on his back disappear.

DEADLY PISTOLS MC, TENNESSEE. Same holy scripture shared on my skin and leather. A skull with wings and two guns blazing on the side.

That's what I'd sworn my life to. That's what owned me. That's the god I'd serve 'til the day I died, and no woman could afford to get in the way of that.

The bathroom door swung open and Blondie stepped out, warm and dripping wet. My cock jerked, begging me to haul her back into bed, especially when she smiled.

"You're *sure* you don't some more?" she whined,

squeezing her tits. "I'm off all day."

"I'm sure it's time for you to get some clothes on and walk the fuck out of here."

"Aw, Fireball." She gave me that sad puppy look as she reached for her clothes, tangled all over the floor. "Well, if you ever change your mind…"

Don't fucking tempt me, woman.

One and done. Those are the fucking rules.

Knew she'd been hanging around the clubhouse long enough to know it. Only a handful of lucky sluts had gotten a couple dozen fucks out of me over the years before I'd dropped 'em.

She'd be getting a lot less than that unless my dick was *very* hungry and *very* desperate. My eyes trailed down her body and noticed the skinny dip in her stomach, the stretch marks, the tired, worn out lines below her eyes a girl only gets in her twenties from too much booze. Maybe some other junk on the side, too.

My guts churned, pissed that the Prez was right again.

I could do better. Thank fuck I'd used a condom. I fucked like a maniac, but I wasn't stupid.

'Course, none of this mattered to my cock. That single-minded sonofabitch got harder just looking at her naked, begging for a hot, anonymous hole to fill.

I turned around to try to settle the hard-on beating my brain stupid. Fucking shit. Even when she was long gone, I'd be riding wherever hell the Prez ordered me at full staff.

How many times did I have to fuck to keep the bastard

between my legs down? Booze didn't do it. Neither did these easy ass sluts.

I'd never admit it to anybody, not even my closest brothers, but I'd had a piece of me shaking loose for a long fucking time.

I waited 'til she had her shit on before I kicked her out. She'd be back to sucking off the prospects next week, probably letting Tinman and Lion rail her at the same time.

Not the kinda woman I'd ever think about filling twice, much less calling my old lady.

Never told the bitch today was my birthday. Thirty-four years riding, kicking ass, and fucking hard above ground, and there was just one thing I was more sure about than my loyalty to the skull.

There wasn't a woman worth keeping. And thank fuck for that.

Every brother who'd ever let cupid ram his sneaky shit into their heart just got something else to worry about. Wasn't a fuckin' chance I'd ever let it happen to me.

* * * *

Dust didn't say shit when I walked out. Just handed me an address written on a napkin in his crabbed handwriting.

Some place in Knoxville. Probably not a dangerous job, or else he'd have briefed us and brought more guys.

No, this was just him and I. Weird, really, but fuck if I was asking any questions I didn't need to.

We rolled through the gate and I followed the Prez along

the highway, letting the fresh spring air rolling off the Smokies fill my lungs.

The mountains loomed large in the distance. Having a clubhouse here felt like living in a castle sometimes. Not that it gave us any hard protection if the Deads down in Georgia or any other mean motherfuckers decided to roll into our territory.

For the first time in years, we had money, and we were starting to get our shit straight. Skin, our Treasurer, was helping jump start the new strip club in town. So was the rich girl he'd taken for an old lady, the stray we'd all helped save.

We'd gotten a piece of her daddy's money in return. *Badly* needed cash, honestly, seeing how the club was running on cheap booze and favors before we fell into it.

Dust rolled down the exit leading into the city and I followed. A couple minutes later, we rounded our way into a cozy neighborhood full of old houses, sleeker and safer than the trailer park where I'd grown up.

His bike slid to a stop next to a small gray house. I watched the Prez tear off his helmet and followed suit, stuffing it into the empty space behind me.

"What the hell we doing here, Cap'n?" I asked.

"Personal favor. If she starts screaming, you just grab her and gag her."

What the fuck? He didn't elaborate, and now I wondered what the hell had crawled up his ass.

I followed him up the concrete steps leading into the house, his hand too close to the holster tucked against his belt for comfort.

Dust knocked on the door while I stood next to him. We both waited, and it seemed like nobody was home.

"Sure hope the man left it unlocked. Otherwise, we'll break it down." He reached for the knob. It popped with a single turn, and the door creaked open into a dark, neat looking house.

Relief should've steamed out my nostrils, knowing we wouldn't have to kick down a suburban door in broad daylight. But I wasn't letting go of shit 'til I found out why the fuck we were here.

"Come on," Dust said, waving me in behind him.

We headed for the kitchen, where I saw a skinny older man dressed up in a tan shirt at the kitchen table, a bottle of Johnnie at his side. Wasn't 'til we were face to face that I saw the brown shirt was a sheriff's, complete with badge, and then I nearly shit my pants.

"Jimmy, goddammit, you're gonna kill yourself." Dust grabbed the half-empty bottle and smacked it on the counter, away from the very drunken cop. "Where is she?"

"Not home yet, Dust. Just give her just a few more minutes. I'll let her in, introduce you guys, and you can be on your merry little way."

"Just like that? Can't believe she'll come along so easy. What the fuck have you told her?" The Prez folded his arms, giving the old buzzard a look straight from hell.

"Nothing, nothing." Must've taken him ten seconds to process the stink eye Dust was giving him. "Fuck, come on, Dusty. Telling her every little thing wasn't part of the deal. I've done my part years ago. Now, you *owe* me."

I waited for the Cap'n's fist to slam into his jaw after the way he'd said it. Nobody talked to our Prez that way – fucking *nobody.*

Instead, Dust pulled out the empty chair across from him, and then yanked out the extra for me to join him.

"Have a seat, Firefly. We're gonna sit here with our friend and wait 'til his pretty daughter shows up."

Prez, what the fuck? It burned my tongue like a damned ghost pepper, but I swallowed back the words, knowing any open questions were only gonna make this shit harder.

"Be good to her, Dusty. Please. It's gonna be hard enough on my girl." The sheriff spun around shakily, looking for his booze. He started to amble up to get it, but his legs wouldn't work, and he fell back into his seat a second later.

"Not even a question, Jimmy. We'll keep her solid. Christ, look at you." Prez stopped and ran a hand across his face, like he could hardly stand to look at the poor bastard. "You gotta sober up. This how you really want to say goodbye to her?"

The wiry cop squinted. Noticed his uniform was missing a few patches for the first time, which probably meant he was off the force. Maybe retired, judging by the wicked deep lines in his face.

"Fuck you. She'll remember all the better times before today. I raised my Cora right. That's all I ever tried to do, everything I promised Emmie the day she died…God! Was it really twelve years ago?" He shook his head, making his greasy hair flop around. "Twelve fucking years. And I'm about to join her."

"Don't start with that shit. You're not going anywhere, Jimmy. Sobering up'll help you when the Feds come to clean you up. I hear the witness protection racket can do wonders these days, get you a whole new name and number. You leave pulling the strings to me. I'll do what I can to make sure you won't have to spend much time looking like an orange-fucking-creamsicle once you spill the beans…"

"No." Jimmy sat up straight, reaching near his belt, struggling for something there. "I'm not going anywhere. I'm going out my way, Dusty. Didn't wanna tell you before…"

His hand came up clutching a gun. I shot up and drew my nine in a split second, all my instincts from the Army coming back like lightning.

"Freeze, fuckin' asshole!" I roared.

"Put it down!" Dust barked, grabbing my arm, wide eyed and crazy. "He doesn't mean any arm. He's…"

The Prez was at a loss for words. He reached out slowly and took the gun from Jimmy without a fight. The two men shared a look across time and space that had me truly fucking baffled.

Nothing about this shit made sense.

Goddammit. Orders were orders, weren't they? Fighting the urge to put a bullet between the drunkard's head before he did the same shit to us, I let my arm fall.

I stuffed my gun back into its holster and sat down, growing madder by the minute at vicious mystery killing us here.

What the fuck was going on? Seriously?

"Hey, never said you could keep it!" Jimmy snarled, reaching across the table. The edge caught him in the guts and he started coughing, toppling over and hacking up a fucking lung.

"You'll get this back when you tell me exactly what you're planning. I'm not letting you die by your own fucking bullet, buddy. We've come too damned far for that."

"Godddamnit, Dusty, you're a bastard to the end." He slumped in his chair, pounding his chest, giving us both a look that made me damned glad the Prez was holding that gun. "Already said – I'm going out my way. I'm a dead man no matter what I do, Dusty. You fucking know it. You think a skinny ass sheriff like me will last a month before getting gutted in the pen? I can't wait for you and the club pulling any strings. I'm screwed, blued, and tattooed."

"All that booze's going to your head, old man. Doesn't have to go down like this." Dust paused before he lobbed the next grenade. "It's gonna be hell on your Cora as it is. You really want me to tell her that her old man died a coward? Offed himself like a fuckin' lemming?"

"Asshole!" Jimmy shot up, tried to punch the Prez.

I was on my feet in a second, ready to grab him, but the Cap'n motioned me. *No. Let it ride.*

So, I did, and watched him fall face first into the table. He lifted himself up slowly, red faced and blubbering like a baby.

Fucking pathetic. Hell, right up there with the most pathetic sights I'd ever burned my eyes on.

I wanted to spit in this fucker's face, and then shake the Prez stupid for dragging my ass out here when I could've been back in bed, balls deep in blonde pussy.

"This is my choice, Dusty. *Mine.*" Jimmy bared his chipped teeth. "You take care of my little girl and leave me fucking be. I'm a dead man anyway with a Torches' hit on my back. I can wait for them to flay my skin off, maybe set me on fire, or I can go out my way. Easy."

What the fuck? My eyes bugged the hell outta their sockets.

The Atlanta Torches were our allies, but only because Prez's old man had given us a shotgun wedding with 'em when things started heating up with the Deadhands MC.

We both hated the Deads, and that was good enough. Dust looked at me while he reached out to Jimmy, and threw him back in his seat so hard I thought he'd push the drunk to the floor.

Not now, his dark gray eyes said. *You can save your stupid questions for when we're done with this sack of shit.*

I was about to roll with 'em anyway. Nothing about this situation made any goddamned sense.

Why were we helping this asshole when he'd fucked up bad enough to cross the Torches in our territory?

We should've rolled out the red carpet to let our buddies put a knife in his throat.

Something stank, so bad my nostrils hurt.

Jimmy shook his head and slumped in his seat, finally defeated. I stood up, ready to get some fucking answers or at least slug the last of that booze. But before I could cross the kitchen, we heard the screen door we'd come through open and bang shut again.

The drunk sat up like he'd seen a ghost. Prez collected himself, and got on his feet, striking the power pose he always did before he had to size some shit up. I froze in my tracks, one hand on the bottle of Johnnie, and the other on my gun.

I only saw her for a second before the brightest blue eyes I'd ever seen locked onto mine.

Fuck. She's…goddamned beautiful.

I'd expected anything between heaven and hell to come walking into the kitchen.

Never expected an angel, if angels were allowed to have racks like strippers and asses like the rising sun, so hot and full and beautiful I went fucking blind for a solid second.

Good thing she was dressed like a pastor's daughter, an old timey skirt reaching to her ankles. I wanted it gone – ripped to shreds. Never mind the fact that it was the only thing stopping me from losing it for a lot longer.

"Daddy? What's going on here?" She dropped her eyes and walked right past me, heading for the table.

I did a double-take as I spun around. No fucking way.

That miserable old drunk yammering about how boned he was shat out this…this sweet, hot, fuckable babe? This walking piece of perfection who got me so damned hard in all of two seconds I forgot why I wanted to put my fist through the nearest wall while chugging Johnnie?

"Cora, girl, you close your sweet mouth and listen," Jimmy rambled, sweat rolling off him like a damned hog.

"I'm…I'm going away for awhile. A good, long while girl. I did some bad things."

Wasn't sure who's mouth hung wider – hers or mine. "What?!"

"Cora, don't…don't you fucking cry on me. I can't take it."

The selfish bastard grabbed her by the arms and pulled her into his chest. Hot, angry tears rolled down his eyes while his daughter fought to get outta his grip.

Cora. I watched her eyes tremble, wishing I could spark a shine in them that would be a whole lot happier.

A pang of guilt rattled my chest. This wasn't the time to think about bending her over and finding out how well that round ass bounced beneath me.

Try not to think about it, you bastard. Try, try, try.
Yeah, good fucking luck.

I put the bottle down and looked on, eyeballing the Prez while she talked to her dad. The disapproving look on his face aimed at me was almost as bad as the one he had for Jimmy.

"These men are here to give you a better life. I know what they look like, and you're going to be scared, but you have to trust them. Do everything they say. They'll keep you safe. Dusty and I go way back. You can trust him, just like I do." Jimmy looked up, his eyes shining like he'd sobered up as he stared at the Prez.

Dust nodded. Very slowly, the cop let his daughter go. She stumbled backward with a look of confusion that almost made me sorry for the hard-on thumping in my denim.

"Firefly." Dust looked at me and motioned to the girl.

My cue to step up. I moved real slow, tried to hide the fact that I wanted to lay her against the nearest surface and fuck her brains out. She must've saw right through it, seeing how she backed herself into the nearest corner like a scared cat.

"It's okay. Prez is talking truth. We're not here to hurt you."

"How do I know that?!" she screamed, looking past me desperately. "Daddy, what the *hell* is going on here? I just came home and you're passing me off to these dirty bikers?"

Dirty? I clenched my teeth. I'd taken a good, long shower before I tapped the slut, scrubbing every damned drop of grease and motor oil off my skin.

"Cora, just listen to me. Just this last time. You don't understand. God willing, one day you will. This is the way it's gotta be. Baby, I'm sorry, but this has to be goodbye. No way around it." He looked away from her, his whole body starting to shake. "I'm going away for a long time. Dusty…give me my gun and get her the hell out of here."

Her eyes lit up like the moon when she heard him say *gun.* Then she started screaming bloody murder.

"Gun? Gun?! Daddy – *why?*" Those tears filling up her pearly blues became waterfalls. "You've lost your mind! I have to get out of here, call the police, before something –"

Fuck no. Only thing happening here was settling her ass down.

I grabbed her, and she smashed her elbow into my stomach, fighting with everything she had to rip me off her. Fuck, fuck.

16

"Cora! Go easy on her, bastard. Easy. Just because I'm leaving this world doesn't mean I won't gouge your fucking eyes out if you hurt my little girl!" Jimmy fumed, throwing his fists against his sides again and again.

"Get her in the garage 'til she calms down! Gag her if you have to. Shit, use the Johnnie..." Prez motioned the bottle, shaking his head. "Fuck you, Jimmy. This is *not* the way I wanted this to go down."

"You owe me, asshole! Last time I'm gonna say it...you think this is easy?" His face creased wicked as he stared at his girl in my arms, kicking an trying her best to scream. "No! It's my choice. The only fucking one I got. I'm a dead man, but Cora...she can live. She's got a chance if you get her the fuck away from me."

Time to leave this shitshow. I left the bottle behind after all.

Last thing this girl needed in her system right now was booze. She'd puke it up if it didn't kill her first, knowing her old man was determined to leave this planet, and leave her to *us*.

"Come on," I whispered, using my softest voice. Still came out like a growl. I let her thrash for a few more seconds, holding her arms against my chest.

I'd keep on doing it 'til she realized her fight was hopeless, or else her arms and legs gave out. That hard-on I'd had earlier?

Fucking thing died in my pants. Even I wasn't a big enough bastard not to feel this shit stabbing me straight through the skull like a dagger.

She was losing everything. Saw herself spiraling down the drain, into a whole new world leading God only knew where. And all because the piece of the shit at the table made her – and the Prez obliged his greedy ass for reasons I wasn't following.

Jimmy and the Prez kept mouthing something to each other I couldn't hear. I held her and rocked her real gentle for a few more seconds, 'til finally that fire in her belly went out.

"Good girl. We'll hang out for a little bit in the garage before we find out where we're going next, yeah?"

She didn't fight when I led her away. Hell, if anything, those blue eyes in her pretty little face reminded me of marbles, so soft and vibrant when they were brand new, and now they were getting tarnished as fuck.

I let her go once we stepped outside, giving her a little space, but never taking my eyes off her.

Couldn't wrap my head around it. Nobody this pretty should've come from that drunk's balls, and she was like a fucking ten.

Early twenties, tits so full they would've overflowed in my hand, an ass just begging to be spanked when she mouthed off. I wanted to wrap her long gold locks around my fingers, feel every fiber tense while those long legs hidden underneath the skirt hugged me.

And that wasn't stopping to think what the hell was up with the schoolteacher garb neither. Fucking shit.

My gaze followed her to her daddy's work bench, where she plopped down and smoothed her hair back, drying the tears on her cheeks with one sleeve.

"What do you do for a living, babe? You look like a real…professional."

Hot piece of ass was what I wanted to say. But something told me a chick like this wouldn't appreciate that kinda compliment the way a club bitch would.

She looked up, her eyes narrowed. "I'll go where you want, but I don't have to answer your questions. Daddy said you wouldn't hurt me. I'm going to trust you'll keep that promise."

My hands formed fists at my side. It was like the little minx was challenging me.

No, of fucking course I wouldn't hurt her. She'd been battered enough for the day, and no man in this club ever got away with roughing up a woman.

But they didn't ordinarily stand there with their dicks hanging out and nothing to say neither, and I took her shit without barking back, just this once.

She deserved a break, as long as she cooperated on the way home to the clubhouse, or wherever the fuck Dust wanted to take her.

"Well? Are you going to stand there or tell me where we're going? If these are daddy's dying wishes, or something, I'd kind of like to know what's in store next." She wrinkled her nose. "What are you, anyway? My bodyguard?"

I turned my back and didn't say shit. *Fuck me.*

For a nervous little girl who looked like she'd just stepped straight outta 1910, she had one helluva mouth behind those plush pink lips.

I turned to her slowly, cherry picking my words. "I'm the guy who's gonna make sure your life doesn't wind up more fucked up than it already is, Cora. If the Prez says I'm your keeper, then that's the way it'll be. You're shot to shit right now because of what your old man just pulled, I get it. That's the only reason why I'm standing here like a good boy instead of marching over and stuffing a gag in your mouth."

She rolled her eyes, and my fingers twitched. If we made it outta here without another fucking scene, I'd be tossing and turning tonight for sure, imagining how good she'd squirm with my big hand slapping her sweet ass 'til she learned some damned respect.

Her mouth popped open, but whatever sass she had planned was drowned out by new commotion inside the house. Prez started screaming at the drunk.

"You stupid toasted asshole – let go! You're not getting a hold of this shit! I'm not standing here while you splatter your damned brains all over your place. Fuck's sake, Jimmy, your little girl's standing right outside. Just breathe."

"Fuck you! I know what I gotta do, there ain't another choice!" The drunk's voice sounded rushed, desperate, angry. "Outta my way, Dusty. Don't make me shoot you, too."

Shit. I stood on the step leading inside, one hand on my nine, ready to bust in if the standoff got ugly. I could feel Cora's tense little eyes all over me, standing behind me, scared for her life.

"You won't. Give it the fuck back!" Dust exploded, his voice so loud it was barely muffled by the wall between us. "Don't be a goddamned idiot. Please. For her sake, if you don't give two fucks about your own anymore. We'll figure shit out with the Torches, take you away and stash you somewhere safe, same as her. Come on. It's not too late, Jimmy. You've been like a brother to me. I'll never walk away easy if I let it go down like —"

One deafening gunshot silenced the Cap'n.

Cora jumped. I pulled my nine, and my fist hit the door, making enough space to peek inside.

"Daddy? Daddy?!" I heard her call behind me, her voice dying in a brutal whisper.

Dust was heading toward me, a grim look on his face. "He fucking did it. Couldn't talk the stupid motherfucker out of shit. Nothing left to do except take care of the girl like we planned," he growled.

Prez punched the button for the garage, and we listened to it creak open. "On it, Prez. Cora?"

I walked toward her, ready to grab her hand and help her up. "Shit. Girl, I'm real sorry for what just went down. You never should've heard any of that. I —"

Felt like I was touching ice when I pushed her fingers through mine. She just stood there, her eyes barely bigger than her open mouth. The girl had gone damned near catatonic, and who could fucking blame her?

I helped her onto my ride. Wrapped her arms around me, and told her to hold on tight, making sure she could at least do that before we moved.

It wasn't 'til she was on the back of my bike and I had a helmet strapped to her head that she started to wail. Dust revved his engine and pointed a finger at the road.

Forward. No delays.

I nodded. It was a long, hellish ride through Knoxville. I made damned sure Cora's arms stayed locked around me, and I held her small, soft hand the whole way home.

If I could've fixed the hole in her old man's head and killed him all over again for putting her through this gruesome bullshit, I'd have done it in a heartbeat.

But the Prez was dead right. Nothing left to do except keep her safe. Well, just one more thing, after the big two.

Protect her.

Keep her sane.

And find out what the ever-living *fuck* was going on here.

II: Wires Crossed (Cora)

The bike's tires spun, loud and dizzy, but they had nothing on my head.

A couple hours ago, I'd been finishing up my paperwork with Mister Fisher, the kind, older teacher helping me intern in his ninth grade math class. Daddy had been sick at home the last few days, so I'd stopped at the drug store on my way home and picked up some cold medicine.

Now, he was dead. I'd heard the gunshot that killed him, put him out of the soul killing misery dripping off him like the sweat and liquor I'd smelled the last time we embraced.

Now, I was pressed up against this hulk in his ink and leather, this utter bastard who looked like a Viking and talked like he'd just stepped out of prison.

Now, I couldn't begin to piece together what was left of my life.

I should've snapped. Shattered. Died on the spot.

Instead, I was riding with this demon. My mind, my soul, my heart in ruins, broken so suddenly they turned me into a zombie, the only thing that kept me from throwing a fit and falling onto the road blurring by beneath us.

It didn't help that the monster who'd forced his way into my life was handsome in a rogue *I'm-going-to-fuck-you-up* or just *fuck-you* kind of way.

Big, brutal shoulders that would've made any linebacker or champion lifter jealous. Ice blue eyes, colder and darker than mine. Light cinnamon colored hair lay thick on his head, connecting with the solid stubble on his chin, sandpaper that looked like it would scratch in all the right ways against a woman's skin.

He looked too good to be bad, but I wasn't a fool. He had the patch, just like the older man riding ahead of us. The winged skull with two guns to the side that told me daddy had buried himself *very* deep, before he'd taken in his life.

I'd teased him about being my bodyguard before I heard the fateful bullet, yes. But to be honest, I knew exactly what he was.

My jailer.

And it wasn't like I had any choice. Something had been eating at daddy for months.

I could never get it out of him. I should've seen the signs when he'd taken up the bottle, hard stuff he hadn't touched since mom left us years ago.

I closed my eyes and grasped the devil tighter, trying not to enjoy his warmth. I'd never ridden a bike before today. Cool spring winds tore at my face, and they were the only thing that reminded me I was alive, except his heat.

My hands smoothed on his rock hard abs – too hard for a man who probably spent his free time chasing skirt and drinking beer. What he did with the rest of his time, I didn't even want to know.

These men were criminals. I'd heard daddy mention the Deadly Pistols MC every so often growing up.

Once, when we were fishing, he'd told me one of them was his friend, before he'd joined the force. Just a neighbor kid he'd stayed in touch with all through his career. He'd grown into a man my father drank with a couple times a year, even after he left the Knoxville PD last winter.

I had a sneaking suspicion the President, Dust, was that friend. Some buddy, letting daddy murder himself in our own kitchen…

Hell, had he *really* killed himself? Or had the biker done him in?

I tried not to cry. Numbness iced my veins, froze my synapses, made it hard to think about anything except how royally screwed I was since I came home to an absolute whirlwind.

My hands instinctively clung tighter to the biker's cut as we approached his clubhouse. Their club logo loomed large, painted on the wall, taunting me with its sick bony smile and vacant eyes.

As soon as Firefly stopped the bike, I jumped off and heard him run after me. I started vomiting underneath a spindly tree before he could grab me.

The bastard held me while I let out all the pain, crying again, splattering my shoes. I couldn't stand to look at him, but God help me, I did it anyway.

I had to see the face of the man who held the key to my

whole future, even if it would set my ruined stomach off a second time.

"What?!" I demanded. "You enjoying this, or something?"

"Fuck you, if that's what you think." His stark blue eyes softened. "I'm figuring out how the hell I'm gonna get your guts back in order so you don't join your old man on the other side. It's been a rough fucking day, darlin'. Been forever since I took care of anybody else."

"I don't need you to take care of me!" I coughed, spat at the ground, and shoved my hands against his chest as hard as I could.

The whole world started to spin. God, I was sick. Dying, maybe. I felt like I'd pass out, and maybe that would be a mercy.

A weak smile pulled at his lips, the last thing I saw before I blacked out. He held me softly, lowered his lips to my ear, and spoke one word.

"Bullshit."

* * * *

Two days in this dirty, cramped room. Two days I should've been studying for my state license, scoring tests, and helping Mister Fisher prep the Geometry lesson next week.

Goddamn it. He'd know by next week I'd dropped off the face of the earth.

These bikers weren't letting me go anytime soon, and I'd be lucky if I wasn't blacklisted across the county for jobs before I got out of here.

Mister Tall, Dark, and Crude wasn't having any protests.

He brought me food, water, and asked me if I needed anything else a couple times a day. Mostly salads and deli wraps from the grocery store across town, about the healthiest stuff I could get him to fetch me without starting a scene.

Eating cost me half the day's energy. When I wasn't thinking about daddy getting himself into trouble and ending his life one wall away from me, I buried my face in the pillow, weeping for the life I'd just had ripped open by a tactical nuke.

Nothing made sense.

The fact that whatever was weighing on him was so bad he'd had me snatched away before he'd put the gun to his head should've scared the hell out of me.

Honestly, it didn't. Nothing hurt worse than losing everything in a single afternoon.

Too sudden. Too savage. Too shocking.

I couldn't get over it. I seriously wondered if I ever would.

No, no, a hundred times no. I wouldn't even roll to face him when I heard the door pop open.

"Chicken ranch with lots of lettuce and kale, babe. Just like you asked." Firefly stood next to me on the bed, holding the bag, until I spun around and snatched it from his hands.

He gave me a death glare as I ripped into the bag, plucked out the wrap, and tore through the deli wrapping paper like a starving raccoon. I took a big bite before I looked into his ice cold eyes.

"How long are you going to keep me in here, living like a bum?"

"As long as the Prez says you staying here is law. You see this shit?" He tapped his chest, a small rectangular patch stitched in blood red beneath his name. ENFORCER, it said, as if I needed a reminder.

"Yeah, I can still read, Fireball. I was going to be a teacher."

His tough face crinkled, anger and amusement warring over a handsome canvass. He seemed to hate it when I used the wrong name.

What kind of name was Firefly for a biker, anyway? At least Fireball would've fit the explosive rage I could sense in him, churning just beneath the surface.

"That's who I am. Enforcer. Sergeant-at-Arms. Means I keep order around here for the club. Usually, that's breaking up drunken brawls and arguments between the brothers, but it extends to you, too, darlin'. Just as long as Prez keeps me posted to keeping your ass fed and watered."

"Uh, huh. How should I salute you, sir? Isn't that how all this pretend soldier stuff works with you biker boys?"

His temples popped as he clenched his jaw. Whatever. I wasn't here to make him happy, and I definitely wasn't here to flirt.

"You don't need to salute shit when you're not wearing a patch. You just gotta respect it. Every group needs discipline, woman. Count yourself lucky. What we've got going on here ain't half as bad as the five years I spent in Kandahar. U.S. Army does a decent job of teaching a man some respect."

Something you could fucking learn, his eyes said, but his lips refrained.

I blinked. No way. *This* six foot something human pitbull was a vet?

"How long were you in?" I said, swallowing my sarcasm with a big gulp of water. "Daddy served too. Short stint in the National Guard. Not that it did him much good."

"Too long to live a normal life. The shit that happened over there – that's a big part of what I'm doing here." His eyes hardened, and he stared me down, as if he'd suddenly said too much. "Don't regret a damned thing. This is the life. Rank means a lot to me, and so does respect. A little peace and order goes a long fuckin' way."

"Yeah, I figured. Daddy was all about the neatness and discipline too, except for the times he hit the bottle." I stared at my shoes, wanting to punch the nearest wall.

He'd been drinking the last time, hadn't he? Right before he…

"You don't need to worry about that shit anymore, babe. It's over. All that matters is keeping you safe. We'll get his ashes out of the county for you when all this is over. You can pay your respects and get on with your life."

If I wasn't so sick to my stomach, I would've laughed in his face. He talked like it was all so easy – like I hadn't just had the whole world torn away from me.

Like dough smashed through a cookie cutter lined with

barbed wire. The old world was gone. I'd entered one that was totally illegal, dangerous, and alien to everything I'd ever known.

Firefly plopped down on the bed next to me, shaking the beaten mattress. I bounced up and down, and for a second, I imagined the sounds we'd make here under very different circumstances.

I bit my lip and blushed. What the hell was wrong with me?

Twenty-two years, and I was still a virgin, that's what. No amount of grief could stop me from thinking all about the things a big man like him could do to me, naked and raw.

"Pay my respects?" I said numbly. "Why?"

"Huh? You loved your old man, right?" His eyes widened.

"Sure. But right now, I hate him for leaving me. I hate him for bringing me here. I hate him for putting me at your mercy, Fireball."

I saw the little tick in his lips every time I butchered his name.

What a bitch I'd become. I wanted to choke and die on my own bitter words, especially when I saw his eyes narrow and his face harden again.

"Fuck this, Cora. You can cool your heels alone and sort this shit out by yourself. I'm the man who's looking after you because I'm told to. I'm not your fuckin' therapist." His look bled murder. Part of me wanted to apologize, if only it wouldn't make me feel worse.

Daddy was the only one who owed anyone an apology – and he was dead.

"You're dealing with a lot, I get it, but a girl only gets so many passes. Only gonna tell you one more time, darlin'. My name's Firefly, and if you keep on going with that Fireball shit, I won't give a damn how fucked in the head you are. I'll bend you over, rip off that skirt, and give your sweet ass the whoopin' it deserves for blowing smoke in my face."

He jumped up, headed for the door, and slammed it so hard behind him the walls shook.

Jaw, meet floor. My mouth hung open for at least a solid minute.

Thank God the only mirror here was in the little bathroom attached the bedroom, or else I'd have seen my face beet red.

If I wanted to stay alive, I couldn't keep messing with this man. I'd have to find another way to stay sane, and deal with my loss, or else I'd only drown deeper in the hell waters rising inch by bitter inch.

* * * *

The next time I woke up, it was late. I'd thought the loud barking was in my dreams, at first, but then I sat up and shook myself awake.

No, it wasn't just my imagination. Someone had brought a dog into the clubhouse. A big one by the sounds of it.

I couldn't sleep through this commotion. It surprised me, since the place had been eerily quiet since I'd arrived. I stood up, straightened my clothes, and walked toward the door, pressing my ear against the banged up wood.

"Fucking shit, brother! I think he's hairier and got a bigger dick than you!" a rough voice said. Then the dog let out three more explosive barks and a whole group of men burst out laughing.

"Prez is gonna shit bricks when he sees this!"

"Club's gonna go broke feeding that mutt, Veep."

"Shut up. He's a pure bred Irish Wolfhound. If you boys think I haven't already cleared it with Dust, you've emptied out your skulls. Only pockets running dry'll be mine because he's my boy. Not the club's."

"I like him, Joker. He's got a good temperament for you." A woman's voice, soft and pleasant, cut through the gruff jeers and bawdy laughter.

Then the dog started barking again and everybody roared.

"Fuck, we've got church in an hour. That hole in the gate won't hold him. Ain't no time to fix it. You'll have to stick him somewhere 'til we're done."

"Yeah, yeah. Already on it."

The door flew open, and I almost fell over. Caught myself just in time against the wall, before I came face-to-face with a tall, dark haired man with even crazier eyes than Firefly. Next to him, the biggest, hairiest gray dog I'd ever seen in my life.

"Shit. Forgot he had you in here. Were you sleeping?"

32

I shook my head, already having an ugly feeling what he wanted. I looked through a small group of biker's and the regal looking brunette, who shot me a look of sympathy and surprise.

"Need a place to park my dog while the brothers meet. It'll only be a couple hours or so. He's a good boy, he won't bother you none." He looked down at the big dog. The animal's mouth was open, his tongue out, and he wagged his furry tail. "Sorry to barge in like this."

"He can keep me company," I said with a sigh, hoping he was right about the giant being well behaved.

"Thanks. I'll be back for him before you know it."

The dog stepped inside. Several rough looking men stared, and the brunette turned to one of them, still eyeballing me before the door closed.

The monster came up to me and laid his head in my lap, letting out a soft whine. No, no monster at all, I guessed, just another lost soul like me.

"Just you and me now, boy," I said nervously.

What had the man with the VP patch called him? An Irish Wolfhound? Jesus, he was half the size of the giant men around here. I reached out tentatively, running my fingers through his thick, gorgeous fur.

The dog licked my hand. Wherever he'd come from, he wasn't as hardened as these men. Something about that made me smile.

This week had been nothing but brutal. For now, I was grateful for the happy distraction.

Didn't take long for the dog to let out a huge yawn, and

then he curled up next to the bed, looking way too comfy for his gigantic frame. I settled in next to him, leaving my hand hanging over the bed, stroking his fur as I drifted off.

A tear ran down my cheek, the last one of the day, maybe. Certainly not the last I'd have as long as I was at the Deadly Pistols' mercy.

The Wolfhound wasn't as distressed as me. He belonged here. I didn't.

But we were both pets to the club now.

If, by some miracle, I survived all this, I vowed I'd move somewhere I never had to hear the roar of a motorcycle again.

III: Zookeeper (Firefly)

"We've been waiting for this damned meeting for three fucking days, Prez, with all due respect. You gonna spill the beans about why the fuck I'm playing babysitter to this chick, and how long I'm gonna have to do it?"

We all sat around the table. Dust hadn't even looked at me since he stepped in. He'd been gone for at least a solid day since he'd come by the clubhouse to make some calls, telling me to make sure Cora stayed locked up and comfortable in my room.

Meanwhile, I swallowed her fucking vinegar as best I could without making good on my threats. Kept my distance, too. When I wasn't bringing her food or checking up on her ungrateful ass, I slept on a bench next to the goddamned bar.

"You're doing her a solid, Firefly. Don't you fucking doubt it." Skin looked at me, smug as ever, his smile twisting the long scar on his cheek.

Bastard thought he was hot shit since he'd got the club's books in orders as Treasurer the last couple months. 'Course, that rich girl he'd claimed as his probably had a lot to do with it.

I'd be grinning ear-to-ear too if I was getting my cock sucked every fucking night by pussy that sweet on my balls.

"Didn't ask for your opinion. I'm talking to the Prez!" My fist slammed the table so hard I could feel my bones rattling in my wrists.

Next to me, Joker looked over, a savage warning in his cold, dark eyes. Shit, that boy had nothing but death glares to hand out. I counted myself the only man here who the Veep didn't intimidate.

"Forget it," Dust said to his right hand man. "He deserves to know. This whole club deserves an answer. An old friend of mine cashed in a favor before he decided to blow his fucking brains out." Prez stared past all of us.

Guess he had every reason to be bitter after failing to stop the selfish, drunken prick from offing himself.

Some friend. The fuck wouldn't even listen when the Prez tried to save his life, and now he'd sent himself and his daughter to hell.

Crawl, Sixty, and a couple other guys looked on at our chief. Their eyes demanded answers. Every man at this table wanted to know why this shit involved the club.

Whatever the fuck was going on, it roped us all in. Knew that much. Dust wouldn't fuck us up like this over any personal biz. Not even black and bloody shit that only mattered to him.

"Jimmy used to be a smart man. Mister Upright Citizen, had himself a badge, a babe, and the nice little daughter who's now playing guest in our clubhouse." Prez looked at us, folded his hands, his gray eyes going cold. "That's the way he sold himself to John Q. Public, anyway. Behind the scenes, he was dirty as hell, taking kickbacks from my old man, Early. He pulled this club's sack outta boiling water dozens of times on the force, covering up our loose ends before any Feds came sniffing. We paid him well for it. Everybody was happy. The boy put his pay to good use, too, raising a family. Did everything there by the book 'til his woman got slammed by the Big C."

A couple guys coughed. Half the boys in this room had lost somebody to cancer at one time or another. I hated that fucking shit. It didn't give a fuck about good or bad, patch or civilian, man or woman.

Jimmy still didn't deserve a shred of sympathy. Too damned bad I started to feel it anyway, pathetic and screwed up as he'd been.

"Don't give me that look, boys. He checked out like a coward, and I know it. Nobody at this table needs to pretend my buddy was a martyr," Dust said, pulling out his lighter. "I ain't blind. He died a fucking idiot. Went off the rails after his wife died. Started to do every sin in the book just to escape being lonely. Poor bastard took up gambling when he wasn't hitting the bottle. Damned fool almost lost his house on gambling debt. That should've been his warning. He didn't listen."

"So, what?" I growled. "Where do the Torches come in? I know they're a part of this, or you wouldn't be talking about this dead asshole here in church."

"They've got legacy money. Fuckers used to pass out loans like candy, especially to crooked cops across Dixie.

Jimmy lapped it up to feed his demon. Bastard made a lot of trips to Atlanta – some Homeland security shit he had to go to after the planes hit the towers – as if any goddamned terrorist would ever go after Knoxville or the Tri Cities."

Sixty snorted, smiled, and then wiped the stupid grin off his face when Dust gave him an ugly look. The Prez leaned back in his chair, fished out his pipe, and lit it before he continued.

"They gave him more than he really needed. Thought it'd do 'em good to stay on the good side of a Tennessee sheriff, right before the Deads rolled in and fucked up their city, giving them something more important to worry about."

Shit. I could see where this was going before the Prez got there, and I balled my fists underneath the table, ready to turn the fucking thing over.

I didn't feel bad anymore for the dead, dumbshit who'd caught his own bullet. He'd walked into hornet's nest and got chewed up bad.

"War costs a lot of money. Lord knows this club's still learning that lesson, getting back on our feet after my old man ran us dry and the Deads caught up to us." Dust looked at Skin, remembering all the shit the club had gone through to get his old lady free from her dirty pimp, plus the even dirtier debt she owed to our biggest rival, the Deadhands MC. "Well, the Torches came calling for every dime. Told him he'd better raid the police department's accounts if he had to, deliver some goods on the side, whatever the fuck it took to dig him almost two hundred-

K out of the hole. Jimmy was stupid, but he wasn't a total fuckin' moron. He wouldn't do it. Resigned instead of raiding county funds."

"Fuck. No wonder the poor bastard shot his brains out," Skin growled.

"Atlanta Torches' mob ties run deep," I said slowly, wheels turning, tying all the dirty strands together in my head. "They wouldn't even need to ride up here themselves to fuck him over. They could get the Cubans or the Irish to slip into town and do it for 'em without us noticing. Fuckers got deep roots going all the way down the Gulf coast, old ties they still keep greased, despite their dicks being trimmed back to Atlanta."

Dust nodded. "They're the only holdouts in Georgia the Deads haven't slaughtered. That's why both our clubs decided to stop shooting at each other years ago and work on killing the Deads instead."

"So what did they want?" Skin asked, running a hand through his thick brown hair.

Prez snorted. "Everything, Skinny boy. Torches would've taken his life, his daughter, and anything worth selling. I'm sure the fucker was damned near broke before he died, with nothing but a police pension paying the bills. They'd have doubled down on the girl for sure. Would've made her earn every fuckin' penny if she'd fallen into their paws."

I pushed a growl down my throat before it could come out. The thought of anybody putting a bag over Cora's head and carting her off to the highest bidder made my fists hungry.

Wanted to smash them into nearest punching bag 'til I put my hands straight through and spat sawdust all over the damned place.

Finally, shit was starting to make some sense. Too bad it only pissed me off more.

"So, how bad are we fucked when they find out your old drinking buddy's dead, and we're hiding his daughter, Prez?" Typical Skin. The man asked all the right questions, and then he never fucking quit.

"About as fucked as you're gonna be if we don't stop worrying about shit that hasn't happened yet," I snapped. "We can handle their pissant joke of a club any day."

"They've got more boys to field than we do," Joker said. His expression lit up like he enjoyed us being outnumbered – more men for the sick puppy to kill.

"You think I don't know that? We kicked the Deads square in the nuts last year, and they're a whole lot bigger than either of us! We can deal. We always find a way."

"Enough." Dust's gavel slapped the wood, banging hard like a gunshot. "We're not fighting the Torches. We're making sure Cora's safe and happy. I'm not planning on locking us into any either-or shit."

Everybody looked at him like he'd just told us we were all getting a year's supply of free booze and supermodel pussy.

"You wanna elaborate?" I asked, edging on disrespect.

Nothing made sense anymore.

Fuck if I didn't want to hit something right now – almost as bad as I wanted to march back to my room and get that girl who'd caused this mess naked, wet, and grinding on my dick.

"You heard me. We'll make it work. Keep her on the down low. The Torches'll be so pissed when they find out Jimmy died before they could get a piece, chances are they won't even worry about his daughter."

"What about her?" I asked, wondering who the fuck was saying those words.

Pussy hadn't ever been my concern before, except how quick it would take me to get up inside it. Something about Cora's case hit me deep, plunged into me like a fucking knife, and twisted itself around 'til I had to ask about shit I'd have never bothered with before.

"We'll keep her close. Give the girl something to do," Dust said, leaning forward and blowing out a long trail of smoke.

That strong, southern shit he smoked could've burned down half of Dixie. Instead, it was trapped in the room with us, reminding us who was boss – even when he went fucking crazy.

"Already got a few ideas," Skin said with a nod. "Talked to my old lady earlier. Why don't we get her a job at the new joint? Meg's going crazy managing all the dumb bitches there. She'd kill for another chick who's had some college and has her head screwed on straight."

I wanted to laugh in his fucking face. That little girl stuffed up in my room probably hadn't thought much about fucking outside the dirty books chicks like her always read.

She'd already gotten fucked outta her teaching job. Sure, she'd jump at the chance to work in a damned strip club, managing a buncha skanks who rode half the guys wearing our patch for extra tips, right? Shit, I'd fucked a few of 'em myself.

Yeah, I thought, *about the same chance as you sobering your ass up, hanging up the cut, and becoming a monk.*

"Something else," I said, locking eyes with the Treasurer. "She's a good girl. No fuckin' way am I gonna tell her she's got a great new job picking out thongs and selling drinks to guys who try to jack off in their seats."

"No need," the Prez growled, aiming his next line of smoke at my face. "I'll handle it, Firefly. The girl deserves that much, a heart-to-heart, seeing how I wasn't able to stop her old man from killing himself, practically in front of her."

"Shit, that's fucked," Sixty murmured, pulling his goatee.

Like we don't all know that, asshole? These were the times when I wanted to walk outta church and find the closest bottle.

The whole damned situation was past recovery, however you cut it. Everybody was sitting here pretending to give a shit while they decided her future. *Fuck.*

"She's doing me a solid, watching my dog." Joker broke the stony silence.

Crawl looked at him and snickered, his long, dark hair flopping over his face. Veep looked like he was ready to whip out that switchblade he always played with and tear him open like a fish.

Sixty punched his closest brother in the side, shutting him up, and redeeming the boy just a little bit in my eyes. Skin, Sixty, and Crawl had their own little posse going. They managed to keep each other from getting their asses kicked.

"Keep laughing," Joker said, a wicked smile spreading across his crazy face.

"No, VP, you've got yourself a pooch to look after. You'd better promise me that animal ain't gonna tear this clubhouse apart. Expect him to learn some respect and behave – just like the rest of you."

Half the guys sank into their seats. Me, I sat up straighter, giving Dust the look he was waiting for.

Are we done?

"Church dismissed. We'll meet again at the pig roast later this week, or else the instant I hear about any Torches fucking around in our neighborhood when they shouldn't be."

Thank fuck. I was outta my chair first, bolting for the door, when somebody locked onto my arm like a damned monkey.

I spun around to see it was the Prez. *Shit!*

He didn't let go 'til all the other guys left the room. Then he emptied the burned tobacco from his pipe into the ash tray and stood up.

"You handle her as best you can, and don't get too attached. Jimmy was all twisted up before he died, but once upon a time, he was my best friend. I'll die before I let his little girl get one iota more fucked up than she already is –

and that includes any man in this club slipping his dick in her when he knows damned well he shouldn't."

Fuck! I could feel an invisible boot nailing me square in the nuts. Bastard must've been psychic, reading my mind so well it chilled my bones something fierce.

"What? You think I don't have pussy lined up right and left? I fuck more than any man here."

"And you'd better keep on doing it, just as long as none of your bitches are named Cora Chase. I'm not blind, Firefly. I've seen how you've been looking at her from the second we pulled her out of that shitshow at the house. You're hungry, boy, and that's dangerous." His hand slid across all the little silver crosses flanking the side rocker on his cut. Some say each one stood for a dozen guys he'd personally put down, and others said only one.

All for the patch. No man wore PRESIDENT on his leather unless he'd killed and bled for it. That went double for Dust, taking the gavel right after Early took a bullet to the guts.

"Dangerous?" I cocked my head, chewing on the word.

"Yeah, asshole. For you."

"Fuck, Prez, you act like I'm some half-starved jackal aching for some cunt that'd probably need training wheels to fuck right. She ain't my type. Not even fucking close."

I'd never told a bigger lie in my life. Prez must've smelled it because he wrinkled his nose.

"Last warning I'm giving you, Firefly. Last and only. You're the only other guy with this patch who put time in with Uncle Sam besides me. You know promises and duty like your own fuckin' asshole. I expect you to keep your word."

"You know I will. I'm here to help her un-fuck herself – not fuck her."

My dick throbbed when I spat each miserable word. Lies, lies, lies.

I'd have to put a fucking choke-chain on the unruly bastard in my pants, the only thing in this world insane enough to make me lie to the Prez's face about my caveman intentions.

"You'd better. I'm not asking you to cross your heart and hope to die, brother." He rounded the table, his eyes falling over the Civil War heirlooms and World War II trinkets he kept framed on the wall, buried in all the club history. Then he stopped, looked up, and pointed at my chest.

"I'm telling you, Firefly. You'll do as I say with this so you don't get your fucking dick snapped off." He turned around, reaching for some fresh tobacco to stuff into his pipe. "Get the hell out of here. Make sure she's all right. Tell her I'll be down tomorrow to talk to her about the job."

"Whatever you say, Cap'n."

I turned around and marched out the door. Hoped to Christ his threat was enough to make me keep it in my pants for once.

Deep down, Cora deserved better. But all I could think about was burying myself in her, sinking my dick so low I fucked away every filthy thing she'd suffered.

Yeah, I'd always had a demon on my shoulder who had the upper hand when it came to conscience. And he vowed he'd burn my dick to ashes if I didn't find a way to fuck this beautiful blonde girl, consequences be damned.

My dick ached, knowing it was a goner by blue ball hellfire or by the Prez's knife. Helluva choice.

* * * *

My room was dark when I stepped inside it. Something big stood up, startling the shit outta me. I almost pulled my gun.

Then I remembered.

"Fuck me and call me wolfie," I muttered under my breath, watching as the Veep's new dog shuffled over to my girl on the bed and licked her face.

My girl? Shit. I gotta stop calling her that.

Cora jolted up and rubbed her eyes when she felt his thick tongue rolling on her cheek. She reached down, scratching the animal's head while she slung her long, beautiful legs over the bed.

She looked at me and scowled. "What do you want?"

"To wake your ass up." I reached for the light switch on the wall and flicked it on.

She covered her eyes as the dim bulbs hummed alive. The pooch whined, walked to the door, and put his huge paw against it, scratching 'til I let him out.

We both watched the big ass dog wander into the clubhouse, searching for his new master.

"Seriously, babe, I'm here to talk."

"I'm not sure there's anything we have to talk about,"

she said, folding her arms around herself protectively.

"Better you hear it from me first than the Prez."

That got her attention. Her big, bright pearly blues rolled with surprise.

I walked to the bed and sat down next to her, ignoring how she shrank away from me. Took a helluva lot more effort to keep my eyes off her chest, her ass, those long legs I couldn't stop thinking about digging into my ass while I railed her stupid…

Cora let out a long sigh and ran a hand over her face. "Well, what now? Let's get this over with."

"You need something to do. Last thing the club wants is to keep you cooped up like a damned prisoner."

She cocked her head. "What? You'll let me go? I thought the whole point of this was to keep me hidden?"

"Keep you away from your house and the old life you knew, fuck yeah. Doesn't mean you're chained to this clubhouse and broke. Prez wants you to get on your feet so you can have a life when all this shit blows over. We've got a job for you."

She looked at me intently. "I'm not good at mixing drinks and I'm not doing anything illegal."

Funny. Real fucking funny. I gave the girl my biggest shit-eating grin and grabbed her shoulder, pressing my fingers into a reassuring squeeze.

"Babe, we're not fucking monsters. Your daddy wouldn't have kept himself close to Dust all these years if he thought we were just thugs and killers. We're not asking you to mule for us with grenades stuffed down your panties or some shit."

"God, you're crude." She wrinkled her nose. Couldn't help but notice the faint trace of a smile on her little lips, before it melted away.

Little Miss Prude liked it nasty – she just didn't want to admit it. I made a mental note that there'd be a lot more where that came from.

"I don't know what my dad knew anymore," she whispered. Familiar sadness sucked the color from her face.

Not this shit again. Change the fucking subject, asshole, I told myself.

"You've got good girl written all over you like the ink on my skin, I know it," I said, sizing her up. "Prez is gonna offer you a job at the Ruby Heel. He wants you to work with Skin's old lady, Meg, on managing business there. Nothing illegal. Nothing crazy. Just good, honest work that'll probably pay you more than that fucking internship."

"Ruby Heel? That's…" She trailed off when it hit her. "Oh my God. I'm *not* taking my clothes off for money. I don't care how much it brings in."

She bolted up, and I went after her, grabbing on her arms. "No, no, no. Nobody's asking you to shake your ass for a buncha horny old buzzards. Don't think anybody's got an arm long enough to pull that stick outta your ass and get you naked for coin. We're asking you to help with the other shit. Business is business, even when it's all about making money on skin. Somebody's gotta handle the logistics."

For a second, she looked at me like I'd just ask her to hand over her first born. Her hand slipped out of my grip, shot up, and a firecracker exploded across my stubble on one cheek.

"I'll do it, asshole," she snapped, pulling away from me. "If everything here looks clean and kosher, I'll try. No promises it'll work, but we'll see. Whatever I decide, don't you *ever* talk to me like I'm some stupid kid who's spent her whole life in libraries. I can handle myself perfectly well in the adult world."

Fucking shit. I barely stopped my inner asshole from blowing smoke out my nostrils and rolling my eyes.

She'd decided to listen to something sensible. That was fuckin' progress.

"You're right," I said, letting my eyes roam all over her body, real slow from top to bottom. "You deserve a chance to show me what you're made of."

"I don't have to impress you. Isn't your President the one who's handling all this? I need to talk to Dust."

"Something like that, darlin'." My cheek still burned. That fire radiated all the way down to my dick, making me hard as granite.

This chick was gonna get eaten alive at the skin shop. Didn't have a clue what the fuck Dust or Meg thought they could use her for. The instant she walked through the horny gaggle of truckers, bikers, and civvies shelling out good money to stare at tits all night, she'd get eaten alive.

And that was if the bitches slinging themselves around the poles didn't chew her up first.

Still, I meant every word I said. She deserved a shot. Anything beat more of her moping around the clubhouse, taking up my room all the damned time, reminding my cock of what it wanted, but couldn't have.

"When do I see Dust?" she asked, turning her beautiful back and giving me a flash of that long, blonde hair. Noticed for the first time it hugged her close, halfway down her back, the perfect distance above that magnificent ass.

"Tomorrow. Never said what time, but if you're up by seven, you'll be good. You like what he says, the job's all yours. Won't be long before I drive you down there to start."

"Oh, awesome, so you're my chauffeur now, too?"

"Sure, long as you admit you like riding bitch on the back of my bike."

Her mouth dropped again. I fought the urge to laugh. Headed the fuck outta there before she could sling more shit, or else pretend her nipples weren't getting hard underneath that nice white blouse.

Even when I walked into the bar and took my seat next to Joker, sucking on a tall beer with one hand on his big dog's head, I couldn't bleach her from my mind.

This girl was something else.

Always shocked and appalled.

Always too fucking hot for her own skin.

Always calling to my dick when we weren't even in the same room.

Always the kinda spitfire I saw myself taming, railing, owning in all my wet dreams – except she really existed in the flesh. Just a fucked up, defiant girl who'd suffered too much shit and seemed too good for a bastard wearing the skull like me.

That made me want her like a fuckin' animal.

Sooner or later, she'd fall. This world tarnished the shit out of the most beautiful souls who tumbled into it. She wouldn't be the shy, upright twenty-something baby face forever.

Tore my heart out to know she'd wind up on my level the longer she hung around here. But the instant she did, I'd be there to catch her, get a piece of that hot, pink, tight perfection wedged between her legs.

I'd risk getting my cock clipped by the Prez for some of that. No, fuck, it wasn't just about the need I had to own her inside-out.

Deep down, somewhere so far and dark I never went there, I wanted the best for this chick. Wanted her to rise above it, to kick some serious ass and make bloody giblets outta this dark, rough universe I called home.

That fantasy was a whole lot more fucked up than imaging all the ways I'd slam her into the mattress after shredding her clothes. *What the hell was she doing to me?*

IV: New Girl (Cora)

"Do your best. Make some money. We've got your meals and the roof over your head covered." The tall, fearsome looking President of the Deadly Pistols MC stood over me, slowly pulling pipe smoke into his lungs every few words. "We'll be out of each other's fucked up sights before we know it, baby girl. You'll be off doing whatever you want, without the club or your old man's spirit dictating what you ought to do with your life."

This man scared me more than Firefly, and it wasn't just because he was older. His eyes had that *don't you dare fuck around* glint in them times a thousand, their gray hue matching the rare ash slivers in his hair when it caught the light.

Jesus. Why did every man here have to look like a killer angel? Beautiful in their own way, but so menacing. Destructive. Frightening.

One question hung on my lips. I'd been fighting it since he'd stepped into my room and sat me down.

"What happened to my father?" I asked, finally mustering up the courage.

"Everything he already told you before he checked out. Jimmy fucked up, got himself into some shit so deep he couldn't dig himself out in time." He took a long toke on his pipe and blew smoke at the floor before answering. "You'd better believe I tried to save him. Did all I could. It ain't easy to wrestle a gun away from a man once he jacks it. Your old man jerked the gun out of my hands and had it waving around like a damned lunatic before I could talk him down. There wasn't any stopping him when he put it to his head and pulled the trigger."

I winced. The fact that I hadn't actually seen it happen was the only thing that saved my sanity.

Now, I imagined everything Dust said, and it tore my heart to pieces. I pinched my eyes shut, fighting back the latest in the endless stream of tears I'd dealt over the last few days.

His face softened when my eyes opened. His fingers touched my chin, and he tipped my face up, giving my jaw a tense squeeze before he let go. Those ash gray eyes bored into my soul.

"Make your daddy proud. This week's been hell on you. Would've twisted anybody in knots, especially a woman who's not used to shoveling this sorta horseshit day in and day out. Let me tell you, no matter how much that blackness inside you keeps trying to stop your heart, it doesn't have to." He paused, almost like he was remembering words someone else had told him a long time ago.

"Live your life, Cora Chase. This club'll keep you safe so

you get a second chance, in time. We can't bring your old man back to life, but fuck if I'm gonna let anything happen to you. You're too damned beautiful for this world. Too young. There's a thousand ways you kick this world right in the fucking sack. Nothing in your past, present, or motherfucking future needs to stop you from doing that."

A hot tear rolled down my cheek. I ripped myself away from him and turned my back, hiding my pain from this stranger.

He sounded disturbingly like my father. So much like all those pep talks daddy had waiting for me after mom died young, a rare tumor in the head taking her life.

"Go with God, girl," Dust growled. "A little divine grace and some help from hell on wheels is all you need. I'll leave you to rest up. Firefly'll drive you down to the Ruby Heel tomorrow. Skin's woman will help you get trained in."

"No. No!" I sputtered, facing him. "I need to know what happened. Why did daddy die? What kind of trouble was he in?"

Dust's face darkened. "That's club business. All you need to know is he died scared. Terrified for himself, and for you. Jimmy cashed in a favor, and it's my job to keep you safe. That's exactly what I'm gonna do, Cora. Details ain't important unless they're all that's between you and some fucker trying to do you harm."

"No? And what if they're the only reason I listen to anything you say?"

His eyes had that scary as hell glint before, but now they turned into deadly stars.

"Little girl, you don't have a choice. I'm keeping you safe if I gotta order my boys to get some rope, a gag, and a funnel to keep you fed. I'll strap you down myself if it keeps you out of trouble. You can either take the only chance I'm dropping into your lap to make something of yourself while you're our guest – or I'll treat you like the VIP you are."

He stopped, pulled the pipe out of his mouth. I just glared at him, even though I was going to pieces inside, trying to stop myself from looking away, afraid.

"This club's run protection rackets before. We've never botched one. It's our way or the fucking highway when it comes to keeping you safe." He smoothed a hand through his hair. "I'm gonna give you some time alone to think, to figure this shit out, before it gets you tied up. Literally. I *will* protect you, Cora, even from yourself. You press me, you won't like what I gotta do to make it happen."

Dust walked out before I could catch him. I wanted to break down the door and go after him, but making a scene out there in the open clubhouse wouldn't do me any good.

Hold on. Just hold the hell on.

Sooner or later, somebody will slip up, and this will all make sense.

These assholes weren't giving me any choice. Much less an explanation.

I wouldn't let go. I had to find out what happened, what kind of danger I was actually in. My hands formed tight, angry fists.

I swore I'd never forget. I'd do what I had to do. I'd work for answers in between pretending I'd settled into some kind of normalcy here.

No, it wouldn't bring my father back to life, but I had to know why he'd died. It couldn't have been for *nothing*.

Hero would never show up in his obituary.

If villain didn't fit there instead, then at least I could let him rest in peace, and bury some of the pain eating at my heart.

* * * *

"We're here," Firefly growled. He killed his engine and helped me off his bike.

It was a bright, sunny morning. The light cut through the haze rolling in over the Smokies. Exactly what I didn't want to see before I headed into the dark, cavernous strip club.

"How long has this place been running?" I asked. The building looked new, or at least it had a fresh coat of paint.

A perfectly gaudy white contrast to the huge glittery neon red heel hanging over the entrance.

"Couple months or so. Took the club awhile to collect the seed money to get her going, but she's rocking it, or so I've heard from Skin. He deals with all the bean counting bullshit. His old lady's got a background in biz, too, and that's who you'll be working with."

"Is she nice?" I should've bit my stupid tongue.

Wonderful. The shy, nervous girl was coming out, despite my best efforts to stuff her into her cage. Doubts and insecurities I'd had all my life before interviews and new classes leaped up, sank their teeth in, and wouldn't let go.

"Fuck if I know." Firefly shrugged. "She keeps Skinny boy happy, and she's a solid girl. That's the end of my dealings with chick shit."

Chick shit, huh? I stared at him, wondering how there could be any justice in the world when this flippant, sexist asshole looked like an Adonis. A very heavily tattooed one, draped in leather, whose hands had seen a lot more dirty work than any model.

It wasn't fair, damn it. A man like this shouldn't ooze sex while he infuriated me more times than I could count. *What the hell was going on?!*

Pursing my lips, I gave him one more glance, without saying anything. It wasn't worth it taking another jab at him, starting a fight before my first day of work.

He really looked like something wild in the spring morning, decked out in his leather, his fearsome patches, the dark inks rolling up his massive arms like tiger's stripes.

Once, he'd been a warrior in the service. Hard as it was to seriously believe.

He'd traded his uniform for a different one, but the soldier look lingered, even behind all the vicious symbols the army wouldn't be caught dead allowing on a soldier.

I'd never wanted to kiss a man, maul him, bite and scratch him to pieces all at once. Until now.

Oh, God. Firefly smiled, pinning my eyes in place with the look that told me something new and wicked was about to leave his mouth.

"Good luck, babe. Give me a call on that burner phone

I gave you when Meg says you're done for the day. I'll be here." He picked up his helmet and whistled, leaving me frozen in my tracks one more time before I headed inside. "You'll do just fine. Get in there and make it rain fuckin' money."

Not what I'd expected. He was so...so nice.

"I will," I said, standing there for a minute, just watching him like a stupid girl gawking at the Prom King blowing by on his hot new ride.

There wasn't any hope he'd heard me over the roar of his bike.

I hadn't asked for any of this – much less a bastard built like a tank, whose every other word was something foul or selfish.

But maybe, just maybe, it wasn't all bad. Maybe Firefly wasn't either.

* * * *

Two hours later, I wanted to take back every word.

The job wasn't bad. It was *awful*.

Meg had been pleasant enough at the start, a curvy brunette roughly my age. The PROPERTY OF SKIN jacket she wore looked strange with her designer skirt and high end shoes, like two different worlds given a shotgun wedding in fashion.

"I'll introduce you to the girls!" she said cheerfully, flicking her hand. I noticed she wore a ring with a tiny dagger in the design. "Don't worry, none of them bite.

We're all about the cash here. Drama free. Getting them out on stage in time's our biggest hurdle."

She flashed me a big white smile and leaned in, covering her mouth so nobody would hear. "It takes a little push to get them going. But once they're out there…well, let's just say every man with a beer in hand would agree it's a sight to behold. Trust me, the bank account agrees."

She led me out of her office into what looked like the backstage dressing room of an old theater. There, in front of the mirrors, I saw four of the most tall, spoiled, looks-obsessed bitches I'd ever meet in my life.

"Tawny, Annabelle, Cindy-rella, and Pix," Meg said, pointing one by one. "Listen up, girls. This is your new production manager, Cora. She'll be handling your tips for accounting and making sure you get out on stage when the bell rings. We've had some issues with that lately. Every wasted second between acts means a few less dollars coming into the Heel and the club."

She looked at the strippers and gestured to me.

One girl rolled her big green eyes, a yelp leaving her lips when she formed a pout. "Oh, please, Miss Wilder. You really had to bring in this little girl to help herd us like sheep? Nobody's dragged themselves out late more than ten or fifteen minutes this month."

"That's ten or fifteen too many. You realize how much revenue we lose when men get bored?"

The four aimed the same catty eyes at their boss, but didn't say a word. Meg turned to me, cleared her throat, and pushed a binder into my hands.

"This has everything you'll need to make sure they're prepped and ready. They can stuff their tips in the envelopes inside. Track everything. We need to. We'd have the IRS bringing this place down in a heartbeat if we left it all to them. Good luck! And holler if you need anything."

Smiling, she headed off with one more wave, her fancy shoes tapping the wooden floor like a train with a few loose wheels disappearing into the night.

The tall, dark, Latin looking woman named Tawny stood up. "Just leave us do our thing, and this'll work out fine. Miss Heels won't do shit if you slack off a little. Hell, she brought you in to keep us in line!"

All the girls laughed, and it echoed all across the stage. I looked at the beat up silver clock hanging over them. We had a few more hours before the place opened up for its first act this evening.

Just enough time to realize I'd been plunged straight into a special kind of hell.

* * * *

When honey didn't work, I tried vinegar.

They ignored me constantly, dragging their stupid, stockinged feet. All the girls spent a few extra minutes smoking and putting on makeup before they even looked at the curtain leading to the stage. Mostly, those bitches just laughed in my face every time I tried to get them going.

Annabelle, the skinny brunette with a club-shaped tramp stamp on her left ass cheek, tried to sneak her tips by me in her bra. She had the cash halfway out and stuffed into her purse before I said anything.

"What?! Stop looking at me like I'm a fucking thief, you little shit," the stripper swore. "Here's your damned money!"

She shoved it into my hands so hard I nearly lost my balance. Before I could so much as shoot her a dirty look, the skank stormed off, a smug little smile dragging on her over-painted lips.

Resisting the urge to run outside and cry, I channeled it into doing my work instead.

No, no, damn it, no.

I had to stay. I couldn't break down on my very first day. Not if I ever wanted to escape this hell forever, and never look back.

"Okay, Tawny, it's your turn," I said, walking up to her with my fakest smile.

"Sure, sure. Whatever you say, bossy-pants." She smiled into the mirror, plucking at her eyelashes.

Scowling at her wouldn't do it. I wanted to rip her lashes off with my bare hands.

"Tawny, come on. Let's get this done. Please."

That was when my brain completely shut down for the evening. I must've stood there begging the bitch to get out and do her job. Overhead, the clock ticked by while she preened.

Twenty minutes and counting past the time when her act should've started. Past the stage, people were getting so restless I could hear it through the curtain, men shuffling around and swearing to themselves.

I was about to start shouting when she yawned. I watched her stand, jerking off her fluffy pink robe. "Well, guess I'd better do a little work today. I've got at least another dance or two in these bones. Don't stress too much, little C. I won't try to sneak a dime past you on my way back here."

She flashed me a wink and tottered toward the stage on her high golden shoes.

Fuck it. Done. That's what I was, and then some.

I crashed out the nearest fire exit and buried my face in my hands, repressing bitter tears while I gulped cool mountain air. It was the only thing that saved me that night from a total meltdown. I stayed out there for ages before I dragged myself in, hoping the cool breeze dried the tears on my cheeks.

Somehow, I blundered on, making the same pathetic pleas.

Chasing them for tips. Feeling more powerless than I ever had in my life, including the last few days when I'd been boxed up in Firefly's room.

My torture lasted two more hours, and the girls walked all over me. When Meg came around to fetch me and let me know my shift was done, the lukewarm smile on her face said it all.

"Hey, don't be too discouraged. These girls are tough. I'm sorry I downplayed it earlier, I didn't want you to panic. We've been having trouble getting them to move since the Heel opened. Give it a week. Get your bearings. You'll figure it all out."

I wanted to quit right on the spot. But then she pressed a small envelope into my hands. My fingers reached in, pulled out a crisp hundred paired with a fifty.

More than I'd expected. Especially for the painful hack job I'd done tonight.

"All under the table, of course," she said. "Skin normally keeps things kosher with payroll here, but he says the Prez told him nobody needs to know you're working here. Firefly's on his way to take you home. See you tomorrow, Cora."

"Y-you too," I stammered, but she'd already left me alone.

I'd never earned that much in a single day at my crappy summer jobs or internships in uni. Too bad I wanted to chuck the money down the nearest toilet, or burn every filthy dollar earned in this twisted job I'd never asked for.

Outside, Firefly was waiting. "How'd it go, darlin'?"

"First day woes. It only gets better from here, right?"

Jesus, please tell me *yes.* It had to.

Hell, *I had* to keep it all together. I wasn't going to give this arrogant bastard one more ounce of my tears.

I definitely wasn't going to open up to him.

"Damned straight." He must've had a sixth sense.

I'd expected a barrage of stupid questions, or crude jokes aimed at my heart, the whole ride to the clubhouse. Instead, he barely said a word, leaving me to my stone cold silence.

He didn't even chase me down when we arrived and I headed straight for my room. Later, there was a heavy knock on the door. It took me at least five minutes to come out of the sick grog from the heavy sleep I'd fallen into the second I buried my face in his beat up pillows.

I padded to the door, wishing he'd gotten whatever crap he wanted to throw at me out of the way earlier. I opened the door.

Nobody there. Just a small white bag at my feet and a tall bottle wrapped up in brown paper.

I looked around, didn't see anybody, and reached down to gather them up. The white bag came from the same deli that fed me all my meals these days. I sat with the bottle in my lap, tore through the paper, and pulled out a nice, thick bottle of wine.

The sticky note attached had the sloppiest handwriting I'd ever seen, but I could make it out.

You're too damned classy for beer, so here's something better. Hope you like red. Sorry, don't know shit about wine. Man at the store said it was solid. Glass is in the bag.

Here's to a better life, or just something to take the fucking edge off.

-Firefly

I didn't realize I was hugging the bottle until I finally moved. I must've drank half of it with my meal before I crashed again, sleeping with a stupid, unexpected smile on my lips.

Nobody had done anything so nice for me since I'd graduated high school, when daddy had a huge German chocolate cake lined up for me and all my friends. The same kind momma used to bake.

The wine was decent, but it wasn't anything amazing. It didn't matter.

That stupid bottle of red with the fake French branding made me happier than the money I'd left crumpled in my pants pocket.

Somebody actually cared. Somebody who spent his days drinking, cursing, and probably chasing the first girl he saw who made his dick stand up.

Maybe there was a little of that here, too. I couldn't just ignore the hot promises in his eyes each time he looked at me. But so what?

I slipped off feeling toasty and loved.

Even if it was an illusion, and only an illusion, it was the one I *needed* just then. The only one that gave me a shred of hope I'd survive another day at the Ruby Heel.

* * * *

For three more days, I kept it together. A tiny glass of wine after work every day helped.

That last little taste, I snuck before leaving for my fourth shift. It only went so far. I'd thanked Firefly for the wine, but I'd been too afraid to say more, scared of letting him see how much he'd really touched me with the crazy surprise.

Meg flipped me to nights, a time that was a little busier. She swore up and down the girls would have more incentive to move, seeing how they made their best tips right between ten and two in the morning.

Men were at their drunkest, their horniest, and their neediest just then. So far, the night crew consisted of three girls I hadn't worked with before – and they were just as bitchy as the evening crew.

All of them talked. They knew I was a pushover before the night even began.

A blonde in her late twenties with fake boobs and a couple inches on me named Trig was up next. Rather, she should've been on the stage getting naked ten minutes ago.

Instead, she sat backstage, taking messy sips off some cheap gin she'd snuck in her purse when she'd showed up about an hour ago.

I clenched my teeth, circling her like a vulture. "You should really put that down. Club rules say no drugs, no cigarettes, and no drinks before your act. It's a big liability to have that stuff in your system when you're up there on stage."

"Oh, you again?" Trig threw her hair back and nasty laughter bellowed out her throat. "Corral or whatever the fuck your name is – *shut up.* I've done this act a zillion times with this stuff kissing my veins. Makes the time go by faster. I don't tell you how to do your job, and you don't need to say shit about mine. Don't know what Meg was thinking when she brought you in. I've seen girls younger and prettier than you who'd do a better job of –"

Shut up? SHUT UP?!

My brain went straight to my hands. Before I knew what was happening, I lunged, and my nails dug deep against the stripper's perfumed scalp. I yanked her hair with my fingers so hard I thought I'd rip it right out.

The bitch screamed. Loud. My eardrums were about one octave away from busting.

I let out a growl, whipping her around with all my strength when she stood up and tried to fight back.

Two other girls backstage started hollering. Luckily, they didn't interfere, just stood there pointing and laughing while Trig got the jump on me and flattened me against the ground.

I went down kicking and scratching. No more nice girl.

She clawed at my face with her long extensions. They were sharper than they looked. I screamed, found her wrist with my teeth, and bit hard. Never stopping until I tasted blood.

Her pain howled through the thick curtain separating us from the stage, and I could hear the commotion out there rising.

Ever since I'd shown up here, I'd been abused, brushed off, and scorned by these dumb girls who probably had half the brain cells I did to rub together.

Whatever, brains wouldn't help me now. I fought with all my strength, rolling and snarling while the other girls screams grew louder.

I didn't realize how far we'd moved until men were jeering all around us. We'd wrestled right through the curtain, out onto stage, and now we were tonight's latest act.

The hot spotlight burned my eyes. Mostly, I just saw red

as Trig's dark silhouette sat on my chest, slapping me across the face over and over again.

Something unnatural tore through my veins, a demon energy pounding in my chest.

I'm already in too deep, and I'm NOT losing. Fuck you, bitch.

I opened my mouth, knew I was screaming bloody murder, but I couldn't hear anything except my own heart pounding in my temples. Sheer adrenaline tensed my muscles, giving me superhuman strength.

I screamed and screamed, pushing her with all my weight. A second later, she was off me, and then I jumped all over her.

Men roared louder, drowning us out. One guy tried to climb onto stage.

"Fucking hell, look at these bimbos go!"

"Why's the hell's the little one still got her damned clothes on?"

"Cat-Fight! Cat-Fight Cat-Fight!"

I gave the stripper's hair another raging pull. I would've done it this time, torn her stupid locks straight out of he head – if only somebody else hadn't yanked on mine.

Frozen, I looked up.

For a second, I swore I'd started hallucinating. Firefly hauled me up into his monstrous arms, threw me over his shoulder, and headed backstage.

"Don't you dare break this up, you bastard!" I snarled, talking through the pain still rattling through my teeth. "Don't. You. Dare!"

NEVER LOVE AN OUTLAW

I pounded his back, cursing up a storm, catching one more glimpse of Skin and a couple other big bikers shuttling Trig through the throngs of screaming drunks.

"Let me go, damn you! Don't you know the other bitch started it?"

"Babe, I don't give a fuck. Right now, I've had it up to *here* with your shit. Any more, and your hot little ass is gonna feel the sunny side of my hand."

My shit? If he didn't have such a strong hold on me, I'd have whipped around and slapped him across the face.

Harder than I'd ever done it before. I wanted to hurt him, just like the past week had torn at me, no matter how insane it seemed.

I didn't care if he made good on his promises to pull my pants down and spank me.

Didn't care if it would've boiled my blood so hot it came pouring out my ears.

Jesus, I didn't fucking care if I'd have loved every second of it. Didn't care if it distracted me from the lunatic anger quaking through my body, imagining his violent hands slapping my ass as red as the neon lights in the club.

Nothing else mattered except finding Trig and finishing what we'd started!

I was still kicking when he put me down. I touched my lip, wincing when I felt the big cut I'd gotten from one of the bitch's punches, and hoped to holy God the skank wasn't carrying any diseases.

Supposedly, Meg tested all the girls regularly for babies and STDs. And right now, a very disappointed looking

Megan Willow Wilder stared me down, her arms folded.

Firefly made damned sure I kept my butt in the chair where he'd planted me.

"I'm disappointed," she said, shaking her head. "Believe it or not, despite what this place is, we're supposed to keep a certain order around here."

Firefly nodded. I looked at them both defiantly.

The way I burned for him – *that* was dangerous – especially when the only thing blazing should've been rage and shame.

"I couldn't take it anymore," I said. "I thought I could, and I'm sorry I let you down. I just hit my limit and…I broke, Meg."

I closed my eyes, feeling the devilish energy seeping out of me, leaving me totally drained. "Honestly, that's what happened. The things those girls said, the way they treated me, letting everything roll off their shoulders."

"Trig won't be working no more, darlin'," Firefly rumbled.

Meg's looked at him, surprised, and so did I.

"Club needs bitches it can rely on to shake their tits and asses. We don't need loose cannons."

"Um, excuse me, do you *know* how hard it is to find girls who test clean in this town?" I'd never heard Meg sound so sour.

"Yeah, doll, as a matter of fact, I do. No, I didn't get an education about manpower in my daddy's business, and I don't know how to crunch numbers like Skin. But I do know any crew's downright fucked with the wrong people

– including this one." He spoke like he'd just launched a billion dollar startup.

I wanted to laugh at his arrogance. Like he knew anything about business?

"Dust'll hear about this shit sooner or later, and I know he'll agree with me. You think this girl went off like a grenade because the stripper bitch looked at her wrong? Fuck that! She had a good reason."

"Firefly, I'm sure she's telling the truth. I *know* who started it. But losing Trig is going to hurt us. We're stretched thin as it is."

"Let me make it up to you," I said, standing. "Look, I don't know this business, this world, the way either one of you do. But I'm not giving up, guys. Not after today. I'm going to do my job right. These girls respect toughness. They won't get away with pushing me around anymore. I won't let them drag themselves out a minute late unless there's a damned good excuse. Give me another chance. I'll *make* them make this club rich!"

"Well, I'll have to talk to Dust," Meg said, staring at the ground before she looked at me. "If it's up to me, I'll give you another chance. Once, I had to adapt to this world, too. Growing pains are the norm, not the exception."

She pulled her leather jacket tight, the one with PROPERTY OF SKIN patched on the backside, like it insulated her from some ugliness she'd lived a long time ago.

"Prez'll leave her be," Firefly said. "Let me talk to him. We'll trump this whole fuckin' incident up to nothing but a skank with a screw loose. I believe in Cora. She's a smart girl."

I blinked. No way. Had I heard him right?

He couldn't really be…complimenting me?

He looked at me then, a reassuring smile shining in his ice blue eyes. "Also believe she'll come around and learn to behave herself."

Asshole. I bit my lip, only giving him a pass because he was on my side tonight.

"Whatever. Just…get her home until I can sort out the chaos," Meg said, frustration overwhelming her. "Ugh. And to think I left daddy's company for this," she muttered to herself.

Firefly stepped up to me and stuck out his big hand. "Walk with me, babe. We'll make sure you're safe from a concussion or some shit, and then I've got a surprise for you. Something that oughta go far to take the edge off that stick up your ass."

"Okay! You're really pressing your luck," I said, taking his hand reluctantly.

More surprises were exactly what I didn't need today. But if it was half as thoughtful as the wine the other night, then maybe he'd prove me wrong.

I caught myself as we headed for his bike, shaking my head. What the hell was happening here?

Firefly shouldn't be rattling around in my head when I'd just survived the fight with a stripper. I'd narrowly avoided losing my job, my only chance to stockpile some cash for the life I wanted after all this.

Every muscle I had tensed up, and I realized with horror what was happening.

The big, arrogant, bossy bastard was kicking his way into my heart, one day at a time. *God help me.*

* * * *

We went by the clubhouse for half an hour. An older woman, Laynie, checked me over while Firefly stood outside the bathroom.

She took my pulse, pressed several points, and asked me to rate the pain. If I hadn't known any better, I'd have sworn she was a nurse or a doctor at one time.

But why would someone like that be working for this club?

Money goes a long way. I reminded myself. *Money is probably what got daddy killed.*

Thankfully, she didn't say much. I needed the peace and quiet.

When it was all over, she turned me out with a clean bill of health. Firefly grabbed my hand again as soon as I stepped out.

"Ow! Just because she says nothing's broken doesn't mean I don't have some scrapes and bruises."

He loosened his grip. "Whatever. They can't be half as bad as the damage growing on your soul. I'm fixing to undo a little of that tonight."

"What are you talking about?'

Firefly flashed me a sharp look, lifted his free hand, and pressed a finger against those big, rough lips surrounded by his stubble. "Quiet, babe. You'll find out soon enough."

Ass. Naturally, I thought about those lips doing dirty, unspeakable things the entire time we were on his bike, riding through Knoxville.

My hands didn't want to press too tightly to his rock hard abs while we rode. This, right here, was starting to feel *very* dangerous.

If I let myself hold onto him the way I really wanted, if I threw common sense to the wolves, then I'd come closer to the awful fantasies about his rough hands, his lips, his muscles, and his piney masculine scent.

I wasn't stupid. Any girl who came too close to this man for her own good was bound to get burned.

That wouldn't happen to me. I wouldn't let myself become the latest tinder to be stamped out the morning after I let him have his way.

* * * *

"Damn, I should've brought a fucking blindfold. Would've made this shit a lot more fun." His cryptic words kept coming as we parked in front of a cozy looking building.

I bit my tongue to keep myself from imagining all the things a bastard like him could do alone with just a girl and a blindfold. He grabbed me, helped me off his bike, and led me toward the door, fishing a key from his pocket for the main entrance.

"Third floor's where we're at. Shame I couldn't get anything lower, but fuck, the view makes up for it."

My heart began pounding as he led me up some stylish

steps, my hand in his.

We stopped in front of a dark wooden door and I watched him change keys on the ring. One push, and we were inside it, standing in an apartment with spartan décor and nice wood finishes. It smelled piney, almost like a lodge.

"Here, darlin'. Catch." Firefly barely gave me a second to turn around before he threw the keys he'd been holding.

My hand darted out. I grabbed them before they hit the floor. "What…what is this?"

He snorted. "What the fuck does it look like, babe? This is your new place. Assuming you wanna cool your heels somewhere else that isn't my bed at night, anyway."

His cocky smile said anything involving me and his bed would've been just fine. Holy crap, that reminded me…

I quickly walked through the apartment, a nice single bedroom unit. Kitchen couldn't have been more than ten years out of date, and it seemed fully furnished – everything except a TV.

In the bedroom, there was a dresser next to a brand new bed, a big furry blanket with an outline of a black bear thrown over it.

"The blanket's a loaner," he said, walking up behind me. "That shit's been in my family for years, but it'll do 'til we can figure something else out. Can't guarantee how long you'll be here, or how long you'll want to be. If trouble comes to town looking for you, then the Prez'll want us to move, and I can't do shit about it."

We locked eyes. I nodded, understanding the strict terms attached. Hell, for a place this nice – *my* place – I'd have put my lips all over him.

I let out a sigh, desperate not to let him see it. Jesus. The hot spot forming between my legs told me that wasn't just a torturous hypothetical.

"You follow me, right, darlin'?" The intense look on his face that said he could've eaten me alive didn't help cool the heat one bit.

I nodded, tilting my face toward the shadowy bedroom, hoping it would hide the flush blossoming on my cheeks. "Yeah. Everything's real tentative, I get it. Any other rules I should know about?"

"You check in with me twice a day. I'll still be driving you to the Heel and back to make sure nothing crazy happens. You got any other big plans to go out, I'm the first one you tell. Remember, same shit the Prez told you holds true 'til this shit blows over – no contact with anybody you knew before the club. Can't have your friends asking any weird questions or dragging you out for drinks when the mean motherfuckers we're worried about could show up any time."

"Do I ever get to find out *who* I should be looking for behind my back?"

He hesitated. "Only when it's over, or when the Prez says so. For now, you see anything that says Torches, you run. Move your ass, and then pick up the phone, stat. Same goes for any guys sniffing around you, acting all suspicious."

"Got it."

"I meant what I said back there," he growled, grabbing me and pulling me close to his chest. "You're a smart girl,

Cora. You play by the rules we've set, and everything'll be just fine. We'll get through this. You'll never have to be up close and personal with yours truly ever again."

Oh, God. Why did that sound so horrible?

The ache between my legs doubled. I gave him a quick squeeze and then tore myself away, before he could find out how badly I wanted to find out where those dark stripes going up his arms went.

"I won't forget this, Firefly. You're...you're a good guy. I think." It sounded so stupid, but there wasn't any other way to say it.

He smiled, ran his fingers through my hair, and then pulled away from me, heading for the door. "You've got drinks, plus a few more wraps and salads in the fridge. Get yourself a fucking pizza or something. I'd have torn my balls off by now if I had your diet, eating the same fat free bullshit all the time."

I was still laughing as the door opened. He disappeared, leaving me alone.

Really, truly alone, for the first time since the awful evening when I'd come home to daddy's suicide.

I closed my eyes, savoring the silence. At the clubhouse, there'd always been someone knocking around, laughing, swearing, or else smashing their empty bottle into a bin full of them. I couldn't count the times glass falling against glass had woken me up all those miserable hours.

I didn't miss it. Nothing about the clubhouse appealed to me except the giant dog. Nothing.

Except that wasn't strictly true, was it?

Don't lie. There's no one here you need to hide it from.

That voice in my head wasn't wrong. If I had to be honest, I was starting to miss him.

Firefly chiseled a little piece of me away every time I climbed on his bike, held his hand, or looked into his crisp blue eyes. I fought to hold onto it, knowing I'd lost too much of myself to hell itself.

But his tools were too precise, too powerful, too prone to smothering me in this insane schoolgirl crush coming on like a fever.

How long before I stopped fighting? *Good God!*

And if I caved, if I let my lips touch his some dark, wild night, when I'd left the sadness behind just long enough to take a risk, where would it take me?

I couldn't handle another tragedy so soon. No more loss.

No matter how deep he stabbed me with his beautiful eyes or the warmth of his rogue embrace, I had to keep it together. I had to keep fighting.

I wouldn't. Couldn't. Didn't dare give in, or else it would be the end of me.

This man had heart breaker written in his soul, and the second I gave him mine, he'd destroy what little I had left.

V: Rules of Engagement (Firefly)

I blew the dummy's head clean off, shattering it like a rotten white pumpkin. Somewhere behind me, Joker's boy barked, halfway to the boom in a lion's roar.

"Shit, bro, can't tell who's fucking louder – that mutt or Firefly's gun!" Sixty laughed, cleaning his rifle. I turned around and saw him staring at the Veep, not-so-patiently waiting for his turn in the little box we'd set up for target practice.

Joker pulled his switchblade out of the stump he'd been carving, his eyes blazing on Sixty. "You call my purebred a mutt again, and I'll find somewhere else to sharpen my blade."

Crazy motherfucker had a look in his eyes like he meant it too. Sixty put his hands up, a shaky grin on his face.

"Aw, hell, Veep. You know I didn't mean it. Maybe if he'd got himself a name by now, I wouldn't be having to grasp at shit to call him."

"Name's Bingo," Joker growled. Behind him, the big dog puffed up, and let out a loud yip.

"Bingo?" I asked, turning around. Sixty rubbed a slow

hand across his face, no doubt suppressing a laugh.

"Grandpa's choice. It fits. The old man spends enough time playing that shit at the home, and the dog took a real shine to him." Joker stuffed his blade back in his pocket and crouched, stroking the wolfhound's massive head.

"What about you, brother? Has that stray we brought in got herself a new name yet from working at the Heel?" Sixty grinned.

I wanted to march right over and wipe that dirty fucking look off his face. "Fuck, no. Told you before, she's not taking her clothes off. She's helping Meg."

"Yeah, well, you know how the culture is. Girl's always end up doing more than they bargained for the longer they deal with skanks and a buncha horny drunks. Money's money, and it starts to get real sweet. 'Specially those nice girls – they act out the most when they get a sniff of their first dick, or maybe just their first dollar…"

Club charter said you never pointed a weapon at a brother without a damned good reason. Right now, I had to fight with everything I had to keep my gun trained on the ground.

"Today's your lucky day, brother. You're getting one good break you don't deserve. I'm gonna give you one chance to get up, apologize, and walk the fuck away before I break your jaw." I took several heavy steps toward him, watching the little shit's goatee twitch.

"Skin would've done it by now, if you'd shat on his old lady as much as you did my girl. You're so damned stupid, you're wrong. These girls aren't dumb fucking sluts – not like the pussy you've got warming your dick every other night."

With a dark look, Sixty stood, clicking the last piece of his rifle into place. He walked inside cradling it without looking back, slinking off to find a bottle and one of his best drinking mates like Crawl.

Joker looked at me, still stroking Bingo. I cocked my head and spoke through clenched teeth.

"What? Brother needs to learn when to shut the fuck up. He's always been bad about running his mouth, leading himself into trouble he oughta know full well to stay the hell away from."

"He ain't the only one."

Ah, shit. Now I'm gonna get a lecture from Mister Crazy Eyes? I thought. *Where the fuck did I sign up for this shit?*

"You wanna elaborate?" I growled, standing back and lifting my gun. I aimed at the last dummy I hadn't blown to smithereens, its paint chipping off, giving it one ugly looking face.

We'd gotten ourselves a small army of the damned things from a junk run for bike parts a couple months ago. All the boys used 'em for target practice now.

"Sixty's better with his face buried in a bottle. So are you, brother," Joker said, his voice a low, guttural whisper. "You're calling her your girl. You're getting too attached. Prez told me he warned you. Doesn't look like you're listening."

My gun barked. *Shit.*

My shot only grazed the dummy, took half its face off, and left the other half staring at us in an even more fucked up, creepy way than it had been before.

"That's my biz, Veep. Nobody else's. I'm man enough to keep my dick from dragging with a mind of its own. What happens between me and Cora, that'll stay behind closed doors. Won't ever become a problem for the club."

"Bullshit!" Joker spat, wiping his blade on one thigh. "You ignore Dust's advice, point blank and stupid, it becomes his problem. That makes it the club's, too."

We shared a long, tense look. Between us, the big, hairy wolfhound looked confused, wondering why two men who shared the patch were suddenly at each other's throats.

Too bad that'd been the norm half the time in this club. Scarce coin and pussy turned men on each other, but we always rallied before the big dogs from outside came in and tore us apart.

Didn't doubt for a second every man who called me brother would take a bullet to save my ass, and I'd do the same for them. We had our disagreements. Big and small and completely fucked up.

But we always rallied. Always. And I told myself I wouldn't let any pussy come between it – even though Joker's words pissed me right off.

I didn't get it. His concerns were bullshit.

Who cares what the fuck happens between me and Cora? He's acting like it'd be any different than all the other times, like when Skin got the whole club behind the whore he rescued.

I looked at him, watching as he cleaned his blade, the only thing he seemed to care about besides club duty and that damned dog.

"Brother, you know I've always put this club first, second, and third. You think that shit'll stop because I'm chasing some skirt the Prez doesn't like me going after, you're wrong. Wrong as fuck." I kicked the empty shell casing on the ground with my boot. "Go ahead and squawk about how I'm after his best friend's daughter. Rat me out to Dust. I don't give a shit. By the time he gets my dick beneath his blade, it'll have been up inside her, and then I'll be done having anything to do with her. I'm gonna fuck this shit outta my system, and then none of us'll have any more distractions."

"I'm no rat," Joker growled, holding up his blade to study it. He laid his hand down flat on the old stump, his dog at his side, and spread his fingers.

Great. I turned away in disgust. He couldn't help giving everybody around him a freakshow, ready to risk his fingers again on his ritual, his trademark, stabbing down into the empty spaces on the wood.

"Prez'll find out sooner or later, whatever the fuck you do. Whatever, ain't my problem. Last time I try to save myself some grief before I gotta find a new Enforcer."

"Save it. I'm not a fucking fool," I snapped. "I'm not going anywhere."

"Truth is, we're all fools here, brother," he said, slowing the thrusts of the knife between his fingers. "I'm not just telling you this shit because I make whatever Prez says law. Just don't want to see you fucked over."

We shared a long, tense look before he spoke again.

"Go away, Firefly. Get away from her. Go back to

pumping iron, boozing, and fucking bitches you won't remember. That's the kinda fool this club needs – anything different is gonna make you dangerous, make you stupid, and weaken us all."

Fuck him. I'd run outta shit to say.

I walked, slinging my shotgun over my shoulder and heading into the clubhouse. The dog whined behind me, drowned out by the steady, quicker *thump-thump-thump* of the crazy Veep's blade on wood. One day, the psycho would take a finger off doing that shit.

Today, it made him feel alive, just about the only thing that ever brought a spark to his eyes and adrenaline into his blood.

Bastard was right about one thing – every man wearing this patch was reckless in one way or another. Up until today, I'd have sworn he was the only fucker here who was certifiably insane.

But as I headed for the weight room we'd set up for a workout, I had to wonder. Veep's words made too much sense. And that made me want to kick holes in the wall.

My brain, my body, my whole fucking system couldn't un-see it. All my weaknesses, the chinks in the armor I'd forged for more than a decade in the trenches.

Shit stuck to my head, and wouldn't fucking leave. Not even when I had my shirt off thirty minutes later, finishing my tenth set of reps with a couple hundred pounds hanging over my head, sweat pouring down me in rivulets.

The girl was fucking me as bad as I wanted to fuck her – maybe worse.

I told myself I'd be done with it as soon as I finally had her. Shoving my cock in the pink and feeling them shake and scream always cured me before. Soon as my seed was dumped and the fire in my nerves got doused, I moved on, never looking back.

Same damned thing had to happen here. Even if she carried a little more risk because the Prez was soft on her outta some bullshit obligation I didn't understand.

I'd own her, dump her, and move the hell on.

Fuck, I had to.

If I started feeling more for this woman than just the urge to lose myself in her tight, untamed cunt, then all the crazy shit Joker warned about was on the table. And if it got to that point, I had an ugly feeling I'd wind up even crazier than him, blind to everything I'd ever worked for by pussy doing its voodoo magic.

"Goddamn." I sat up and swore.

Lifting usually calmed my ass down, but today, it wasn't doing shit. I toweled off and fought the urge to rush the punching bag, sweat myself stupid 'til I passed out by throwing punch after punch at the sleek, black leather.

I settled for five more reps, increasing the weight 'til it took my whole body to stop my biceps from popping outta my skin. I grit my teeth 'til they nearly shattered and counted out each blinding, heavy load I pressed.

One. That was for the first day I saw her, the wounded little dove, sexy and sassy on the darkest day of her life.

Two, three. That was forgetting to wash my pillows, breathing in her scent all night, and waking up with my dick so swollen and hard I could've used it to bust concrete.

Four. That was for threatening to spank her, imaging how she'd squirm, scream, and squeak when my palm crashed against her skin. She'd probably come when I tanned her ass without me even touching her clit, and then I'd lose my fucking load in my pants. *Fuck.*

Five. Those goo-goo eyes she made at me last night, when I gave her the apartment. Couldn't stop imagining those ocean blue eyes staring up at me while her lips were wrapped around my cock, sucking me off like she needed my seed in her belly to stay sane.

"Fuck!" Snarling, I pushed the barbell overhead one more time, barely shoving it back into place before it smashed my ribs.

Every damned muscle in my body died, save one. My hungry, crazy dick stood up in my shorts like a missile ready to fly.

I had to stamp this girl outta my head, sooner or later. There were only two ways to do that – fuck her, or level with her.

Option A would've been a whole lot more fun.

But option B – that evil, boring motherfucker – might be the only thing in the world that'd stop me from bedding her and screwing up my head forever.

I ignored the blood pounding in my dick the whole way through my shower. Then I dressed, stuffed the extra shit in my locker, and got on my bike.

In a couple hours, I'd be picking Cora up and driving her home after another late shift at the Heel. Hadn't heard from her since she'd checked in this morning.

The whole long ride through the Smokies, staring down at Knoxville's lights winking through the night, I swore I'd get this square.

Tonight was the last night Cora fucking Chase was gonna be rattling around in my head like a wet dream I'd had for a thousand years.

Tonight, I'd tell her where the fuck we stood. Then I'd find the nearest bottle of Jack, Johnnie, or Jim and two dirty sluts who'd slobber on me all night.

I'd drink, fuck, and burn her outta my head forever.

* * * *

"Trish, Velvet, Cream – you're all up! Three girl act. Move your asses." The light caught Cora's blonde hair something beautiful as she clapped her hands.

She slapped her palms together in a steady, loud clamor 'til the dancers moved. Their heels clicked across the floor. If they grumbled, they kept that shit to themselves, high tailing it through the curtain to the stage, where a rush of horny catcalls greeted 'em.

None of the bitches mouthed off. Whatever the fuck she'd become, it clearly worked. I barely recognized the anxious little caterpillar we'd picked up about a week ago. She'd come outta her cocoon all spitfire.

Maybe Sixty was right about this place changing girls. Just not the way he said.

Whatever was happening here, it was dangerous. Seeing

the shy girl slink away and the woman emerged made me want to bite her damned sexy lip even more.

"You about done?" I said, putting my hand on her shoulder.

She whipped around and smiled when she saw me. "Firefly!"

Fuck. Seeing this honey all over her lips wasn't gonna make tonight easier. I'd have preferred vinegar for what I had coming – plus it would've anchored my cock down better.

"Yeah, sorry, I was just wrapping up. Night manager was a little late, and all the girls move faster when I tell them, ever since the fight." She grinned. "Feels good, to be honest. I never thought I'd be great at this job, but that's changing."

"Yeah, babe, you're doing well. No fuckin' doubt about it."

Goddamn, I've gotta stop calling her babe, I reminded myself.

"Listen, we'd better hit the road so I can get you back to your place. Weather says it's gonna be storming tonight."

"So what?" She wrinkled her nose and pushed a hand through her hair, fluffing it, like giving the threat of getting soaked the finger. "We can wait it out. Let's have a drink at the bar across the street. If it's still raining when we head out, I don't mind. I've got a nice, warm shower waiting at home, thanks to you."

She did it. Before I knew what the fuck was happening, her little arms were around me, her nails digging into my muscle like I'd just handed her the moon.

Fuck. Shit. I had to put a stop to this now, dammit, or I never would.

"No more of that," I growled, pushing her away. That lead ball in my chest did a fucking nosedive, and my dick demanded to know *what the fuck* I was doing.

"Huh?" Confusion clouded her beautiful face. Didn't make me want her one bit less.

Nothing about this shit was easy.

"This crush, Cora. Don't bullshit me. We've both got something going between us, clear as lightning cutting through the summer sky. Just as dangerous too because we ain't grounded. I know the Prez told you to stay the fuck away from me. He said the same to me. Means we can't have this flirting and teasing."

I didn't tell her he'd threatened to cut my dick off. Wasn't sure it'd have mattered anyway with the way she shook her head, stepped up to me, that defiant smile pulling at her lips.

Christ. Was she wearing gloss? I wanted to bury those hot little lips in mine, set them on fire 'til they burned right off her pretty face.

"And you're just going to let him push you around?"

"Nobody's telling me to do shit, darlin'. This is *my* decision. I helped you out, and as far as I'm concerned, my job's done. Any man in this club with a little free time can drive you home. From now on, you'll be riding with our prospects, Tinman and Lion. I've got other shit to shovel."

"That's too bad. Really." She tried to sound upbeat, but I could hear the hurt invading her voice. That sassy look on her face became pure poison. "I'll have to get drinks with them, I guess. Maybe they'll be more fun than you, Firefly."

Fuck. More fun? What kind of goddamned fun was she talking about?

"Shit, I've been looking all over for you, brother." I was ready to open up on her, tell her the prospects didn't know shit about having a good time, when a voice boomed behind us.

Skin waited for me to turn around, wearing the same smug ass smile he always had. "What do you want?"

"Two things. Meg says you're doing great, Cora. The shit that happened the other night was nothing but a speed bump, and now we're riding smooth as a sheep's tongue."

"Sheep's tongue," I snorted. "Yeah, and you'd fucking know."

"Yeah, yeah, motherfucker," He shook me off without even losing his smile. "Second, Prez told me to come by to deliver the news in person. He says you've got a good thing going with this girl, and you've really helped diffuse what could've been a damned bad stick of dynamite."

Cora pursed her lips. We both wanted a piece of the jackal in front of us, acting like he was judge and jury.

I clenched my jaw. *Just get to the fucking point, asshole,* I growled inwardly.

"Shitty part is, he's hearing rumblings from Atlanta. Says the Torches have found out all about her old man, and their informants have already been sniffing around his old place. Crawl went by there earlier and said it was fucking ransacked. Somebody went through the police tape and turned it upside down, busted a few windows, looking for shit."

I looked at Cora. Her eyes were on the floor; sad, hurt, and angry as all hell.

Goddamn, I wanted to hold her. Not because my cock was telling me to for once.

Bad enough those assholes had driven her old man to blow his brains out. Worse that they'd sent somebody to turn her old home upside down, put holes through the walls and windows like a fucking dive.

"Prez is talking to Red Beard tomorrow," Skin continued. "He's mad as shit. Wants to know why our club isn't helping theirs track down the shit they say they're owed – including Jimmy's pretty little daughter."

She couldn't take it. Cora broke, covered her face, and walked away.

"She was standing right next to us, you fuck." My fists tensed hard at my sides. Didn't give a shit how dead they were from the workout a couple hours ago. Damn if they wouldn't have loved to bounce off Skinny boy's face just then.

"I know," he whispered. "Had to get her away because it's better she hears the rest of it coming from you, rather than me."

"What? Why's that? Brother, why you gotta be so fucking cryptic all the damned time?"

He smiled. "Cora needs one of our boys posted to her full time as long as the Torches are searching high and low. Prez's orders. Can't have her slipping outta sight, into a trap."

Oh, fuck. Fuck me with a screwdriver.

Asshole didn't even say it, but I read it loud and clear, felt it hit me right between my damned eyes. "Me."

"You got it." Skin nodded, scratching the stubble on his cheek. "Shit, don't look so fucking glum, brother. It's not like he's asking you to do anything more than up the time you're already spending with her, hauling her ass around."

"You're telling me this is a twenty-four hour op? When the fuck am I supposed to make sure the club's secure? I'm still the Enforcer. If we've got a snake closing in around us, then we've gotta have the guns and guys ready to make sure we don't get bit."

"We'll up security here at the Heel, too. You can leave her alone when she's working. But Prez says on the road, in the bed, outside the fucking bathroom – you stay on her." He looked at me, the trademark scar on his cheek catching the light. "Good thing the club pitched in to get her that nice place. It'll be a whole lot bigger for the two of you than your room at the clubhouse would've been."

"Fuck this. I'll talk to Dust myself," I growled, reaching for my burner phone.

"Go ahead. He'll tell you the same shit I just did. Then he'll wonder why the fuck you're wasting his time asking twice." Skin reached for my shoulder, slapped a brotherly hand on it, and risked me breaking his goddamned wrist. "Easy, brother. Just treat her right. All this'll blow over before you know it, and you'll be right back to fucking nameless whores who call you 'Fireball.'"

Enough bullshit.

I threw his hand off me and walked toward the exit, stuffing my phone back into my pocket. My shit-eating arrogant brother was right. Didn't doubt for a second what he passed along from Dust was truth.

I had to find Cora. She wasn't taking this shit any better than me – especially after what I'd started laying on her before Skinny boy showed up.

My hand slammed into the dented metal fire escape leading outside. Cold mountain air hit me in the face. I looked left, right, and finally found her by the dumpster, sitting on a cracked wooden post.

"You shouldn't be out here alone," I growled, coming to a stop behind her.

"And you should learn to mind your own business, Firefly." She slowly looked at me with her lips all twisted.

"Firefly," she snorted, shaking her head. "What the hell kind of name is that for a biker, anyway?"

She squealed when I reached down, swept her up, and pressed her into the wall. "Got it early on in this club, the night I took the prospect patch. We had twenty fucking Deads in a ten foot grave, except all the fucks were still breathing. They'd come to fuck us into line, assuming they didn't kill every one of us first. Thought they were smart motherfuckers for taking the Prez's ma, Laynie, holding her for ransom, having their way with her before we got her back. None of 'em had any brains left after I poured gasoline all over their evil asses and threw the match. All the brothers thought I enjoyed the screams almost as much as the Prez. My face glowed like the devil, listening to those assholes screaming, heading straight for hell…"

"You're all monsters," she whispered, the smart ass look on her face completely obliterated.

"Yeah, well, you're about to be seeing a lot more of this monster." I thumped my chest, waiting 'til her big blue eyes swirled with curiosity. "Much as I wanted to turn you over to the prospects, Prez says that ain't an option. You heard what Skin said – you've got bigger devils than us looking for you. Long as they're on your ass, I stay closer."

Her eyes rolled in her head like marbles as the full horror sunk in. Then they locked onto me, and her lips opened slowly.

"Oh. Awesome. If only I'd have known working my butt off here would just get me a constant babysitter. I'd have picked a few more fights."

"Watch it, woman," I snarled, making sure she could feel the heat of my words against her ear. "You're treading on seriously fucked up ground. You think I like this?"

I gripped her shoulders tighter, digging my fingers in 'til she shook her head. My dick jerked in my pants, pure instinct igniting, every inch of me up against her. So close.

Close enough to inhale her scent.

Close enough to feel her bristle.

Close enough to see every fractured part of those sweet blue eyes I wanted to go nova when I buried myself in her to the hilt.

Too. Fucking. Close.

"I'm just following orders here, same as you, darlin'," I said, easing up on her a little. "We've both gotta get through this, one day at a time. Breathing fire all over me won't do you any favors, and it sure as fuck won't make this easier. Let's call a damned truce and deal with it."

She looked at me, sharp and serious. For a second, I thought I'd actually talked some sense into the head attached to that perfect gold hair I wanted in my fist.

Then she rolled her eyes, and I heard her tongue cluck against the roof of her mouth. "Whatever you say, Fireball."

"Fuck."

Fuck! Every dark, animal instinct I'd been pinning down whenever I was with her tore through my bones and came ripping outta me.

I didn't stop to think. Just spun her around, ripped down her jeans, and had her soft panties in my hand a split second later. Fucking fabric nearly ripped as I jerked it down her thighs, snapping around her knees, lining her up just perfect for my aching palm.

"Don't you get it, darlin'? I'm trying to save your fucking life, and you're *still* calling me the wrong goddamned name after I warned you a thousand times!"

My hand struck her firm, sweet ass. Once, twice, three blistering times before she pointed her head at the sky and whimpered.

Oh, fuck.

Oh, mama.

What the fuck you doing? Hell, what's SHE doing?

My brain was too screwed up to figure out what was happening with any reason. That shit had gone straight out the window. I just had her pressed against the wall, half naked, squirming under my hand as I delivered five hard strikes against her skin, so rough each time her ass bounced.

On the fourth and fifth whacks, her knees bent forward. She bit her lip and made a muffled noise I'd heard on women a hundred times before – that little sound they made before they blew.

Every muscle must've tensed up in her body. The girl was about to come, and there was no fuckin' stopping it.

Cora came. Little minx convulsed, losing it on the spot, leaning against me and sucking in a rush of air. It burst out a second later in a sexy whine that nearly blew my dick up in a single heartbeat.

So wrong. So wild. So fucking *hot.*

My cock drove me fucking mad, filling up with lightning. I slammed her into the wall and held her as she came for me, one hand grabbing her ass, confirming I'd cracked her body's code in one vicious, fucked up moment…

Arching her back, she moaned louder, her little ass grinding against the bulge about to go nuclear in my pants. By some miracle, I held it in.

Resisting the urge to whip it out right there and force my way inside her hot, wet, wanting cunt was an even bigger miracle. Fuckin' water to wine level.

I stroked her hair as she came down from it, letting my hold on her soften. My lips pressed against her red hot ear, whispering the only thing I could think to say.

"Shit. Goddamn. Cora, fuck, I'm sorry."

Apologizing for finally doing what I'd wanted sounded

hollow as all hell. Too bad the little bitch on my shoulder I called a conscience forced it outta me.

Deep down, my cock cried for more. He wasn't the least bit sorry for the psycho shit that just happened out here. He just wanted me to pull her legs apart, fuck her 'til this torture blazing through every part of me was done.

My hands clasped her pants, her panties, feeling the wet spot that must've been brewing in the middle since before I'd stepped outside. *Fuck.*

She wanted me. Bad. And I'd just put the Berlin-fucking-wall between us.

I made a decision. Slowly, I pulled them up over her cool skin, gritting my teeth.

"Babe, are you —"

"Yeah." She cut me off before I could say okay. "Just…take me home. I don't want to talk about any of this."

Whatever. I knew I'd fucked up when she wouldn't even look at me on our way through the parking lot. She wedged her helmet tight to her head when I handed it to her, like she wanted to blot out the whole damned world.

No, probably just me. Fuck if I didn't deserve it, as much as she'd deserved my hand against her ass.

I rode through Knoxville's dark streets, conflicted the whole fucking trip to her building. Her grip on me was surprisingly tight for what just went down. She must've been fighting every urge in her to recoil, to run, to get the fuck away from me and this dirty underworld before it chewed her all the way up.

Cora's building came into sight. Turning my bike to the curb, I slowed down and killed my engine, standing up before she could pluck off her helmet and go.

"Wait." I stood up straight, and leaned down, my ice blue eyes meeting hers. "My job's to protect you. I can't have you holding any grudges, or thinking I'm gonna go off like a loose fuckin' cannon every time we're together. Whatever happened back there, I can't take it back. So, I'm giving you a chance to suck some of the poison outta your system."

She looked at me like I didn't understand. Had to spell it out for her.

"Babe, punch me in the damned face, as hard as you can, if you feel like it'll help."

Cora blinked. "You want me to hit you?"

"Yeah." I nodded. "Therapy or some shit. Hitting things always makes me feel better, especially if it's the fuckers I'm pissed at."

With a sigh, she ripped her helmet off, and then shoved it against my chest. "You really don't have a clue, do you? I need to go. You do your job, Firefly, and I'll do mine. That's all we need to worry about to get through this. There's no point in dwelling on anything else, just like you said."

Before I could stop her, she was gone, fumbling with her keys and slipping into building. I stood there in the cool Knoxville night. Tried to see the mountains looming over the city, but the thick gray clouds overhead painted them dark, invisible.

"Fuck," I grunted, tucking my helmet back on my head

and climbing on my bike.

I tore the hell outta there without a second glance.

I'd fucked up bad tonight, and I knew it.

All I'd wanted to do was march in with my goodbyes, hand her off to somebody else, and scrape her out of my goddamned life forever.

Prez's plans fucked that all away. My own raging lust did the rest.

Cora didn't realize it yet – or maybe she did, and just didn't show it. One way or another, we were both completely, irreparably fucked.

I couldn't keep this shit purely professional. Neither could she. I'd never had a chick come so fast without even stroking between her legs, and she went off like a goddamned landmine.

My cock wouldn't forget that shit. Neither would my mind, my body, my soul. No matter how much I'd hurt her or twisted her up tonight, neither would Cora.

Didn't need the cold mountain wind rifling through my hair to know we were on a collision course. Everything conspired to smash us together 'til we kissed, fucked, and suffered the consequences.

I took a long detour before I found my way back at the clubhouse that night. Spent at least a couple hours roaring through the dark, twisted mountain roads, screaming into the night. Probably damaged my fuckin' vocal cords cursing myself, the club, and God for what was steaming up ahead like a raging train.

Took half the night to make peace with it all.

By the time I dragged myself home, the first blue tint of day flickered on the horizon. I fished the spare key outta my pocket and slowly made my way into the apartment.

Thank fuck she was dead asleep in her room. I crashed out on the old sofa the club had pitched in to buy, and slept like mad, every part of me knowing she was just one wall away.

This wasn't just about the crazy ass push and pull between me and Cora anymore.

Shit, it wasn't even about fucking her, pinning her to the nearest flat surface, and emptying the fire in my balls a hundred times over.

Truth was, I'd fought like to hell to get her away. And I'd only brought her closer, came up close and personal with the silver bullet she'd planted in my heart.

Fuck it, the truth hurt. But I wasn't running no more.

I had to keep this girl safe.

I had to own her.

I had to make her mine 'til it didn't take my hand thumping against her ass to make her look at me with respect shining in those bright, pearly blues.

I wanted her to want me for real, to wear my brand and be proud of it. I'd make it all happen. God willing.

Fuckin' had to, sure as a maniac. Didn't give a single shit who I had to kill or what I had to suffer to do it.

The gloves were off, and they'd never go back on as long as my hands were hungry to finish what they'd started with Cora's sweet little ass.

VI: Stalked (Cora)

My ass stung the next day. Truly, the only reminder that the night before wasn't just a crazy dream.

Firefly did it. He'd spanked me. He'd thrown me against the wall, pulled down my pants, and put his palm to my flesh like he had a right to it.

I should've been horrified. But my body responded with a mind of its own, giving me the most explosive orgasm I'd ever had in my life.

The bitter aftermath hit nearly as hard.

I was shaking, exhausted, and ashamed when I walked into my apartment that night. I was strangely satisfied, too, as if he'd given me something I'd been craving and trying to fight forever.

Sick. Scary. *Wrong* on so many levels.

I couldn't begin to count them all. Hell, I couldn't even handle all the different things I had rushing through my brain, threatening to tear me in two.

I loved what he did to me, and I shouldn't have. I hated him – so I told myself, knowing it was a feeble lie.

Also knew I was more mixed up than I'd ever been

before, and the big question weighing on my mind as I tossed and turned that night felt like an anchor around my neck.

What now?

I couldn't begin to guess. There wasn't any fighting the order Skin sent down from Dust, to serve and protect, guarding me until the mysterious threat faded for good.

I'd gotten myself a full time bodyguard I never wanted. I couldn't tell which urge was strong – to kiss him, or slap him across his smug, gorgeous face.

My body knew exactly what I wanted. Desire hummed in every nerve, reminding me how amazing it had been to feel his dangerous strength pressed against me, striking hot, almost inside me.

Just…fuck. As if this wasn't hard enough.

The more time I spent with him, the more my need grew. That's why it stung a thousand times worse than the spanking when he'd threatened to rip it all away.

I needed the big, crude bastard in my life. Needed him even worse than the saner part of me needed him to stay the hell away.

There wasn't a manual here. There was no telling how I'd survive, but I had to try, one day at a time.

If the bad guys nobody would tell me about didn't get to me first, then maybe my own wild desire would. Whatever happened from here, I couldn't ignore the magnetism aiming my body and my mouth straight at him.

I couldn't just run, much less stay away, now that he'd been assigned to deal with me. When I heard him knocking on my bedroom door, I sat up, and pulled the blanket around me extra tight.

No more escaping it. I had to face my destiny.

* * * *

The Heel was a madhouse the next day. It almost took the edge off the quiet, awkward ride through town with Firefly. None of us said anything after he asked me about breakfast, and I told him I'd find something to order at the club.

A big group of firemen were in town for some kind of conference. The handsome, rowdy bunch of men buying lap dances left and right nearly gave some of the Pistols guys a run for their looks.

I stared out at the big men laughing while Tawny squirmed in front of them through the small crack in the curtain, making sure everything ran smoothly. So far, so good.

"Hey, don't stare too long. You might go blind – or else you'll make Firefly jealous." Meg came up behind me so suddenly I jumped.

"What do you mean? He's just my bodyguard," I lied, hoping the dark light backstage would hide the redness creeping across my cheeks.

"Whatever you say. No worries, we can keep it between us girls. Nobody needs to know you were eye-fucking all the man candy out there." She winked.

"No, it's not like that," I insisted. "I was just taking a quick look, doing my job, thinking."

"Mm-hmm. You do a lot of that, don't you?"

"My father was a lot like them once. Different branch of public service, sure, but he wore a uniform and would probably sneak off to places like this with his friends back when he was on the force. After my mother died, I mean."

Jesus, what the hell was wrong with me? Why was I thinking about what daddy did in his off hours, much less going to strip clubs?

"That's the way it goes with real men. They might wear different uniforms, but if the heart underneath it's true, then that's what really matters." Meg nodded sagely, as if she had a burning need to reinforce her own words so I'd believe them. She eyed the small ring on her hand.

Yeah, about that…daddy hadn't been true underneath. He'd gotten himself in deep trouble, handed me to these rough men who wore a different sort of uniform before I got killed, and left this world like a coward.

It still hurt to think of him that way. I hadn't even asked about his ashes, or what happened to our old house after I'd heard about the men on my trail ransacking it. Everything hurt too much.

"I'm talking about the outlaws," Meg said, studying the pain in my eyes. "They're good men, even Firefly. I wouldn't be walking around wearing Skin's name if it weren't true."

"These are the guys I was always told to stay away from. I respected the badge, and always did what my father told me." I shook my head, turning toward the loud hollers coming through the curtain. "I still can't believe it sometimes, the fact that I'm stuck living like this. Can you think of anything worse?"

"Easily." Her face darkened, and she turned around, walking toward the little office she used for running the place.

Something urged me to follow her. She didn't shut me out, and waved me into an empty chair when I followed her into the small, cluttered brain controlling the Ruby Heel.

"What happened to you?" It just came out of my mouth. "I see the kind of clothes you wear and the way you talk...you're a rich, educated woman. You're a misfit in this world, just like I am, aren't you?"

"I was thrown into it, the same as you. My family gave me everything. Easy, when you're born to the most powerful businessman in East Tennessee. I grew up spoiled, and acted out plenty. It got me in deep shit when I ran into the wrong man in the mountains." She looked down at her finely painted nails, always hot red or jade green, except they were a little chipped today.

"He took me. Enslaved me. Forced me to do despicable things with strangers. I was going to be auctioned off. The bastard whored me out, ruined my hope, made me wish every day I'd die in my sleep. Until one day a big, beautiful biker man came, and promised me the world. Skin saved me, Cora, in more ways than one."

My heart sank. I hurt for the pain in her voice, the half-forgotten agony just oozing out of her.

I bled for myself, too.

Suddenly, I had an inkling how much worse it could be.

My tragedy wasn't unique, and I *hated it.*

Nobody was looking out for me. Nobody cared. Dust, he made a lot of moves to keep me from dying because of his promises to my father, but he didn't know me.

He didn't care, beyond carrying out his mission. No one did, save for one man.

"And you decided to stay?" I asked. "After he helped you, I mean?"

"Well, obviously." Meg smiled. "This is my world now. Sure, growing up in a nice family and screwing around without a care in the world seemed like heaven, a long, long time ago. But this is where I really belong, running my own life, at the side of a man I love and owe my life to. We're engaged to be married soon. It's going to be the best day of my life."

"Why are you telling me all this?"

She folded her hands and leaned forward, staring into my eyes. "Because I want you to be more than just a drone. There's more to this life than just working and going home with the same sour look on your face, Cora."

"Uh, it's not like I'm able to go bar hopping all over town with the target that's on my back. Supposedly."

"I know," Meg said quietly. "But it won't be forever. One day, you'll be a free woman. You can hang this up, go back to teaching, and forget all the punches you've taken this past month. Or you can own this world, carve a piece of it for yourself, and find out what you're truly made of. You can kick ass, but you don't have to do it alone. The choice is yours."

I fought the urge to stand up, walk right out of her office, and slam the door so fucking hard my wrist snapped. I didn't come here looking for sisterly advice from this woman who was barely older than me, and wasn't much closer than a stranger.

Still, I respected what she'd suffered. I promised myself I wouldn't leave making a scene.

"Are we done here?" I said slowly, tasting the bitter cut of every word.

"Yeah. Go finish your shift and ride home with the man who's protecting you. If anything I said here today matters, don't tell me about it. Show me."

I stepped outside and gently closed the door behind me, resisting the urge to smash it. It would've been a nice substitute for the urge to obliterate all the screwed up shards of my life.

I wasn't fooling anyone, though. Not even myself.

Being a bitch to Meg after she'd tried to have a heart-to-heart wouldn't make things easier. It wouldn't drain the feelings I had for Firefly, or set me free.

That was up to me, and nobody else. My shift went by in a blur, hustling the girls out to the firefighters and the other drunks. By the end of the night, I was smiling.

I couldn't wait for him. Almost looked forward to hearing the growl of Firefly's motorcycle, or maybe just the rumble of his voice.

We'd sort this out, little by little, just like the mess in my own head.

* * * *

"Ma'am, I only had one backstage, honest!" A skinny brunette named Velvet clutched her cigarettes to her chest, as if I'd reach for her bare tits and snatch them away.

That's exactly what I did a second later. The girls had all bought my legend since I'd lashed out at Trig. I stuffed them into my pocket and let her tumble backwards before I shot her a sharp look.

"Take it up with Megan. You know the rules – no junk, not even the legal stuff, while you're on the clock. The club could also get fined. Employment regulations, and all that. I'll keep these for now. If Meg says you can have them back, well, that's up to her. Go!"

I pointed toward my boss' office. Velvet pouted, but she moved, clicking her high heels against the wooden floor.

The clock overhead ticked on. *Fifteen more minutes.*

"Holy shit. Cora fuckin' Chase?"

I whirled around and faced the gravely, slurred voice. A tall, older man I didn't recognize at first stood backstage, a tall beer in his hand.

Not his first, judging by the way he swayed while he looked at me.

"Tony Pearson?" I squeaked, vaguely recognizing the deadbeat dad. Mister Fisher had a lot of trouble with him in class, always getting into parent-teacher shouting matches over the phone when his kid, Billy, flunked quizzes.

"Yeah, fuck yeah. When did you turn into such a big

slut? Shit, Billy said you'd disappeared, stopped teaching altogether. Real big mystery…"

I pursed my lips. "That isn't what's going on here. Hey – stay back!"

I held out my hands. The drunk wasn't deterred. He moved, coming towards me, backing me against the tall dresser Velvet had just abandoned.

"Hot little cunt. Always knew you had a nasty side when I saw you, coming to the school to deal with that prick over Billy's shit. Fuck, how 'bout a couple kisses, princess? We'll call it payback for all those times you made me shit my pants over those fuckin' Fs you slapped on his papers!"

"You shouldn't be back here! Get out, before I call security."

The bastard grabbed me. His hands went all over, moving rough and sloppy. He went for my breasts, between my legs, through my hair.

Help! I looked around desperately, but I was all alone. The girls were all on break or else out on the floor, doing their acts.

He reached under my shirt, tearing at the blouse so hard I lost several buttons. I screamed, but the beat of the music through the curtain was too loud, drowning out everything except raw bass and wailing guitars.

"Get. Off!" I pushed him as hard as I could, but there wasn't any leverage. He'd thrown me across the dresser and his gut was too big, holding me down, slowly pushing his way between my legs while he felt up my skirt.

"Shuddup. You like it rough, we can play rough!" He

pulled my hair so hard it nearly ripped.

Goddamn it. This was going to ruin everything.

Even if somebody came back here and stopped him before something awful happened, I'd lose everything I'd built with the girls. Gossip ran deep in these circles. They wouldn't listen to a woman who'd been shredded by a drunken, stupid, dirty old bastard like him.

I wasn't going down like this. *Hell no!*

My teeth sank into his arm. He reared up, shaking me off with a roar, bringing his entire arm into the blow that landed on my cheek.

He hit me three times – or at least that's what I could count before I felt myself being dragged under.

Then the heavy weight against me lifted. I blinked, staring through the darkness, and saw Tony's bulk lifted high into the air like he had wires pulling him up from the ceiling.

He flew through the air and hit the floor. His body made several loud snaps. The broken ribs must've winded him. When he opened his mouth to scream, nothing would come out, and it was too late by the time Firefly's boot started ramming his gut.

"Drunken sack of shit! You stay the fuck off her and apologize if you wanna crawl outta here alive!" His hatred was the only thing harsh enough to cut through the music growling all around us.

The deadbeat choked, sputtered, and wrinkled his face into a brutal grimace with every kick. Against my better instincts, I ran up, desperately wrapping myself around

Firefly's neck, trying to reach him before he killed the asshole.

"Firefly, don't! You'll get us all in deep trouble if you don't just let him go." I pulled on his shoulders hard, digging my nails in, trying to get his attention. "You hurt him. Bad. That's what he deserves. I'm satisfied."

"Yeah? Well, fuck, babe, I'm not!" Another brutal hook hit in the drunkard's gut.

Tony was barely conscious now, staring up at me over Firefly's shoulder. Begging, without words.

Please. Stop him. He's gonna fucking kill me.

"What the *hell* is going on out here?" Meg came storming out with Velvet at her side, her phone in one hand. "Jesus, Firefly, stop! This man needs an ambulance."

"Stop kicking the shit outta the sorry, stupid fuck who tried to hurt Cora, you mean?"

My boss' eyes went wide. She looked at me while the stripper at her side wisely slunk away.

"It's true. He snuck backstage. Asshole was already drunk by the time he wandered back here. He recognized me. His kid used to be in one of the classes I helped with…he pushed me up against the dresser over there, tried to force himself on me…"

Firefly's fists twitched. I could tell he was just a second away from tackling the beaten demon on the ground, finishing him off. I grabbed his arm, jerked it into me, and mouthed a phrase when he finally looked at me, his blue eyes on fire.

No! You've hurt him enough. Please hold back, Firefly. For me.

I couldn't find the strength to say the words. So, I thought them, and hoped he'd understand, if only I touched him the right way.

With a growl, he nodded. Meg's shoe hit the ground with a resounding whack, and we both looked at her.

"God. Damn. It!" She furiously tapped her phone, eyeballing us every other second. "I'm going to have to let Skin know. It won't be easy talking our way out of this one, if this man decides to press charges, or does something worse."

On the ground, Tony groaned, rolling into a fetal position. Firefly crouched, gave him a slap across the face, and looked dead into his eyes.

"You hear the woman, asshole? Huh?" He wrapped his fingers around the asshole's neck, and didn't let up until Tony nodded. "Good. I'll tell you exactly what's gonna happen here. We'll have you hauled off breathing in a little bit. You'll have some down time and some big fucking bills for me busting you up. I swear to Christ, you'll smile at every one of 'em, without so much as a peep about how you can't handle it. You're never stepping foot in this club again, motherfucker. If you so much as see an attorney for a free consult, you *will* see me again. I'll finish everything we started tonight. And you'll lose your chances to drink another fuckin' drop of booze when I cut your tongue out, or jack that worthless little stump between your legs when my blade takes it off, too."

Firefly reached near his belt. In a flash, his switchblade came out. He held it firm, cold, and menacing against the drunkard's throat.

"We got an understanding? Tell me now. I need to know, before the medics our girl's calling make their way here. Hurry the fuck up!"

Tony nodded, vigorously, his eyes bulging. I'd never seen panic dancing so wildly in anyone's eyes before. Not since daddy, but this time there was no sympathy. No mercy.

Satisfied, Firefly put the knife away, and stood up, giving the beaten animal on the ground one more look of utter contempt.

"Best fucking timing in the whole damned world. Showed up a little early to pick you up, trying to smooth things over."

I nodded, and walked with him past Meg. They ushered us away with a furious wave, desperate to get us out of there so she could handle the backstage mess we'd left her.

It wasn't until we were outside that I noticed I still had my arm linked tight with Firefly's. He'd saved me for the second time. All the worries and fears I'd had just hours ago melted away in a shot of adrenaline and a chaser of warm, manly body heat.

The thunder in his eyes flashed again as he reluctantly let go, helping me onto his bike. We'd have words at the apartment, no two ways about it.

Unlike before, I was ready.

Lord, I was ready for *anything*.

* * * *

"You hungry? Saw this morning we're running low on groceries. We can stop off in town and pick a few things up, if you want."

I shook my head, hugging him close as we rode down the dark, shadowy streets. It seemed like summer would never come. These spring nights still chilled me to the bone.

I'd have frozen if it weren't for his body heat. I put my face into his shoulder and breathed his rough, masculine scent, wondering what the hell I was doing.

None of this was right. Sheriffs' daughters weren't meant to savor outlaws' heat.

No matter how crooked daddy was, I shouldn't have been riding so close, imagining all the ways he could fling my body around on the bed. I'd never craved anyone as badly as I did Firefly that moment, and it scared the hell out of me.

The ride went by in no time flat. When I opened my eyes, we were back at the apartment, his engine rumbling to a cold stop. He stood up, reached for my hand, and yanked the helmet off my head.

"Last call for better food, or it's pizza tonight, babe."

"Whatever works." I felt like a schoolgirl with a stupid crush following him inside.

Damn, why did I feel *anything* after he'd tried to push me away earlier this week? After he jerked down my pants like he owned my body, smashed his hand against my ass, growling in my ear...

Wet didn't begin to describe the ache between my thighs. No, this desire leaked out of me, caused me to lick my lips secretly while my pussy throbbed, praying to be filled.

Everything pulsed open, slick and wanting, even when I watched him do something mundane like climb up the stairs in front of me. The big, beautiful biker always towered over me. I watched his muscles flex while he climbed, his skin scrawled with the menacing inks I'd see in my most feverish dreams.

Jesus, girl. Keep it together, I told myself. *You were almost taken against your will back there.*

Nothing sexy about it. I don't care if the sexiest man alive just saved you from getting tainted by a nasty goblin...

Aw, shit. Maybe it matters after all.

Yes, yes I do.

I care. I care about feeling him, tasting him, having him, dammit. More than I'll ever admit.

Down the little hallway, Firefly stopped, jamming his key into the lock and popping the door. He gave me a sharp look, caught me chewing my lip.

I wanted to sink right through the floor. My veins were still swimming in adrenaline, all the shocks I'd suffered over this unbelievable month stacked against me, plus the latest humiliations tonight.

The door jerked open, and he ushered me in. I headed right for the couch while he pulled out his phone, trying to find somewhere to grab dinner from.

He snorted, and I stared, causing him to look up. "Text from Skin. Says that worthless piece of shit I stomped at the Heel's been carted off. Stupid motherfuck had better remember what I said about keeping his damned lips shut…"

"You did plenty, Firefly. You saved me." I only realized how big and watery my eyes felt when he gave the floor a soft kick.

"Shit, I'm no hero, Cora. Quit looking at me like that." He paused, locking my eyes in his. "Did the only decent thing a man should when he walks in on something like that. If Skin's old lady hadn't showed up in time, I'd have killed the fuck and dropped his sorry carcass in the woods. Wrong timing."

"No." I stood up, walked over, and put my hands gently on his shoulders. "You did everything you could, Firefly. The timing was perfect. You've given me a second chance, or maybe this is my third. Honestly, I've lost count, but I appreciate all you've tried to do for me. I know I haven't been the most pleasant…"

"Babe, you've been fine." He reached up, grabbed my hand, and pulled it to his face.

Before either of us knew what was happening, his stubble grazed my skin. He kissed my hand, pressing those lips I'd wondered about a thousand times on my flesh.

A jolt ran through me.

Crazy. Electric. Sensational.

I'd never believed in love at first sight, much less first kiss, and that definitely wasn't happening here. Lust, on the other hand…

His teeth grazed my tender skin before he pulled it away, thrusting my hand back against his shoulder. *Oh, God.*

Some miracle stopped me from turning into a puddle on

the spot. Small favor, really, because now I had a lot more on my mind than lukewarm virgin fantasies.

I saw his lips all over me at once, igniting my skin, pushing me over the edge with just his touch, like the night he'd spanked me stupid.

They were finally coming. I'd have his rough, incredible lips on mine.

Conquering my mouth.

Moving down my throat.

Worshiping my nipples.

Turning my pussy into a hot, taut, sopping wet mess.

"You got something on your mind, or what?" he growled, tangling his fingers around my wrists to keep my hands glued to him.

"Nothing, really. Just thinking about circumstance."

Yeah. Right.

"What? The shit that brought you here?"

I nodded. With a growl, he jerked me closer with both hands, hanging mine across his shoulders. I didn't resist – quite the contrary when I let go and fell against him – begging to be closer.

"Dust has got me on you full time for good reason. All the dark and deadly fuckery heats up from here, Cora. You know it, don't you? Tell me you feel that shit coming, sure as a mountain wind."

Yes. Something was coming, anyway. Melting me from the inside-out.

A chill ran up my spine, cutting through the heat. Yeah, I knew it.

Of course I did. And it didn't matter, none of it did, just as long as I had him protecting me.

"I don't know anything," I whispered. "You won't tell me what I'm really running from, and neither will the other guys. What else can I do except listen to everything you say?"

Crap. I realized how much my voice was trembling.

Firefly looked up. Sparks of amusement flashed in his eyes, before they winked out in the icy blue fire that always smothered them, the same glow that filled his whole face.

"I don't share club biz unless it means keeping you safe." He drew a long breath, guiding me to move in front of him by the hands. "Looks I finally have to. Fuck."

He stood, guiding us both to the couch, where he sat down first, jerking me onto his lap. "Your old man got himself in some bad shit, and left everybody else to clean it up. Same thing Dust told you. Had a real hard-on for gambling, and he borrowed some money from another MC called the Torches, down in Atlanta."

My heart beat a hundred miles an hour. He softly fisted my hair, pulling me deeper into his lap, twisting my head so my ear was aimed at his lips.

I tried not to sweat from the one-two punch of being laid across Firefly's magnificent body like this, while he whispered all the secrets I'd yearned for deep in my ear.

Then he spoke again. His hot breath caressed my earlobe, racing down my neck, almost causing me to explode, just as much as his hand grabbing at my thigh. He held me where he wanted me, open for whatever he wanted to say – *or do.*

"Babe, listen to me real fuckin' careful. More than you've ever paid attention to anyone, about anything." I tried not to tremble, feeling his hand moving up my thigh, stroking and teasing. "The Torches want everything your daddy ever owned to pay his debt. That means you, too. You're collateral, Cora. They'll kill you, fuck you, sell you – whatever they think's gonna bring them the most coin, or else the most satisfaction."

I shook my head, sadness mingling with my lust. Two emotions waging war.

"Jesus. I can't believe he left me like this. Still, *why'd* he have to do it?" Firefly's hold fanning the smoldering desire in my blood was the only thing that stopped me from crying yet again.

"Dunno, Cora. Everybody screws themselves one way or another, some worse than others, especially in this world." He paused, kissing at my neck, before he brought his lips back for talking. "Your old man's not the only one who fucked up. Truth is, I did, too. Tried to fight this shit happening between us. Treated it like a miserable goddamned hangover I could shake off by distracting myself with booze or work or getting my dick wet in other girls…"

I tensed up.

Oh, God, now was not the time to tell me about other women he'd slept with. If he was about to announce how he'd been screwing around the whole time I'd known him…my hand went stiff, ready to hit him across the face with all my might.

"Don't even think it, babe," he growled, sensing what was coming. "Haven't fucked anybody since you showed up. This is all I'm after. All I fuckin' need."

His hand crisscrossed the top of my thigh and then wedged between my legs. I sucked my bottom lip hard, desperate to stop myself from crying out. He'd start rubbing anytime, or else pull my panties aside and take everything he wanted.

"Yeah?" I whimpered, all I could manage when his fingers felt the wetness.

Oh. Oh, holy shit!

"Yeah. This pussy's all I've been thinking about getting up inside since the day I saw you, sad and suffering in that shitty garage. You're all I wanna taste on my tongue, babe. All I want that's hot and pink and wrapped around me. I can't do the shit I loved before since you walked into my life. Not without thinking about first, second, and last. I'm goddamned obsessed." He sucked in a harsh breath, slowly cupped my mound through slick fabric, and squeezed.

I practically died.

"You want the truth? My full fuckin' confession?" Firefly's stare went full primal. "I'm gonna go fucking nuts if I don't get you under me, on top of me, legs wide open and begging for my cock."

Total. Goner.

I couldn't stop the moan hissing out my lips when he put his strength into his fingers. He squeezed my pussy in his hand so hard I thought I'd explode on the spot.

It took everything I had not to buck against him, just

NEVER LOVE AN OUTLAW

hump his fingers like an animal in heat.

"You mustn't have a lot to think about," I whispered, wishing I could chew off my own smart tongue. "All just me? All the time? Really?"

His free hand caught my hair, twisted my face, until I looked at him, eyeball-to-eyeball.

"I've got plenty. Already thinking about the fucking shield I'm gonna have to stuff down my pants to keep Prez from taking my dick off after it's been inside you." Two stiff fingers reached around the center of my panties and began to pull, dragging them down my thighs, exposing me completely. "Before, I just wondered what the fuck was wrong with me. Why I couldn't let go of the urge to lay you down and fuck you with everything I've got, baby girl. You've got a mouth like dynamite and that's what drags me in like bait. That sweet fuckin' ass I felt the other day, and those tight, beautiful tits do the rest. You're a lucky girl, darlin', and I hope you know it. Everybody else I ever fucked, I was lucky to know their names before I tasted 'em. Damned lucky if I wanted a second round. All that's turned upside-fucking-down since you, Cora. I want you. Again and again and a-fuckin'-gain…"

Sweet. Baby. Jesus.

His fingers found my naked slit and began to play. Every muscle in my body contracted.

If there was ever an urge to get away, or fight him off me, it totally died when his thumb glided through my wet folds, found my clit, and started to stroke me to high heaven.

Those whimpers leaving my mouth became howls. I couldn't pretend I wasn't enjoying this, too shocked by how stupid good it felt to have his hands where they'd belonged since forever.

"Goddamn, you want this bad, don't you, woman?"

"Yes!" I squeaked. Barely.

His fingers teased my entrance, collected my wetness, and used it to fuck me raw. My thighs quivered. The hold he had on my hair strengthened, feeding fire through my roots, igniting cinders through me, from top to bottom.

"Shouldn't be doing a lick of this shit, babe," he growled. "You're too good for this. Too damned good for me…"

"No, no, no," I panted, pinching my eyes shut as he fingered me faster.

"It's bullshit!" He spat. "All of it. You come off so fuckin' innocent, and you ain't, darlin'. You've just been begging for my hands, my mouth, my cock up inside, balls deep, all along. Fuck!"

Firefly's breath hitched, and his hard-on rubbed against my ass, straight through his jeans. "Lucky you, Cora. So fuckin' lucky. I'm gonna taste everything when you come your brains out all over me tonight."

His mouth crashed down on mine. Our first scalding hot kiss happened with his hands pushing me over the edge.

My clit swelled, hummed, and burned against his thumb. *Damn!*

No more holding back. My back arched as much as it could with his death grip on my hair, jerking my face to his.

I came, screaming into his mouth.

His tongue probed deep, twining with mine, sucking each time pleasure pulsed through me. A whole new world was blown wide open.

Twenty-two years a virgin, gone. Now I needed him to take my cherry good and proper.

My nipples throbbed hard as stones beneath my bra, my blouse. The fabric became pure torture, when they ached to be in his mouth.

Hell, every single part of me wanted to him. Surrounding him, or surrounded by him.

Licked, fingered, fucked, filled so deep I'd finally have the itch welling up inside me for what seemed like a million years scratched.

Pleasure pulsed through my brain for a small eternity before I wilted. When I did, his kiss softened. The bad boy's lips roamed mine more gently, almost tender.

"Fuck the couch," he said, standing and lifting me up in his arms. "We're moving somewhere I can get you naked and horizontal."

I moaned as he threw me over his shoulder, jerked up my skirt, and took my panties away over my feet. It was only a few footsteps to the bedroom.

He'd already forced me to come twice, and I still blushed like the shy, silly virgin I was when he threw me down on the bed.

I moved a shaky hand toward the lamp because the room was dark. He crossed the bedroom faster, kicked the door closed, and punched the light switch before I could do anything.

"Don't even think we're doing this in the dark, under the blankets, like fuckin' monks. I wanna see you squirm every second I'm licking your pussy. Gotta see your face when you start screaming, darlin'." His hands moved to his belt, and I heard the buckle clatter as he jerked it through his denim loops.

"Firefly…" I lost my words, everything except his name, heavy on my lips.

"Take the rest of that shit covering you and throw it on the goddamned floor. Now. 'Cause if you leave it up to me, I'm gonna shred half your fuckin' wardrobe."

I watched the leather cut that always lined his chest fall. His shirt peeled away next, and I could barely remember my own name.

My eyes were glued to the huge, rock hard, heavily tattooed torso coming into view. A body built like an angle, a statue, nature's best craftsman.

His chest swelled when he inhaled. The winged skull with two blazing pistols next to it poured fire across his muscles. Every part of him rippled, glistened.

This body wasn't cut from pumping iron in the gym or running – though I knew he did plenty of that too – he'd earned his strength by actually *using* those muscles.

For fucking. For killing. For dropping men with ease, wiping the arrogant smirks off their faces, just like he'd done earlier tonight with Tony the drunk.

He smiled. "Fuckin' knew you'd like what you see. Go ahead and touch. Follow the inks as far as you want."

He never asked twice. Firefly grabbed my hands, spread

my fingers, and put them on his abs, the same strong ridges I'd hung onto all along, riding on the back of his bike.

Now, they beckoned under my fingertips. Naked, magnificent, and hard.

God! Would it be wrong to just stick out my tongue and lick this man?

Firefly reached out with the same two fingers that brought me to heaven a few minutes ago. He gently pushed them beneath my chin, tipped my face up, capturing my eyes for the millionth time with those stern blue eyes.

"Dig your nails in," he growled, shoving my hands against him. "Might as well get used to it, baby. You'll be drawing blood when I'm between your legs, fucking you over and over…we're fuckin' 'til kingdom come. Been wanting it forever."

My fingertips bent. I reached up to his breast, pivoted my nails into his skin, and dragged them down. I whimpered as they fell, tracing the dark, deadly symbols scrawled all over him like a dark, human canvass.

Holy, holy shit. How can a man be built just like a god? How was it fair that me – Cora – was about to give myself to him?

My fingertips fell, all the way to his unbuttoned jeans. Then he leaned down, moving his hand behind my head, jerking me into a brand new kiss.

His lips moved against mine for what felt like forever. Every twitch and twirl of his tongue made me realize I was dripping wet, begging to be opened, teased, and filled by this man.

Seizing my wrist, he yanked my hand down to the bulge in his jeans. I moaned when I felt it, ready to pop out the crevice in his half-open zipper.

"That's for you," Firefly said, holding my eyes just inches from his. "Every fucking inch. That's the cock that's gonna take you, fuck you, own you, Cora. That's the part of me that's gonna make us one, make you cry in ways you can't even imagine."

"Yes, yes," I said, trying not to get too giddy.

Everything between my legs ached. My core folded in on itself, so ready to be opened up again by his power, it hurt.

Damn it, this wasn't a choice anymore. There weren't any brakes on the naked, sweaty want rushing through my system.

I *needed* him in me. Had to have him split me open, make me a woman, show me all the ways that massive, scary body of his could make me quake and scream.

"Already told you once – take off your clothes. Now, babe. Neither one of us needs a trip to the fucking store tomorrow to replace everything I destroyed."

I looked at him and nodded. Just sat up, undoing my blouse, peeling away everything as quickly as I could. Meanwhile, the sneaky bastard dropped his pants, his boxers, and left his back facing me when I toppled into bed, bare and leaking.

Ready for him to take whatever he wanted.

Slowly, he turned. I fought the urge to push my hand between my legs when I caught a glimpse of what he'd been hiding in those jeans.

If God ever put a bigger cock on a man, then I'd be afraid to see it. Firefly was *huge.* It wasn't just the raw length and girth that got to me, but the way it swelled when he pushed his fist around it, pulsing with a mad, potent energy, angry and alive as the rest of him.

"Fuck," he growled, squeezing his length until the thick head ballooned, spilling a small trickle of crystal clear fluid to the floor. "There's no way you'll be able to take this without getting a whole lot looser and wetter first."

Wetter? Looser? Had he lost his loving mind?

He climbed onto the bed, growling while he pushed my legs apart. His mouth dashed all my doubts when it took mine all over again.

He kissed me, harder than before. I sucked his lips and trembled, loving how he rammed his tongue against mine. Hungry, feral, just like a wild animal.

Sometimes, he pulled back, forcing me to lean into him, and struggle for another kiss. He always held me down, making me work for it with that smug, trademark smile.

"Bastard," I whispered.

"Beautiful," he growled. "Every fucking foot of you."

He showed me. His mouth stamped hot, playful kisses down my throat, nipping at my ear, before he sank down to my breasts. My nipples rolled between his fingertips, and then he brought his lips over them, softening each bud against his tongue with the same aggression he'd given me in every kiss.

"Oh!" I whimpered, wondering if I could come from nothing except his mouth all over my tits.

I'd heard the strippers talk about sex before. They were numb to it. Jaded, maybe.

But even they got off to a strong, highly experienced man.

Tonight, I had that man to myself. I had it all. Looks, experience, and a spark between us unlike anything I'd ever had for another human being.

Every growl reminded me he must've felt something too. He manhandled me like he wanted, squeezing my breasts as his head sank lower, moving between my thighs.

Fuck. Shit. He's really going to take me with his tongue!
And he did.

Firefly pulled my thighs apart, kissing each one, brushing his rough stubble across my smooth skin. His mouth moved upward, and I heard him stop, rumble, inhaling my scent.

"Fuck, you smell good. You're wet as a damned garden hose. Too bad it ain't wet enough." My legs began to tremble as he reared up, staring at me, his eyes fiery blue and determined as hell. "I'm gonna make you soak these fuckin' sheets, darlin'."

My pussy throbbed before his tongue even met it. When it did, I struggled to take hold of the sheets, the only thing that would keep us on planet earth while he ravaged me like never before.

Firefly's fingers had been amazing, but his mouth. Shit, *his mouth!*

Lips, teeth, and tongue opened me, stroked deep, wrapped around my clit. He sucked, licked, pulled, and nibbled, teasing muscles I hadn't even known about before he laid me on this bed.

My virgin pussy had been starved for years, too sheltered and afraid to open itself to pleasure. Firefly made up for years in a sexless desert, sending his lightning through me in every lick.

My mouth widened a little at a time, forming a perfect ring. My whole body wound up like a spring, so close, inching toward the edge with every rough tickle of his stubble, every lash of his tongue.

The more I squirmed, the harder he held me down. His tongue scrawled more filthy words across my clit in every wet, powerful jerk than he could've ever spoken.

Come for me, babe.

Come for me hot.

Come for me wild.

Come for me like your whole fucking life has led you to having my face between your legs. You know it has.

Come for me like the beautiful, damaged girl you are.

Come for me NOW.

My hips jerked. I clutched the sheets and screamed, involuntarily riding his face. Thunder left his throat. He pulled me against his mouth, locking me in while my pussy rubbed his chin again and again.

"Firefly, Firefly, fuck me, Firefly!" These were my last words for the next five minutes.

I came so hard I almost passed out. Time became a blur, only kept constant by his tongue stroking my clit. He pulled it taut between his teeth, all the better to be whipped over and over again with his mad, mad laps.

He feasted on me like a total beast. He owned me.

And I loved it. *Loved it.*

I'd never been so alive and awestruck as I was than when Firefly's tongue worked me over. If only it could've lasted forever!

My muscles twitched, every single one of them, a full body orgasm so intense I saw stars.

Blood red, orange like headlights, blistering white.

I swam in the hot void and lost a little sanity, giving it all up to Firefly.

When I could force my eyes open, his tongue strokes had softened. So had his grip.

I realized my pussy must've creamed the entire time in his mouth. His tongue cleaned me, stroked me alive again, tasting every drop like I was some rare delicacy.

"Fucking shit, baby girl," he growled, coming up and wiping his mouth. "Never had pussy this good before. You're soft and wet and so fuckin' sweet. Don't know how you do it."

I smiled, pushing hot beads of sweat off my brow as he pulled me into his big arms. "What you do is pretty mysterious too," I said.

"Yeah, whatever. Don't need to understand it. Just need more. We're barely getting started. I'm gonna own every goddamned beautiful inch of you tonight, and then every night I'm walking this earth."

His words did something strange and marvelous. My nipples puckered, swelling and hardening with his promises. Or were they threats?

Whatever they were, I wanted him to carry out every single one of them, and then some.

I flattened my hands against his chest, running my fingertips over his broad, strong shoulders. Our eyes locked. Raw fire pulsed in his, a single-minded need to take me before he totally lost it to the animal urge to hold me down and fuck me.

My legs opened as he moved between them. I watched him dip below the bed for a second, reaching for something, and then heard a condom's wrapper tear a second later.

"Put it the fuck on me," he growled, pushing it into my hands.

I sat up, marveling at the big, insanely hard erection throbbing between his legs. He wrapped it in a fist and more pre-come surged, drooling with savage want, ready to be inside me.

"I've never done this before," I whispered, my cheeks burning. I tried to steady my hands as he guided me, positioning the small, circular condom over his throbbing tip.

He stroked it down his length, my hand going with it. I felt him quiver, even through the latex. My pussy clenched, and I fought the urge to suck him off then and there.

There'd be another time for that. Tonight, he had to take what belonged to him, what I'd decided to surrender to my tall, dark, brutal Prince.

"Lay back. Open wide. Bite down on my arm." He held it against my throat and pushed me down while he moved between my legs.

"Bite you? Why?"

"Trust me, darlin', you're gonna need something when this cock splits you open. You've never had a man before, have you?"

I shook my head, blushing with embarrassment.

"Yeah, that's what I thought. You'll be coming again in no time once you get through the burn. Promise."

My hands pulled at his arm and I held on tight. His hips moved, one thrust away from pushing into me, aggressive and deep.

"Take me, Firefly. Make me yours. Just for tonight."

"Just tonight? Bullshit, babe." New fires roared in his eyes. "I'm taking this pussy. Fuckin' owning it forever. You understand?"

His ass rolled forward. My pussy tingled, stretched, and burned as he pushed into me, making me feel the full power of those last two words.

You understand, babe?

Yes. I did. I finally fucking did, and I grit my teeth as a sharp sensation bit into me.

It hurt just a little, being opened like this, but there was a deeper pleasure behind it, something fiercer than what I'd felt being worked over by his hands and mouth.

"So fuckin' tight. All fuckin' mine." He bared his teeth, pushing deeper, deeper, then holding himself there like he needed a moment just to believe it. "Shit. Fuck. Cora, you were *made* for this dick."

I believed him. Hell, I truly started believing I'd been designed for him when he reared back, almost pulling out, and then crashed into me again.

This time, with more force, more feeling, more power.

My ass dipped deep into the mattress and then sprang back up, sliding onto his cock, giving my body even more leverage on his. The burn between my legs crested. There was one wicked second where clenching my jaw wasn't enough, and I had to bite into his arm, digging my teeth into his skin as he taught me how to fuck.

"That's it, babe. Fuck me back. Fuck me, hard as you can take it."

Moaning, I threw my hand across his neck, digging my nails in. My legs moved, locking around his. I pulled him into me, begging him with every muscle to drive deeper.

Fuck me through the burn.

Fuck me through everything I've suffered.

Fuck me until I forget everything except this bed, this body, and everything I love about you, Firefly.

Just fuck me.

I swore he read my thoughts. His hips pistoned faster, picking up speed, slamming me into the mattress a little harder with each and every thrust.

A fireball built around my womb, the same one I'd had before, except bigger and hotter now. Firefly fucked me harder, making us into two engines humming against each other in perfect harmony.

Sweating, clenching, begging for release. Our bodies formed a rhythm each time he crashed down, plunging all the way to my womb, skin slapping skin.

One, two, three.

Fuck, fuck, fuck.

Filthy F-words filled my brain like a mantra. Nothing else kept time except that count in the back of my head and the patter of my own heartbeat.

His dark inks looked more furious, the skull and the guns, matching the expression on his face. I realized it just as he swore for the millionth time, picked my legs up, and threw them over his shoulders.

"Fucking-A, baby girl. You're gonna kill with this tight little cunt if I don't put out the fire. Come for me again. Come all over my dick."

He could make me do anything.

My body responded like he'd reached inside me, flipping a switch. I was already approaching another toe curling climax, but this took me there faster, sweeping me into light and heat and fire.

Holy. Shit.

His cock stabbed into me three more times, each stroke faster and harder than the last. His pubic bone had just the right tuft of hair to scratch me where it mattered. I felt him, grinding against my clit, bringing me off with the same expertise he must've used on a hundred girls.

Except tonight, the bastard was all mine, and what a big, beautiful man he was. I believed him when he said those dirty, possessive things, all the stuff about wanting me more than anybody else.

He couldn't fake the rough edge in his voice. He couldn't fool anyone, not with the way he threw himself into me, fucking me with his whole body, determined to bring us both to heaven.

I came so hard my entire vision filled with speckled stars, too many colors to count.

Everything below my waist blazed, and up above, my hair stretched in his fist as he pulled it tight. His mouth crashed down on mine before I could scream, swallowing my pleasure, owning my tongue like he overwhelmed the rest of me.

Oh, Firefly. Oh, God.

Oh, oh, oh so fucking incredible.

Every finger and toe hurt when I could finally come up from it because they were bent. He hadn't stopped, hadn't even slowed himself down. The biker's massive body just kept thrusting, coming like a locomotive, the greatest machine nature had ever built for explosive, relentless sex.

I couldn't breathe, and I didn't even care. That fire in my pussy slowed to a simmer, and the pain was all gone now.

Nothing except volcanic desire kissed my veins through my blood. My desire was only taking a short break before I knew it'd erupt all over again.

"You're goddamned beautiful when you come," he growled, pushing the words out through ragged breaths. "You know I'll never stop making you, right?"

His thrusts slowed, and he ran a calloused hand across my face. I purred, my lips trembling, feeling my pleasure cresting high again.

"Never?"

"Fuck, no. Not 'til I've tamed this pussy and my name's

stamped all over your sweet ass, baby. Now, turn the hell over. Let me see the rest of what's mine."

He pulled out just long enough to change positions, helping me roll onto my knees. My arms stretched above my head. I grasped the pillows, precious support I knew I'd need the second he mounted me from behind.

Doggie. That was what they called this, wasn't it?

I felt like a bitch in heat when he started pounding. His cock angled differently, bringing me a more delicious feeling than before, fanning the fire inside me lightning hot.

"Damn it all!" My voice choked off as he slammed into me faster. I buried my face into the sheets, feeling the wave within coming, ready to sweep me up and smash me against the rocks named Firefly.

"Give it the fuck up," he growled. "Give it all to me. Wanna see this ass shake like every other inch of you when I bust inside you, darlin' baby girl."

He smacked me, right on the ass, bringing me back to the first night I'd lost control beneath his palm.

Firefly wrapped one hand around my thigh, shoved it between my legs, and found my clit. His free hand moved upward, fisting my hair, pulling me back onto those rough thrusts threatening to break me in two.

Everything sweet, bitter, and sinful overloaded me. I lost it.

This time, I came hardest, screaming into the sheets until they were between my teeth. My hands tore desperately at the pillows.

I sweated, I ached, I fucked him with every bone in my body.

My ass bucked into Firefly's thrusts, desperate to feel him join me in the rough firestorm he'd lit below my waist. His hips crashed against me, such a manic frenzy I thought he'd break the box spring underneath us.

"Fuck, baby girl, I'm coming. Gonna give your tight little cunt everything it's been crying for since the day we met!" Both his mean hands pushed through my hair, slick with sweat.

He pulled, jerking me up from the sheets, and he didn't stop. Roaring, he held on, twisting my hair like reigns as his cock swelled deep inside me.

Even through the condom, I could feel the explosion.

One second, there was nothing but his hard, masculine strength inside me,. Then a flood of molten fire, drowning me, his throat filling the room with an animal's growl.

"Fuck, fuck fuck!" He sounded inhuman, like he'd channeled pure lust. Let it take him over.

I didn't think it was possible, but shit, I came *harder.*

My breasts pulsed. My pussy throbbed. My clit swelled, screaming for his seed, the only thing in the universe that would put out the inferno raging inside me.

Our bodies both crashed together, two glaciers falling apart. Numb to everything except our own pleasure, blind to the entire screwed up world.

Moaning, shaking, sweating. My brain short-circuited again and again, alive with his fury, his passion, his guttural release. We fucked for what seemed like forever, never letting up until my arms and legs gave out.

Another growl, and he slowly pulled out of me, cursing

when he did like someone had just called closing time at the bar.

Lord, I could've used a shot of something after Firefly. Maybe even a cigarette.

"Shit!" I jerked up to see what had him so upset.

Crouching on the bed, he held the condom between two fingers, a steady trickle of his come pouring out of it.

My heart stopped.

I watched him stand, dump it in the trash, and come back, running one hand over his handsome face.

"Fuck, Cora, I'm sorry. You're not on the pill or some shit?"

"No." It was like the whole world condensed into the room, suddenly alive with possibilities I'd never considered before I'd bedded this bad boy.

"Goddamn. Never had one of those things break like that before. We gotta go. Get you some shit at the pharmacy. We'll make this right." He grabbed my hand.

"No." I said it again, squeezing his fingers tight. "We can wait until morning. There's stuff that's good for twenty-four hours."

His eyes narrowed. He looked at me like I'd lost my mind, but I saw his cock swelling out of the corner of my vision.

"Get back here and take me again. No condom. The damage is already done. Whatever happens…we'll deal with it. We'll be all right." I crawled to the edge of the bed and threw my arms around him, running one hand down the nape of his neck. "You're all I need, Firefly. *This* is all I've needed, all I've been thinking about since the day you spanked me."

"Fuck, babe, you know what you're asking for?"

"Yeah." Slowly smiling, I licked my lips. "I'm asking you to fuck me harder next time. And don't you *dare* pull out."

I stabbed my finger playfully into his chest. For a second, he stood paralyzed, like he'd lost the ability to comprehend what was coming out of my mouth.

Then there was nothing but the loudest growl I'd ever heard vibrating in my ears as he threw me down, spread my legs, and pushed into me.

VII: Sunrise (Firefly)

Day's first sunlight seeped through the blinds, and I still had her under me.

The little minx didn't know what the fuck she'd gotten herself into after I tossed the busted condom, asking me to fuck her, fill her, pretending to knock her the fuck up without even saying it.

She whimpered as I held her feet up, gripping her sleek ankles with my hands. Perfect angle for going balls deep. I'd have every tight, wet inch of her. She'd get every damned millimeter of the only dick she'd ever be allowed to fuck.

Cora whined underneath me as I railed her harder. The girl was a natural at taking it good and hard. I'd corrupted her half the fuckin' evening, and my balls still needed to pump fire.

"Fifth goddamned load of the night," I growled. "Shit, you're gonna milk me dry, woman, making up for lost time with that pussy of yours."

She whimpered. Louder when I sank to the hilt, touching the entrance to her womb with my tip, hard as nails despite all the come I'd already pumped into her.

Lava churned at my cock's base. I'd keep fucking her 'til she gave up the ghost and passed the fuck out. She'd been insatiable so far, and I'd put everything I had into keeping up.

I'd been blessed with all the stamina in the world, dammit. I'd eat my fucking bike one piece at a time if I left a virgin wanting.

Another moan. I threw myself into her, plunging into that perfect heat surrounding my dick. Fuck, she felt good.

Good? Fuck, no. *Amazing.*

Lightning crackled my spine, tore through me, and pinched me like a fiend. I had to fuck her harder.

She took every thrust, good and open for me now that I'd loosened her up. Angry blood hammered in my dick, calling my cock deeper, deeper.

We fucked 'til I shook the bed, rattled my brain, her bones, the whole fuckin' room.

"Firefly!" she purred, the only word hanging on her lips when I had her in the zone.

I reared up and slapped her ass, ramming her onto my cock, loving how my balls slapped all over her ass. "That's the fuckin' name that owns you, darlin'. Say it again."

"Firefly!" Her eyelids fluttered. She'd be over the edge soon.

Not fast enough. If she was still doing anything but screaming, I wasn't going hard enough.

Reaching underneath her ass, I pulled her up, rolled, and sat her right on my cock. I stood, picked her up, and fucked her in mid-air. Girl bounced in my arms as we stood over the bed, hotter and wilder by the fuckin' second.

Watched her pussy drip all over the place between my strokes. *Fuck, fuck.*

Her little cunt sucked, yanked, and stroked me all the way to my balls each time I drove deep. Christ, I wouldn't last like this. I had to finish, had to feel her pulling my come outta me.

I slowed my strokes, teasing her 'til her sweet blue eyes opened. "Put your hands around my neck and hold the fuck on tight. We're going to the goddamned moon."

Maybe I should've said the sun. That sick motherfucker chose just then to come over the mountains, cut through the blinds, and burn my eyes.

Fuck if it stopped me. I walked her over to the nearest wall as she held on. Pushed her up against it, one hand on her ass, the other tugging those bright gold locks.

My dick thrust faster. Harder. I fucked her like the raging, snorting bull I'd become.

Hellbent on ruining her, rebuilding her, owning her.

She wailed so loud I knew the sorry fucks in the other apartment must've gotten a rude awakening. Thought made me grin, so I fucked her even harder.

A couple seconds in, and that tight velvet between her legs I was already addicted to convulsed around my cock. She lost her voice and sucked hard at the air, anything to keep her lungs going while I short-circuited her sweet bod.

I watched her come, rippling like sex incarnate on my dick. Everything I'd been imagining all night since she told me to drop the condom blazed through my head like a wet dream.

Couldn't stop thrusting. Couldn't stop fucking her. Couldn't shut down the fantasy of me spilling my come inside her, curling her toes as she took every drop, burying my kid inside her.

Fuck, fuck, mother of fuck!

I buried myself to the hilt and let my nut come. Every fucking part of me ached and boiled over. My face craned up to the ceiling and I growled hellfire, letting her pussy milk my balls, pouring everything I had into her.

My cock should've been dry by now, but her body jerked new ropes of come outta me.

Hot, wet pussy drenched every inch of me, hot as sin because I'd flooded it for the umpteenth time.

That's it, darlin'. Fuck me senseless.

Took a million years to come down from the high. Her tits were bouncing and I was about to rip her hair outta her head by the time it eased up.

When my eyeballs stopped clenching shut, I held my dick in her, loosening my grip. She leaned up for a kiss. I pulled her hair a little tighter before I smothered those lips.

Kissing this woman was all I could do to deal with how completely fucked I was. No bullshit, I'd meant every word I growled to her before.

This shit wasn't stopping tonight. I had to fuck her more. Over and over and over 'til I broke my fucking dick off.

I held her close, guided her to the bed, and lay her down. Held her flat against my chest, stroking that sexy blonde hair. Fuckin' loved how it caught the sun, changing from fifteen to twenty-four karat gold.

The girl zonked out in less than five minutes. I watched her slip into some sorely needed dreams, planting one more kiss on her forehead.

She'd need that beauty sleep. Cora suffered, worked her ass off, and her list of shit to deal with was only growing fatter and meaner by the day.

'Course, I'd added riding my dick to her daily routine, not to mention coming so hard those bright blue eyes snapped shut. That had to make up for the bad shit.

We'd shared two rooms since her old man's mistakes forced us both through the wringer.

Sharing the same space didn't do a damned thing anymore. I needed more. Staring up at the ceiling, I swore I'd keep her in my bed, and I didn't give a single shit what it took to make it happen.

She was mine, dammit, and nothing in this world would force me to let go.

* * * *

Fucking phone started vibrating sometime just before noon. I rolled outta our empty bed and heard Cora showering before I grabbed it.

"Yeah?"

"Where the fuck are you, bro?" Sixty growled. "We're up to our asses in work today. Those old farts from Kingston brought their fancy play bikes in for a tune up. Good money. Could really use an extra hand out here."

"Yeah, yeah, keep your dick in your pants, brother. I'll be there soon."

I hung up. After all the shit we'd been dealing with lately, it was a small relief to be called in for grease and ratchets in the shop instead of throwing fists or bullets.

My stomach growled. Hungry as fuck after all the energy we'd burned last night, never stopping for dinner.

My cock still had a furious craving too. Damned thing throbbed as I stuffed it into my shorts, pulled up my jeans, and turned around.

Seeing Cora didn't help one fucking bit. Especially when she was bent over, digging in the closet, the towel wrapped around her waist drooping dangerously low.

Fucking shit. Took every fiber of discipline not to head on over, rip that thing off, and drag her back to bed.

"Morning," I said, as soon a she saw me, holding a fresh set of work clothes. Those bare, beautiful tits I'd sucked all night hung on her chest, calling my lips like goddamned sirens.

"Thought I'd better let you sleep in just a few more minutes," she said, flashing me the smile I wanted to wipe away, kiss by flaming kiss. "I'm normally up by now. Morning dove, you know. Consider yourself lucky that you might be the first thing helping me sleep in since…"

Her smile melted. I held up a finger and shook it like a club.

"Don't say it, babe. Just get dressed, and let's find ourselves some breakfast. Or lunch. Or what the fuck ever."

My guts rumbled again. Shit. She heard the growl and

laughed. Couldn't suppress the grin rolling across my face.

"Next time, remember to take a break and eat," Cora said, pulling up her panties. "Wouldn't want you to starve because we were…you know."

"Fucking?" Smiling, I stepped toward her, shirt and cut under my arm. "We've got work to do, baby girl. You're gonna learn to talk dirty. And you can shoot me square in the chest if you ever catch me chasing after a damned burger more than this pussy. I'd rather have your hot little cunt against my teeth than anything some fucker over a grill could ever serve…"

My arms went around her back, jerked her into me, and we kissed like vipers wrestling.

Fuck, she tasted good. My hand swung low, squeezed her ass, and then my fingers were down her panties. Had that shit ripped down in half a heart beat, feeling her wetness, fresh and clean and just begging to be fucked.

"No, no, no…" She pushed weakly against my chest. "We have to go to work, Firefly. It's going to be a long day. Oh, please, don't make this more difficult…"

"Difficult?" I growled. "You think it's gonna be easy on me? Shit, I'll probably put my fist through the fucking clock when I know I oughta be here in bed all day, holding your legs apart, making you come on my dick ten more times."

"Ten?" Her eyes went wide. "I'd die! Surely, you're joking…"

"Try me, darlin'." I winked. "You'll be glad as fuck you did."

She laughed, and my ears rang happy. Goddamn, I

could've listened to that sound all day, second only to how she sounded before her body gave it all up to me.

"Tonight. After you pick me up." Cora motioned across her heart, crossing it like a kid.

"I'm gonna trust you on your word, babe. You oughta know by now I take promises *very* fucking seriously. And if these little lips ever mislead me, well, you know how that goes." My hand circled behind her, rolling down the small of her back. Then I lifted it and let it crack firmly across her ass.

She squirmed against me, pushing her sweet, suckable tits flush against my chest.

Fucking tease. I love it.

"Firefly – I promise!" she squeaked, struggling in my arms. I laughed and held her tighter, lowering my face against her, 'til our foreheads touched like something outta a damned chick flick.

"All right, whatever. Give me one more kiss for collateral."

She did. I tasted her as long as I could.

Long as I could stand before my cock ripped through my jeans was more like it, but fuck, I knew I had all the time in the world. I'd staked a claim, and I'd only drive it deeper, harder, and longer from here.

This little minx was gonna sing for me tonight. Then every fuckin' night we had.

No end in sight, and that should've freaked me out.

I'd just taken the first pussy I wanted to keep coming back to over and over. Not just because it felt like gold wrapped around my cock neither. Because I craved it, needed it, called it *mine.*

What the hell was going on?

* * * *

Cora blew me another kiss when she got off my bike. We'd grabbed a quick breakfast at a diner before I dropped her at work.

Hard to believe the night we'd had after all the hell that had been raised at the Heel less than twenty-four hours ago.

I drove away with the mountain wind in my face, pulling off my helmet when my bike got on the home stretch. It was finally warming up. The Great Smoky Mountains were coming alive, pouring their green scent across the landscape like God himself holding a damned spritzer.

My lungs sucked in every drop. Couldn't stop smiling, wondering if there'd ever been a more glorious day.

These old lungs were gonna need every molecule of cool, clean air they could get, too. I'd be pulling double duty soon, fucking my girl as much as I could stand, on top of busting ass for the club.

Too bad the club had her claws in like a banshee as soon as I rolled into the chop shop we had just on the edge of town.

The boys were all there, their bikes parked in a neat row.

Weird, since it was normally just Sixty, Crawl, and me. Sometimes we invited the prospects and hangarounds to help with the grunt work if they had a mechanics' smarts, but today all the boys were there in the lot, including the guys who didn't know shit about digging deep in an engine's guts.

When I saw Prez's bike, I knew something stank to high hell. *Fuck!*

Parked my ride, climbed off it, and put my hand over my nine in its holster. I walked quietly, heading straight by the empty register, then through the deserted garage to the rear.

Walked in on the most tense shit I'd seen since the last time we were knife-to-knife with the Deads.

"You're making a big mistake, friend," Dust growled, an angry half-moon of men wearing different patches around him on both sides.

"Fuck you, Dusty. *Fuck. You.*"

In the center, a big man with a scarred face and a huge, bushy ginger beard had the Prez up against the wall. Red Beard, leader of the Atlanta Torches. Motherfucker had a legendary temper, too, and it threatened my boss' life.

Didn't even hesitate to pull my gun and point it at the fucker's rotten skull. "Get the fuck off him!"

"Sharp." Red Beard nodded at a lean, lantern-jawed bastard standing by his shoulder.

The asshole, who I saw was wearing a V. PRESIDENT patch, pushed his way through the crowd and aimed a big shotgun at my chest. "Put that popgun down," he snarled.

"Not 'til your Prez gets the hell off mine."

"Everybody relax!" Red Beard shouted. "Any of you Pistols fuckers punch your triggers in a single millimeter, it's gonna be a bloodbath, and we'll all lose our dicks."

"Firefly, listen!" Dust looked at me, his angry gray eyes shining big and bright over Red Beard's shoulder. "It's ain't worth it. Let it ride. Bad fucking timing."

"You don't get to talk about timing, asshole!" Red Beard roared in his face. "You knew that fuckin' cocksucker was stinking and rotting in his house for days. Shit, you knew the city hauled his carcass off to get fuckin' cremated – and you didn't say shit about it! Fuck's sake, we're supposed to be allies!"

"Yeah, supposed to be. Fuck me for picking jackals for friends," Dust said, shoving the rival Prez hard in the chest.

Red Beard pushed back. Miracle he didn't put a fuckin' bullet in Dust's brain. They scuffled, rolling against the wall, the other guys around them anxiously fingering their guns.

Prez wasn't lying about a potential bloodbath coming. My eyes flicked through my boys. Joker, Skin, Sixty, Crawl, and the prospects were all lined up against the Torches.

Our crews were roughly equal in numbers. Nobody had a solid position, an advantage, and that sucked serious balls.

Every man here had an equal chance at putting a few holes in the sorry fuck across from him, and receiving a few in turn. Sharp smiled across from me, just itching for a chance to let his rounds blow my ribs apart.

"Alliance is over, fuckface. We'll deal with the Deads on our own," Red Beard growled. "Whether or not you cough up the guns we settled on and Jimmy's cunt daughter is what's gonna decide whether or not we start killing Pistols, too."

"No!" I shouted, stepping right into Sharp's muzzle. Fucking thing drove against my chest like a tank, so close to death I could feel every hair on my body standing on end.

I was tempting fate, and I fucking knew it. But that 'cunt daughter' meant Cora. I'd die to keep her safe. Some mad dog redness clouded my vision, mad and primal shit fiercer than all the times it had ever went through my veins before.

"You'll get your guns, asshole," Dust thundered. "Just as soon as you lower yours and send your men back to their bikes. You already broke standard operating procedure, showing up here instead of the fucking clubhouse. This is our goddamned business – civilian biz. Too fuckin' public for an exchange."

"Shut up!" Red Beard slammed Dust into the wall, his beer gut helping pin the Prez down. "You fucked us over, and you goddamned know it! We had a good thing going on. We were trading, fighting, sharing intel on the Deads. Now, all that's fucked, and it's your fault. Not ours. I'm not gonna stand here while you try to fuckin' tell me otherwise, shithead."

When I heard the familiar click of a switchblade opening, it took everything in my power not to start a shooting war that'd get us all killed. *Fuck.*

Had a sudden flashback to the mountains outside Kandahar. Me and my guys were pinned down, taking a Taliban mortar attack straight up the ass. A couple troops next to me got their arms blown off, and one man lost his head. Fuckers were behind the rocks, shooting at us while their bombs exploded everywhere. All we could do was lay, wait, and put down suppressing fire 'til the cavalry came.

Airstrikes took the terrorist pukes out a couple minutes later. I'd been helpless then, just hoping for a miracle.

This day, this shit…this was worse. Watching Red Beard shove his knife against my Prez's throat fucking gutted me.

Joker moved first. Wrapped his rough hands around another Torches' throat, holding him in a brutal headlock, the kind that'd choke the fuck totally to death if we didn't diffuse this shit quick.

"Rawdog!" Sharp yelled, pulling his gun outta my ribs and turning around. "Prez, that asshole's gonna kill him!"

"Not if I do Dusty first," Red Beard snarled, his hand gripping the knife like the handle of his bike, one flick away from ending Dust's life. "We're way past heart-to-heart bullshit. I want our cut of the fuckin' guns. I know they're here – you moved 'em when you heard we were rolling into town. Gonna give you once chance to bring 'em. Right fuckin' now. Do it. Before I decide to push this hungry dagger straight through your goddamned throat."

"Prez, just say the word," Skin said coldly, his gun aimed at Sharp's face. "We'll go down fighting, or we'll give these fuckers what they came for. Your choice."

The crown had never been heavier for our fearless leader.

Every Prez in an outlaw MC dealt out life and death, heaven and hell, plus everything in between like fucking cards. Dust would either order us to our deaths, or he'd give these fuckstains what they wanted, buying us the time we needed to figure out how to kill 'em good and proper.

I expected to hear the Prez bark, the string of words that would either end this rough ass rocket ride I'd called a life, or else let me breathe the biggest sigh of relief since Afghanistan.

Instead, the crazy fucker did Plan C. Pistols and Torches alike nearly shat their pants as we watched our Prez push himself into Red's blade, blood pouring out around the crack where his throat connected with the knife.

"What the fuck?! You lost your mind, you dumb sonofabitch?" Red Beard roared, falling backward in shock, his hands shaking. The knife dropped outta his hands and clattered on the busted concrete.

He wanted to threaten us. He didn't want to kill the Prez in front of us and trigger the shooting that'd get us all killed.

It worked. Dust bent his head, put one hand across the wound in his throat, and looked the bastard straight in the eye.

"You ain't giving any orders here," Prez rasped. "I am. Joker, Firefly, go get their fuckin' guns. Then make sure they get their asses off of our property."

I moved. None of the Torches stopped us as I caught up with the Veep. We headed for the garages, where the boys had an old drag racer missing its wheels up on blocks, a tarp draped over it. Joker looked at me, nodded, and we both grabbed opposite corners.

Ripped the tarp right off. There, through the missing windows, were several familiar black crates stacked high.

"Let's get this shit loaded in their truck." Joker spoke

like we were doing a damned chore, rather than narrowly saving this club's ass.

We had to move our asses. Couldn't think about the risk, the danger, or the Prez bleeding all over the fuckin' ground after the cut he'd taken.

Everything moved on autopilot after that. Small miracle I swallowed the urge to rip every one of those fucks with the rival colors apart, soaking the glowing torches sewn on their cuts in their own dirty blood.

When everybody saw the Veep and me carrying their crates, the whole atmosphere relaxed. Just barely.

Prez leaned against the wall, still covering his throat, blood drying on his hands as fresh red soaked through.

"Put them down," he said, his voice getting weaker by the second. "Let these fuckers take their shit to the trucks."

We did. Red Beard nodded, and a few of his burly brothers picked the crates up, disappearing through the gate from our view.

"We're not leaving 'til we check this shit over," he growled at Dust. "Not 'til we find out where Jimmy's little bitch has gone, neither."

"Already told you, we don't have a fuckin' clue. She ain't our problem. We've had this alliance for fighting the Deads, sharing intel, doing deals. That's all shot to shit now. Consider it dissolved and get the fuck out. We're done here."

There was a long pause. I kept one hand on my nine, ready to blow Red's brains out and start a shooting war if he so much as took another step toward Dust with that blade in one hand.

Prez was hurt. Fucking incredible he could just stand there like the stone cold bastard he was, bleeding out his neck, staring all these mean motherfuckers down with his life oozing outta him.

"He right, Prez?" The one named Rawdog looked at their leader, and I noticed one of his eyes was just glass.

"Yeah. For today." Red Beard turned his back and started walking, pushing past me with two of his boys flanking him. The rest trailed behind them.

I took several steps toward the Prez, and froze when I heard the Torches' stop by the gate and shout.

"Nice doing business with you pricks! We'll be doing our homework, fuckers, and don't you forget it. If I find out you've been lying about out that bitch who scurried off or anything else, you *will* see us again. Don't give a shit if it means killing some Deads along the way. We'd rather have an army of crazy fuckers breathing down our necks rather than friends like you." He stopped, looked me dead in the eye, and let a mean smile twist his lips. "Shit, looks like the reaper's breathing down his. Better get that boy a tourniquet, or else I'll be busting somebody else's balls next time I come back."

Asshole. I formed fists so hard my fucking knuckles cracked. Blinked my eyes, just staring through the redness, 'til they were gone.

Nobody moved 'til we heard their engines roar. Then everybody ran toward Dust. I got to him first.

Prez halfway collapsed. I took over where he'd left off,

squeezing one hand against his throat, feeling hot blood gushing against my fingers.

"Oh, fuck." I looked up, staring at Skin and Joker. "We gotta get him the fuck outta here. He's been bleeding like this for at least five minutes. Poor bastard must've lost a fuckin' gallon by now."

I looked down. The dirty red puddle beneath my boots said it was no exaggeration.

"Joker. Firefly. You boys…you're taking the lead now. Hold the club together while I try to un-fuck myself. I…" Prez tried to talk more, but his eyes rolled back in his head.

Shit. Fuck.

"Fuck trying to drive him. We need Laynie out here *now,* dammit!" I barked orders.

"On it." Joker had his burner phone out, dialing her number.

Meanwhile, the prospects tore off their shirts, ripping them into neat strips so we could try to stop the bleeding. Behind us, we heard laughter, the rumble of the last few Torches' bikes.

Rage flashed red on Skin's face when we heard the fence surrounding our garage get bowled over. The whole crew of fuckers must've flattened it on the way out, judging by the rattle.

I looked at Dust and grit my teeth. His eyes were closed, and his pulse was slowing in my hands, but he held on.

"Just keep it together a little bit longer, brother," I whispered, gingerly squeezing his hand.

We'd get him patched up. Then Joker and me would

figure out how the fuck we'd kill every last one of the miserable shits who'd jumped us.

They'd made it personal, too, the stupid fucks, the very second they'd mentioned Cora. And pushing our Prez against the wall, causing him to slice his own fuckin' throat?

They were already dead.

God willing, we'd smoke 'em without any more of our boys suffering for it.

* * * *

We stood around while Laynie show up, worked her magic, and then got him into her car. The woman was always a beast under pressure, patching guys up and saving lives, but she worked like a double demon on her own son.

Soon as she had him stable, riding with her to the clinic, we got on our bikes and rode straight to the clubhouse. The old mustangs with their bikes in the shop would have to wait. Club business trumped civilian shit any day of the week, and it had never been this serious.

Half an hour later, we were all in the meeting room. Felt strange to see the Prez's chair empty – or close enough.

Bingo sat in it like a fuckin' person, his massive, hairy body taking up the full seat. Everybody watched the big dog, his lazy tongue hanging outta his mouth, ignorant to the heavy cloud hanging over the club.

"Think you oughta let him sit there?" Sixty said, lighting a smoke.

"Prez ain't dead. Better him than any of us. He's keeping

it warm." Joker looked at me, and I nodded, putting my fists on the table.

"We've gotta figure out how we're gonna handle this shit. No telling how long Dust'll be out of commission 'til Laynie fills us in."

"We can't go after 'em. Fuckers own Atlanta with their mob connections. Outstate Georgia's Deads' territory. They've got themselves a moat surrounding their asses, made of our worst enemies." Skin tried to reason, like he always did.

"Yeah," I said, wishing like hell it weren't true. Brother was right. "We don't have the numbers and we don't know the territory well enough to hit 'em where they live. Chances are their old school ties to every mafia and gang in Dixie would tell 'em we're coming, too."

"What do we do?" Crawl pushed his shaggy black hair back. "Don't give a shit what we decide, just as long as it means they die."

"Everybody's on the same page there, brother. We can't be fuckin' idiots. Need to watch our asses," I said. "Let's look at the situation. We've bought ourselves some time, giving 'em their guns. They came in all pissed about that dead fuck, Jimmy, foaming at the mouth so much they didn't give a shit about tearing up our partnership."

"Go on." Joker had his knife out, holding it by the blade. Crazy fucker looked like he wanted to push his fingers down on it, slice them clean off.

Who the hell ever knew what was rolling through his head?

"We'll lure them onto our turf for another round. This time, we'll find out when they're back. We won't be caught with our pants around our ankles again."

"Lure them?" Sixty snorted. "Shit, bro, it won't take much. Red Beard said he'd be back if he found out we fucked 'em on anything else."

"Yeah, and we have." Everybody looked at me. "Cora. They're gonna find out about her sooner or later. It's my job to keep her safe. Seeing the Prez take a hit made me realize I can't do it as long as they're breathing. I'll let 'em find out she's ours – *mine* – but I'll make damned sure they don't come within ten miles of where I've got her holed up."

"Fuck me – you're using your girl as bait?" Skin's eyes narrowed. He looked at me, then at Joker.

The Veep looked up, suddenly done playing Russian roulette with his knife. "He's right. Girl's the only lure we got."

Steam nearly shot out my fuckin' ears. I hated hearing her talked about like a goddamned piece of meat. I *really* fuckin' hated that this was the only way to keep her safe and do justice.

My fist hit the table. "Look, I'm the last fuckin' guy at this table who wants to do any of this. Red Beard's an arrogant piece of shit with a temper like a damned volcano. You saw what he did to Prez."

"Yeah," Skin growled. "We all saw."

"How do you think he'll react when he hears we've got Jimmy's girl? Bastard thinks we double-crossed him once. Twice – he'll flip his shit. The Torches'll come roaring into town for blood. We'll have a bear trap ready to snap their fucking legs off. Cora's never gonna be in a lick of danger, if I've got anything to say about it."

And fuck me, I did. Had it all mapped out in my head, every grim, dirty detail coming together to protect her, avenge the Prez, restore the club's honor after the kick in the balls they'd given us.

"What the fuck are you thinking, Firefly?" Skin growled. "I'm gonna trust you on keeping her safe. You know the special treatment the Prez has given this girl from day one. Don't know how the hell you think you're gonna announce her, bring them into our ambush, without leading 'em smack into her."

I stood, looking over all my brothers, one by one. "We're gonna piss off Red real bad. Let the fucker know we lied right to his face. Announce it in the open."

I paused. They all looked at me, waiting. I flexed my fists, finally ready to speak the words chewing at my insides.

"Truth is, I'm claiming Cora. She's getting my brand slapped on her skin and a ring on her finger before shit flies. Torches' spies'll hear all about it. We'll hit 'em hard when they come charging in, assuming big Red doesn't have a fuckin' stroke first…"

"Shit!"

"Fuck!"

"Goddamn!"

Several brothers bellowed at once, laughter and shock filling up the room. Joker's knife slammed into the table, adding one more gouge to his spot, already knifed to kingdom come. Bingo sat up and barked, cutting through the commotion. We all piped down as the Veep stood, ruffling Bingo's furry head with one hand.

"Fuck, and they call me crazy," he said, giving me an ice cold look. "You're gonna lose your dick when the Prez finds out."

"Then we'd better move fast. I plan on keeping my pisser. Dust'll be mighty forgiving when he finds out we've mopped up the Atlanta assholes while he's laid out in recovery. Besides, this shit goes deeper than just keeping her safe and cleaning up this fuckin' heap. Cora and me, we're together now. For real."

Sixty grinned, his goatee twitching. "You poor bastard. You sure you're ready to be a *married* fucking man?"

"I'm more worried about her," Skin growled, the long scar on his cheek catching the light. "She has to want this, brother. She doesn't, I'm gonna make damned sure she's got an out the instant we've got the Torches' guts smeared across the Smokies."

"She will," I said, giving him a look from hell. Bastard was probably bent out of shape because he'd been the first brother engaged to his old lady, and now I'd beat him to the altar. "Cora wants me. She needs me. She's fuckin' suffered for everything she's got, and I'm gonna make sure she never has to do it again."

"Whatever, bro. Joker's right. It's your cock on the line." Sixty laughed, and Bingo barked again.

"You heard him. Church adjourned," Joker said, slamming the Prez's gavel down on hard wood. "Report back when you've got this shit in motion."

I nodded, ready as hell to head out and do what I had to do. Saving the club and killing all the Torches was gonna be easy as a run through the Tri-Cities, if I kept this manic energy going.

Getting Cora to go along with it, a little harder.

I'd find a way. Lived my whole life just drifting by like a fucking zombie. Only way I thought I could live after the shit I'd seen overseas. Men dying, villages burning, mass graves of poor sorry bastards killed in cold blood by terrorist fucks. We'd always stumble on that shit whenever we got too deep in the killing.

No man fit easy in civvie life after being on a battlefield. It stayed with him, made him wild, stole his soul and all his drive for anything except the next adrenaline fix.

Drinking, boozing, chasing down pussy to keep me company for just one night.

Before Cora, pussy never got to my head. It was something to fuck, something to feel wrapped around every throbbing inch of me, good for just a shot or two. No different than what I did when I hit the bottle.

Before Cora, I couldn't have dreamed about chasing down pussy for more than just a fuck. Owning a woman past more than the pink was as alien as the big yellow moon in the sky.

Now, I craved it. I wanted it so bad I could feel it smoking in my veins like fire.

I need her. Bad. Needed to keep her. It fuckin' scared me.

Every brother sharing my patch knew how I fought. The unlucky motherfuckers who'd been on the receiving ends of my fists, my shots, or my matches and kerosene knew I *never* backed down. I never winced. I never quit 'til I'd buried the bastards lined up against me and my club alive.

Fighting, killing, torturing…none of that shit raised a single hair on my neck.

Cora, on the other hand…my life after Cora…what the *hell* did that look like? Not a damned clue, but I wanted it.

I rode hard through town, heading for my girl. I could taste her on my lips already, feel her soft gold hair in my hands as they gripped my bike's handlebars.

Before, this free life of blazing down the road and setting panties on fire while I bombed my guts with booze was plenty.

I still wanted some of that – the riding, the freedom, the fresh mountain air sucked between my teeth. But it didn't hold a flame against my screaming need to see my brand on her ass while she called me her old man.

I'd own this girl. I'd make it work, however many fucks I had to fight.

I'd have it all, everything I'd dreamed about, coming into reach. Or I'd be dead.

VIII: By the Hook (Cora)

"Here." Tawny pushed crumpled cash into my hands, wiping the last beads of sweat off her brow.

"Thanks. Go get yourself some water." I smiled, stuffing the bills into my special binder for Meg, before I carted them back to the safe in her office.

The stripper nodded, turned around, and scurried away. I swore she stopped just short of a salute.

They never even tested me anymore. The brush with Tony had only fed the legend. Several girls saw Firefly pounce at just the right time. Now, everybody feared dealing with him, if they took a jab at me.

Sweet victory, I thought, an extra spring in my step as I sat down for accounting.

In the office, I did a quick tally of everything I'd collected this shift. My mouth dropped open when Tawny's tips took it over thirty five hundred.

A new record for my shift!

"Hey, babe." Firefly chose the best timing in the world to walk through the door. Rather, his huge, rock hard body stopped and filled the entire frame, resting his hands on the sides.

"You're just in time!" And I meant it. I got up, ran to him, and threw my arms around his gorgeous neck.

We kissed. So hard, hot, and sticky I thought he'd kick the door shut and take me right there.

Honestly, I wouldn't have resisted, so high on success I'd let him have anything, anywhere.

The unimaginable was happening. The club got richer thanks to me. I'd found something I was actually good at. Hauling in this kind of cash every night told me that maybe this life wasn't so strange after all – and just maybe, I could make it.

"Fuck, you taste good. What's all that for?" he asked, breaking the kiss reluctantly. His strong hands held on to me.

"I'm happy to see you, silly. It's been a great night for money. Meg and Skin are going to be *really* happy."

He grunted. "Yeah, Skinny boy can use some of that shit after the kinda day we've had."

I looked at him and cocked my head. He didn't elaborate.

Instead, he pushed me gently inside, shut the door, and sat in the chair across from Meg's desk. The normal office chair looked tiny with him filling it, and I couldn't help but smile.

It was either that, or think about everything that mountain he called a body did to me.

"Finish up. We've gotta hit the road."

"Okay! We should stop by the store later. I'd like to pick up a few things for the place, especially now that we're both getting settled in."

I didn't notice his face had darkened until I looked up. Those soft blue eyes were like icy stones. He had the same stare as the one when he'd knocked out Tony Pearson the other night.

"That's gonna have to wait, babe. We're staying at my sister's place for the next week or two, or however the fuck long it takes to wrap up important club biz."

My fingers came to a dead stop on Meg's keyboard, logging the day's profits on the spreadsheet. *What?!*

"Sister? I didn't even know you had one! What business? What are you talking about, Firefly?"

"All the boys got into a bad fight with the Torches today. They came here, pissed off about your old man, looking for you. Prez shrugged them the fuck off. They tucked their tails and ran, but that shit won't last long. They're dangerous. Outta control. They'll be back. Means we're gonna deal with 'em on our own terms.."

"But I mean…our place…" I looked down at the dusty computer screen, my heart sinking. "Jesus, my work here…"

"Meg'll hear it soon. She'll work around it, have somebody cover your shifts 'til hell blows over. God willing, you'll only be outta commission for a little while." He stood, crossed the small space to my desk, and put his hands down flat, gazing straight into my eyes. "No bullshitting, babe. I'm trying to save your life."

I wanted to cry. Just when I'd started to relax, feel at home with him, and this strange, dirty underworld…

"What's the plan?" I said softly, wondering if I even wanted to know.

"Like I said, my sis is giving us her place for the next week or two. Hannah's a hotshot traveler for the banks, spends half the fuckin' year over in Switzerland or the Virgins or some shit. Her house is nice. Lot bigger than the apartment."

His teeth clenched when he said the last part. I came up behind him, and laid my hand softly on his shoulders. Thought it was just because there was a gaping hole between him and his sister, and he'd let me in on it, in his own little way.

"There's more, darlin'. We're not just hiding the fuck out 'til this all blows over. I gotta be honest. Can't lie to you."

I looked at him, narrowing my eyes. For the millionth time since I'd been thrown into all of this, my heart raced, thumping along with a steady, revving tempo, ready to tear me in two.

"I can't take the mystery here. Tell me."

"No. I'll show you. Come on." He grabbed my hand, rough and insistent.

Before I knew what was happening, we were leaving the office. Firefly pulled me toward the curtain. I started dragging my feet – what the hell was he doing? Didn't he know they were right in the middle of Honey-Bee's late night act?

"Firefly, no!" There wasn't any stopping him.

He was too strong, too persistent, and the lights blinded me the second we stepped out on stage. Huge, glaring spotlights and neon red would've wrecked anyone's eyesight after spending eight hours in the gloomy blackness backstage.

The music came to a screeching halt. Honey-Bee swung from a giant sling above us, wearing nothing except tall white heels and those fake crystal angel wings she always slipped on before her act. She looked down on us, totally confused, a ball of feathers in her hand she'd been ready to blow to the horny men as part of her tease.

Then the catcalls started.

"Take it the fuck off, baby! All the waaaay!"

"What the hell's this big biker asswipe doin' on stage? Didn't know this place was licensed for hardcore fuck shows..."

"Honey-Beee!"

I pushed myself into him, desperately pushing my nails into his neck, holding his eyes. "Firefly – please! We can't be out here."

"No, babe. Keep breathing. I've got something for you."

He reached into his pocket. His hand took mine, held it up, and I watched the bright gold ring in the club's bright lights slide onto my finger as he shoved it in place.

"Everybody listen up!" Firefly boomed, roaring through the crowd. When he spoke, their chatter stopped, like a hurricane silencing the ocean. "Came out here tonight to let ya'll know I'm claiming this girl. Cora Chase is about to be the best goddamned old lady a man could ever ask for, and an even better wife. One round for everybody on me!"

The crowd erupted, hooting and hollering. The few lone women stuffed between the clammy, horny bastards screamed like they'd just won the lottery. Free booze meant the world to old bar flies so desperate for booze they came here with their husbands just to drink.

Hell, I wanted to join them. I could've used a tall, stiff drink right now. Maybe ten of them.

The entire club blurred. I couldn't follow what was happening. That ring around my finger felt like a leash, a noose, a choke point trying to smother my whole world for the second time in a month.

"Crank the fuckin' music up when I'm done," Firefly growled, grinning to the crowd, still holding up the new ring on my hand triumphantly with his. "Play something sappy and loud about love, I don't give a shit, DJ. I just want this whole fuckin' town to know that Cora's Property of Firefly now. I'm gonna love her, keep her, and never, ever let her go."

The crowd exploded. Firefly moved in, pulling me to his chest. His tight arms around my waist were just about the only thing stopping me from passing out.

"Kiss me, baby girl," he whispered in my ear. "Meant every fuckin' word I just said here, Cora. This is about protecting you, yeah, but it's more than that. Don't expect you to understand. Don't care if you ever do. You're mine now, babe. Forever."

Too much. Too soon. *Too crazy.*

No mistake. This was *CRAZY!*

I tried to claw him, to scream, but I couldn't do anything when the bass started blasting through the club. Honey-Bee chirped happily above us, shouting down congratulations, showering us in huge handfuls of cheap feathers like snow.

His lips moved up my neck. Rage, confusion, and desire wrestled like snakes inside me, making my skin crawl until I swooned.

He held me, kept me from collapsing. Our eyes locked, and those dark, blue seas in his face held a thousand wild promises.

I didn't know what to do. Didn't know if I'd step out of here without having a heart attack.

Then the gorgeous lunatic pulled me toward him, burying his lips against mine. I sank into his kiss and bit him. Hard.

Firefly never took his mouth off mine until he decided it was finally time to move. Not even when I tasted his blood.

* * * *

Eventually, the delirium on stage swept me away. At first, I thought I'd passed out, and he'd carried me to the small, dingy church just outside Knoxville. But then, if I was unconscious, I couldn't have ridden with him on his bike, draped around him like a ragdoll, clinging tight to him through the sharp turns he took on those high mountain roads.

"This wasn't the way I wanted this shit to go down, darlin'. It'll have to do. Ain't no time to throw you in lily white and invite all your friends and family. It'll be a small ceremony. We'll make up for it in all the years to come. Do bigger bashes when we renew our vows."

"You're…you're out of your mind," I whispered, trying not to stumble as he led me up the steps.

I was still woozy from the ride in. My brain temporarily shut down, processing the latest trauma.

God. How could he do this to me?

Nothing about this made sense. Well, maybe the part about keeping me safe, but did it really take this to do it? Marriage?

Talk about extreme. Irrational. Ridiculous!

And just when I'd just started to like him, too.

Firefly gave the old double doors a hard shove, and we stepped inside. I did a double take when I saw Skin and Meg standing near the altar, alongside an old, wiry looking preacher man with silver hair and owlish spectacles.

"You two *knew?*" I hissed at Meg as he dragged me down the aisle.

"Just found out. Skin said the ceremony needs witnesses to be official…sorry, Cora. I'm just trying to help." She lowered her eyes, shooting her lover a sharp look that said it all. *Are you sure about this?*

Skin embraced his woman, pulled her tight to his chest. Right now, she was the only one being comforted in this freak show.

"It's gonna be okay, babe," he whispered softly, before he looked up at me. "Gonna be all right for you, too, Cora. Nobody wanted it to get this real, but we've gotta keep you safe. Firefly won't let anything bad happen to you. He promised."

We stopped next to the altar, and the two men shared a vicious look. Firefly took my hand, held it to his lips, and kissed it. I felt the scar I'd left from the harsh love bite, and tasting his blood in my mouth.

"Everybody ready?" Preacher man asked, his voice as soft and out of place as everything else here. He didn't even flinch when he looked at me, smiled, and saw the sickening look on my face.

Jesus, he looked official, too. I wondered what drove him to do this kind of favor for the club.

"Babe, don't fight it," Firefly said, pulling me into his warm embrace. "Hold on. This'll all be over before you can...what the fuck?"

I head-butted him. My face sank into his warm, powerful chest, igniting a whole new storm of emotions I couldn't begin to handle.

Nothing in my life was going down like I'd planned it.

But this...this weird, sudden, terrifying joke of a wedding tore away the shielding on my heart. All the pain and humiliation I'd suffered came pouring out. Inhaling his rich, masculine scent made me want to stay there forever. Die there, if I had to.

Even now, it calmed me. Even when I hated him. I should've put up a fight, gone out kicking and screaming and shouting, but what little I'd had left died on the Ruby Heel's bright stage.

He'd decided I was going to be his old lady, his *fucking wife,* and there wasn't a single thing I could do about it.

"Wait." The word dropped out of his mouth like a

hammer hitting concrete, and everything else stopped, including the crappy organ music flowing through the speakers.

"Brother?" Skin sounded so unsure.

I looked up, and saw Firefly's attention shift from him to me. "You're confused as shit right now, aren't you? Fuck yeah, you are, and you've got every damned right to be. I swore a promise to the club before we got all this in motion. Told the man standing here I'd do whatever the hell it took to keep you safe. I thought you'd be on the same page."

My eyes were prisoners in his. He leaned in, licked his lips, and whispered words that gutted me.

"I'm sorry, darlin'. I fucked up."

His beautiful blue eyes softened, mirroring the change in his energy from hot and excited to melancholy. Suddenly, my sympathy swelled for him – so insane and unexpected I wanted to scream.

"Wedding's off. For today. We'll settle this shit when you're good and ready, Cora," he said, stopping to put his warm, firm lips on my forehead. "Skin, you let the brothers know it's done, without a hitch. She's still getting my brand and wearing my ring, but we're stopping just short of making this shit legal. I gotta do what's right for everybody here."

Meg sighed. I saw her out of the corner of my eye, tugging on Skin's hand, a soft smile pulling at her cheeks.

"Good," Skin growled. "I'd have stopped this shit myself with the way she's acting. You're taking a wife, Firefly, not a slave."

NICOLE SNOW

"What? You think I don't fuckin' know that? Why the hell you think I'm putting a hold on the only shit I ever wanted?"

"For fuck's sake, brother, that's exactly what I'm saying. You don't need a lecture from me. You're a good man." Skin bowed his head just slightly, a respectful gesture I never would've imagined coming from these rough, hard men in leather.

They shook hands, before Firefly turned his attention back to me, pulling me deeper into his embrace, big as the southern sky. His arms held me tighter than before, solid like oak.

My heart swelled. He'd sounded so serious, so loving. He'd surprised me for the millionth time today, and I wasn't going to be able to handle any more.

Preacher man shuffled awkwardly behind us, coughing into his hand. "I'll keep the papers in my office, just in case anybody decides to change their mind."

"No need," Firefly told him.

For just a split second, I regretted the fact that we weren't going through with it. Then he shook me awake, cupping my chin in his hand, and tilting my face up to meet his eyes.

"Darlin', you look at me, and listen good. Far as you and everybody else knows, we're hitched. I announced it at the Heel because the Torches have got spies all over town. They need to know you're mine. They need to get pissed about it, so they'll roll right into the hell we've planned for 'em."

"Firefly, I –"

"I ain't done yet," he growled, moving his face closer to mine, until I could feel his hot breath on my lips. "I meant every fuckin' thing I said back there. Everything I told you tonight. I want you to be *mine,* dammit, but not like this. This wedding's on hold. Doesn't change the fact that I'm making you my old lady tonight."

My heart stopped. I gasped. His hand snaked down my back, grabbed my ass, and jerked me into him, turning me into a buttery, knee-shaking mess.

"You've got about twenty minutes to decide how you wanna wear my ink. We're going to get you branded. Right now." He brushed his lips against mine, teasing me until it hurt. "This is the place to take God as my witness for everything I'm telling you next. Make no mistake, Cora, *you are mine.* Get used to it. There's no taking it back. Second my name goes on your skin, I own your sweet ass, plus every other inch of you, darlin'. Mine tonight, 'til the end of fuckin' time."

Oh, God. His words hit me like dark biker poetry, rough and conflicted as everything I felt for him, igniting a hundred more raw emotions.

I wasn't looking at a man anymore, or feeling him. He was a human tornado, conquering me with his eyes, telling me with nothing more than a long, hard glance that this was real. All of it.

Just like a raging storm, he'd pick me up, fling me around, and fuck me with those huge, feral muscles until I was bruised and dripping wet.

Love? Hate? I didn't know the meaning anymore.

That wicked, mysterious place where they met was Firefly incarnate, and he vowed to make me feel every mad inch of him.

I actually bit my bottom lip as he took my hand and spun me around, pulling me toward the church doors.

Skin whispered a few words to the preacher man, something about how he'd better not breathe a word of this to anybody. Nothing except the lie we'd all been told to say.

We were married.

Back on Firefly's bike, I hugged him tighter, breathing the warm night air hanging down over the city from the Great Smokies.

No, I hadn't been ready for a flash wedding ceremony. Daddy wanted something beautiful for me, long ago, and I did, too. But I wasn't fighting him on the old lady thing.

A delicious tingle pulled on my nipples, firing between my legs. Whenever I thought about him owning me with ink before he claimed my ass, I shuddered, and held on tighter.

We tore through the backstreets, his bike kicking up puddles of rain settling on the streets. My heart raced faster, and that savage pulse between my legs quickened when I saw the glowing red sign.

SKULL'S INK, it said in neon, with a smaller sign beneath it. NO F*CKIN' CRYBABIES ALLOWED!

"Last stop before we hit my sis' place," he said, drinking me in with his eyes. "Let's make the most of it. Fuck if these fingers aren't itching like hell to put my name all over you."

"Don't know about *all* over me," I said, sticking out my

tongue. "One spot. That's all I need to make it official, right?"

"Yeah, darlin'," he said. "That's the goal. Long as I see my name stamped in your ass, you're getting fucked 'til you can't even walk. Promise."

Holy Shit. I shivered, the anticipation building like a fever.

We walked into the deserted shop. I'd expected an artist to come out and do the work, some freaky man with dark shapes scrawled on him from head to toe.

"Sit down," Firefly said, gesturing to the nearest bench in the back. He jerked on the lamp overhead, aiming it.

"No way. You're a tattoo artist too?"

He just smiled, laying out his tools. "Pants off, babe. We'll talk it over as we go. You'll be more relaxed than usual because you've already had my hands all over your ass."

However true, that didn't stop me from blushing like a prom girl as I dropped my khakis. On the table, his rough hand snatched at my waistband, ripping my panties down.

I heard him breathe deep, taking in my scent, everything I couldn't hide from how hot and wet and conflicted I'd been for at least the last hour.

"Fuck. You're lucky I learned a thing or two about discipline with Uncle Sam, alongside these inks. Otherwise, I'd be slamming into you hard and deep, right the fuck here. You'd be out before we even got started."

His hand touched the small of my back, swept downward, zipping over my bare ass cheeks. Arching my back, I sucked in a breath, held it, and let it steam out my lips.

"Soon, baby girl. Keep that fire hot. Hold it just for me."
He leaned down, numbing my ass with one hand, pouring
hot breath into my ear. "Quicker we get this over with,
quicker you get this dick inside you. This ain't officially our
honeymoon, but I'm fucking you like it is."

Then his hand slapped my ass, making a clap so loud
and harsh I jerked on the leather bench. "Ah! Did you really
need to do that to check if I'm numb?"

He chuckled. "Nah. It'll be a few days before I can give
you a proper spanking after this shit, and I know you're
gonna mouth off sooner or later. Preemptive strike."

Asshole. I buried my face in the leather underneath me,
the only thing I could do to hide my smile.

* * * *

By the time he'd finished, I was out of my mind with pure
desire. No, no, that didn't begin to describe it, and neither
did all the other euphemisms for *dying because I wasn't
getting fucked this instant.*

Dripping wet. Horny-as-hell. Heat.

They all plucked my nerves. Painted my skin soft, wet,
and full of goosebumps.

My own reflection seemed foreign when the mirror
twirled in front of me, then angled down so I could see my
butt.

"Good?" he growled. "Looks pretty fuckin' amazing
from where I'm standing, but it's your ass, darlin'."

I looked into the mirror. A winged skull with pistols

smoking on both sides lay on my upper ass cheek. A proper tramp stamp.

Everything I thought I'd never have on my body, and yet, it seemed right. So strange, wonderful, and wild I couldn't stop smiling.

The text inscribed on the skull's forehead in flaming, tapered black said it all. PROPERTY OF FIREFLY, DEADLY PISTOLS MC, TENNESSEE.

"Wow. You've got some serious talent," I said, sliding off the bench so I could finally pull up my panties. "I like it."

"Fuck yeah, you do. Had a feeling you've been wanting to wear my name since the first night I got my hands all over you, babe."

I stared at the ground, searching for my khakis, saying nothing. He knew me too damned well for his own good.

For some reason, I thought about his time in the service, trying to imagine this big, savage bastard as a soldier. He'd had his share of names, numbers, and tags throughout his life. He'd turned them over for a patch, and a road name, not so different from the transformation happening to me.

It's proof stung gently on my butt cheek as I fastened my belt. He was cleaning up, putting his tools away and pivoting the lamp, when he caught me staring.

"What've you got going in that pretty head?" he asked, giving the bench I'd just lain on a quick wipe.

It needed it, too. I'd laid there for what seemed like a small eternity while he did his work, shaking and sweating, slick between my legs.

I tried to take my mind off it. I walked up to him, laid a hand on his shoulder, and followed his huge bulk as he rose to full height.

"What's your name? I only know you as Firefly. That can't be your real name."

"Huck," he said. "Huck Davis. Ma was a real sucker for Mark Twain."

Huck. Huck?!

I burst out laughing. Wracking my brain to remember the stories I'd read when I was a kid, I came back with all the hijinks and good humor from a simpler time.

Surprise aside, it fit him. Just like a glove.

"Fucking shit," he growled. "You'd better believe Firefly's the name that I wear proudly. Far as we're concerned, that's the one you're gonna keep calling me, baby."

"No, no, it isn't that." I squeezed his shoulder, swept it up, letting my hand wander across his cheek, feeling his rough dark stubble. "I like it. I like it a lot, Huck. You shouldn't be ashamed. It's a wonderful name. It tells me something about the good man behind all the leather and skulls."

"Yeah, well," he grunted, collecting his words. "You'd better keep that shit to yourself, unless we're behind closed doors. Don't give a damn what you say when it's just me, you, and a surface for fucking. You can call me fuckin' Shakespeare for all I care, once I'm up inside you, Cora."

He pushed the small cart with his tattoo tools away, rounded the bench to my side, and jerked me into his arms.

We kissed while his hands roamed my back. He fingered the loops around my belt in my khakis, teasing one hand on the upper edge of my ass, so close to the new brand he'd stamped on me.

The tingling sensation teasing me all evening sparked into an open fire. I pinched my thighs together, struggling to contain the heat between my legs.

Fighting for control, and failing.

Just burning, burning, burning.

"Fuck," he growled into my mouth, refusing to pull his lips away. "Gonna teach you to suck cock good now that you're mine. You'll love it, yeah?"

Yeah. I moaned into his mouth, doing a terrible job of hiding just how hot it made me.

Just thinking about gliding up and down his long, hard, wild length with my tongue, taking him in my mouth, almost caused me to lose it on the spot.

Firefly's hand caressed up, taking my breast in one hand. He squeezed it hard through my shirt and bra, begging me to throw my clothes off again.

I squirmed against him, pushing my hips on his, forcing my pussy to feel his rock hard bulge against my belly. I swore it was about to tear through his pants, and then he'd flip me around, slam me against the leather bench, and own me all the ways we both wanted.

But he stopped. I blinked, opened my eyes, struggling to see through the lust clouding my vision.

"What?"

"That ring," he growled, grabbing my hand. His eyes

had caught it while we kissed, when I'd moved my hand across his face. "Take it off now, babe. We only needed you wearing it as a prop at the Heel, so we could make everybody believe."

Ouch. My heart sank. For some reason, it hurt.

I knew damned well that it shouldn't. Didn't change the painful reality.

Stepping away from him, I held my hand to my chest, gazing at the small golden loop he'd given me. Our eyes met across the small space between us.

"No," I said, forming a fist. "Let me wear it, Huck. I want to. I know it seems insane after the way I acted earlier tonight, but it was all so sudden, so crazy, being forced into something like this."

"You mean wed to me?" His eyes burned, and I nodded. "Yeah, I get it. Darlin', if you wanna keep that shit sitting pretty on your little hand, I'm down. You'll be under my lock and key for the next week or two anyway. Nobody's gonna see it, except me."

I smiled. "I like the sound of that."

"Good," he rumbled, throwing his arms around me all over again. "Because you're gonna look twice as fuckin' sexy wearing my brand and my ring. Don't care if one of those things means something fake. I'm gonna fuck you like it's real, give you everything you're begging for in those hot little lips."

He buried me in another kiss before I could even speak. All I could think about was having him on top of me, driving into my core while my legs clung to his.

Sweating, shaking, creaming all over his cock. *Oh, hell.*

Giving it up for him. All to him. Letting him guide me.

Fucking us both toward a future I'd just begun to seriously think about.

Emotions collided in my brain like comets, sending more fire streaking through my blood. I pushed my tongue against his, sucking at his mouth, biting into his bottom lip for the second time that night.

He bit me back this time. Before I knew what was happening, he had me against the wall, ripping pants to the floor.

The fresh tattoo tingled as my ass ground against the brick wall, but I didn't care. Firefly pushed his jeans down, rubbing his cock against my melting slit, hungrier than ever to take what he'd laid claim to.

Then he was inside me. One rough, insistent, unforgettable thrust.

His hand went up my shirt, fondling the breast he'd started on earlier, without holding anything back. Snarling, he jerked his hand against the partition in my shirt, tearing it open.

Buttons flew all over the place, clattering on the ground like pebbles. He held me down, crushed my mouth beneath his before I could squeak any protest. His hips moved, pinning me to the wall, fucking me so hard my bones shook with every stroke.

Oh, shit. Holy, holy, holy shit!

"Give it the fuck up to me, Cora Chase. Know you want to real goddamned bad. Saw you dripping the whole fuckin' time while I put my ink in you."

His strokes came faster. Harder, like a human piston.

His hips pulled back and rammed into me, rougher every time, an honest-to-God earthquake that wouldn't stop until I gave him everything he wanted.

My shirt ripped again in his hand. Another hand moved behind me, snatching at my hair, curling it in his fingers. He pulled, setting off a whole new series of explosions inside me.

I was going to be naked, without any clothes, if he kept this up. And I couldn't bring myself to care.

Not while I was slumped against the wall, overwhelmed, captured by his kiss.

Not while he crammed me full of his cock, stretching me a little more with every stroke, training my pussy to fit him like we were made to join.

Not while I was about to have the most furious orgasm I'd ever had in my entire life.

"Ah, fuck, you feel too good. Too goddamned good for every inch of this, woman. Gonna fill you up. Come with me, Cora! Fuckin' come, come, come…"

His cock stabbed into me one more time. My feet found their way behind his, and they pinched at his body desperately, while my nails clung to his neck, clinging for support.

"Oh, oh…oh hell!"

Hella good. Fire and brimstone lashed my body in waves when I lost it.

Snarling, he came, filling me with his heat. His seed

flooded me, and he drove his cock deeper, grinding that short, sweet crop of hair on his pubic bone just perfectly against my clit.

I thought I'd died and gone to a new dimension where there was nothing but blinding, hot pleasure. Full bodied fire licked me again and again from head to toe. Everything below my waist curled in on itself, pulsing magnificently, just yawning and clutching and throbbing with passion.

In the middle of it all, something wet exploded from my center. I could feel myself coming so hard I gushed all over his cock, wondering if he'd truly torn me open and emptied part of my soul all over him.

"Fuck, fuck, fuck!" Firefly held me down as time slowed.

Still coming, still fucking me, shooting his come as deep as it would go. My pussy clenched so hard to his cock I thought I'd pass out, high on his lightning shooting through me.

We lost ourselves in that mad, mad rhythm for what seemed like half the night. When I could finally blink again, and open my eyes without wincing from the shock, he looked at me.

I saw my blue eyes reflected in his, two seas on fire, storming in ways I could barely even fathom as our two very different worlds came together. Or, at the very least, our bodies. Flesh on flesh, burning and pounding as one.

"Easier than I figured to make you squirt," he growled, running his hand across my pussy as he pulled out, holding it up so I could see the wetness. "Don't you dare blush, darlin'. Get used to it. I fuckin' love it, and that means you're gonna be doing it a whole lot more."

I couldn't help it. My cheeks turned beet red, perfect targets for him to smother me in a whole new series of scalding hot kisses.

"Let's get you cleaned up so we can ride," he said, bending over and pulling up his pants. "Sooner we get to Hannah's place, the harder we can fuck in peace and quiet. Helluva a lot nicer than this fuckin' dump, too."

I smiled as he handed me a towel. I let him wipe the excess coming out of me before I put my clothes back in place, a strangely intimate thing almost as intense as letting him inside me.

He conquered me. It wouldn't be long before I begged him to finish what we'd started in that screwy little church.

It scared me. But fear hadn't held derailed me during any of this. My desire to claw my way through every inch of this dark, dangerous underworld only grew, the closer I got to Firefly.

Before, I'd been worried I'd end up a slave forever to the Deadly Pistols MC. Now, I just had to worry about being his – and a willing one.

He conquered me. Piece by piece, night by night, kiss by steaming kiss.

God help me, I loved it. Every time another part of me pulled away in his hands, or my heart collapsed in another avalanche, I quietly rejoiced.

This man, this unreal pleasure he brought, was everything I'd denied myself under daddy's thumb. Firefly's heat burned away the lies, no different than how his crude words stripped things to their truths.

So I walked with him. Rode with him. Gave him my everything as my protector, my lover, my guide.

Where he'd take us in the end, I wasn't sure. But I was ready for the journey.

When we stepped outside and climbed on his bike, I held him tight, smiling as I rested my chin on his shoulder. His motorcycle cut through the darkness, and I marveled at how quickly I'd learned to love its reassuring growl.

His life was complicated and scary sometimes, but it had a certain charm. Firefly owned who he was. He lived *honestly,* and right now, after all the confusion, that meant the world.

Maybe one day, it wouldn't be so bad being an outlaw's bride.

It had to be better than being a dead, crooked sheriff's daughter. Hell, it might be everything.

* * * *

My mouth dropped when we rolled through the huge iron gates outside Knoxville. The house was beautiful, tidy, and ginormous.

Its high brick walls glowed in the moonlight behind the lovely gardens, vines and flowers just beginning to poke their buds out after the winter. Huge roman columns held up the roof, and when he took my helmet and guided me toward the double-doored entrance, I wanted to check to make sure we were really at the right place.

Fifteen minutes later, we sat in front of a roaring fire, a glass of wine in my hand and a beer in his. He'd snorted when he looked at the fancy glasses lined up, ripping off the cap with his bare hands and drinking from the bottle instead.

"Sis keeps this place stocked to the fucking brim for all her rich friends. None of that shit ever appealed much to me," he explained, taking another long pull on his brew.

I put my wine glass down, careful not to spill any. It felt like a wine tasting at a lodge, with all the fancy trimmings and Turkish rugs beneath us. I feared I'd break something just sitting there.

"How did she make so much money?" I asked. "I mean, if you don't mind me asking. I didn't picture you coming from this kind of family, Firefly."

He swallowed the last of his beer and grinned, slamming his bottle down on the table. "I didn't. We never grew up rich, Hannah and me. She only turned into a hotshot entrepreneur about five years ago, when shit really started going her way. We both chose our trenches. Mine were in Afghanistan, and then all over Dixie, riding with the Pistols. Hers were spreadsheets, computer fuckery, kissing the asses of angel investors for a couple years before she got her app launched. Fuckin' thing must've made a cool million over a month or more, and then some."

"Wow." I sipped my wine, loving the quality.

"Yeah. She's got herself a nice little deal with that Ty kid up in Alaska now. You know, the rich techie Sterner fuck you see all over the gossip rags from time to time. Boy married his fuckin' stepsister, you know."

I laughed and nodded. Of course everybody knew about the Sterner family and all their antics. For every dollar they earned, there must've been a gene for crazy. Except that girl he'd married, Claire, had gotten the fairy tale romance almost every girl dreams about. So the tabloids said, anyway.

"Truth is, I'm happy for her. Both of us grew up in a damned trailer park, our folks living check-to-check, never enough to go around. We barely talk anymore, me being so fuckin' busy with the club, and her being all biz. But we were close once. We both grew up dirt poor. Sis is doing me a solid, letting us hang here like this." He looked up, the fire next to us dancing in his eyes. "You'd better believe she's the only chick I'd die for besides you, darlin'."

I smiled, staring into the flames, watching them rolling softly in the fireplace.

"I hope you never have to," I said. My heart ached when I thought about any pain coming to him because of me.

"Shit, girl, so do I. But I'm ready." He stood, crossing to the little loveseat where I sat, joining me. "Nobody's ever gonna lay a finger on what's mine. I'm a jealous sonofabitch, yeah. Know how to take good care of everything I own, too. You're safe, babe, long as you stick with me. I'm not letting you go anywhere."

His arm went around me, and I buried my face in his chest. Enjoying the cozy, warm, masculine cocoon around me was all I wanted for a night like this.

Well, except for one more thing…

My thighs tingled deliciously, meeting in the center where a whole new fire burned. I nestled in his arms, hiding my face against his perfect chest, until I couldn't take it anymore.

When I finally looked up, he read my mind. Firefly held my chin, letting me feel his strength as he pressed his fingers gently into my face. He held it there, poised for his kiss, which came hot, slow, and teasing as he brushed his lips against mine.

I couldn't stop the moan coming out when his mouth covered mine.

"Come on," he said, lifting me up, into his arms. "Your eyes are bugging out at all this fuckin' glitz and glamor just sitting here. You're really gonna flip your shit when you see the bedroom."

Oh, God.

* * * *

He wasn't kidding. Jesus, did this man ever crack a joke? Ever exaggerate anything?

The room where we stayed was bigger than the apartment, and I'd thought that seemed like a lot of space for just him and I.

Here, we had our own sauna, a small bar, and a gigantic canopy bed all to ourselves.

He undressed me before we stepped into it and I watched him pull the curtains shut. A small, blue lamp switched on above us when he touched a button. We were suddenly deep in our own pure world of luxury and desire.

My mind raced a hundred miles an hour, and my heart tried to keep pace, enjoying the wild clash of this bad boy against the sophisticated backdrop. The Ruby Heel tried to emulate this atmosphere, sometimes. Only it came off ten times cheaper by its very nature as a strip club and watering hole for dirty men.

This was authentic. A prince was about to take me, and it didn't take much imagination to complete the illusion. Only this prince was harder, way more tattooed, and probably had a much filthier mouth than any spoiled bastard who'd ever worn a crown.

"Open those fuckin' legs, baby girl," he growled, pushing my thighs apart. I hesitated for too long, lost in my thoughts.

His hands moved rougher, opening me, his lips laying kisses against my soft belly. "Pay attention. If I gotta start asking twice, I'm gonna tie you the fuck up in these silk sheets and bend you around any way I want."

Yes! Yes, please!

My back arched, perfectly timed to his lips moving lower. He sank down near my knees, kissing his way up, up, stamping warm heat across my thighs. His breath poured over my pussy, teasing me.

Muscles I didn't know I had wound unbelievably tight. I tried to wiggle toward his face, but he stopped me, holding me back, forcing me to suffer the anticipation.

"You get my tongue when you tell me you love wearing my name *and* my ring," he growled. "Say it, Cora. Make me believe it."

Holy fucking shit. Didn't he have a clue what he was asking?

I squirmed in his hands, desperate to be licked, fingered, fucked. But he was asking me to open all the way, to let him into the deepest part of me.

Oh, God. I hadn't realized he was an expert psychologist along with being an outlaw and a tattoo artist. Lucky me!

"I love wearing whatever you give me, Huck. Everything," I whimpered, feeling him pulse more fiery breath across my pussy, focusing around my clit. "Really, I do. I want it all. I want you to take me."

"Fuck, you're a good actress. Almost believe you. Almost." His thumb started in my thin strip of pubic hair, slid down, and pushed into my folds, moving dangerously close to my clit.

But not close enough!

I bit down, clenching my teeth. Going insane from the raw need stabbing me didn't begin to describe this torture.

"What more do you want?" I snapped, wishing he wasn't able to hold me down like this. Good thing I loved it. "I told you, I'm serious. I love you, you bastard. I. Love. You."

No! I didn't realize what I'd said until it was out of my mouth and in his ears.

Shit. My lips trembled. I was about to try to claw it back, come to my senses, stop the sopping wet sex fever from drowning me in words I really shouldn't say.

But Firefly never gave me that chance. His fingers pulled my pussy lips open and his face moved into me. Licking, sucking, devouring, shoving me into frantic pleasure.

His thumb barely moved when my body gave it up. Electric currents hit hard, and he slid two fingers into me, jerking them like mad across my soft, quivering wall.

My clit went between his teeth. He sucked it, wiped it with his tongue until it swelled and pulsed in his mouth.

Fuck it. There was nothing left to do in the lunatic heat roasting me alive except own it.

"Don't stop, love. Never, never fucking stop! I love you, Firefly. *Love. You.*"

His free hand grabbed my ass, pulling me into his face. He made me ride him with an intensity that didn't even seem human.

I came so hard I thought I'd go blind. The words screaming out of my mouth wilted into nonsense, shrieks and moans and sounds I couldn't classify.

Firefly licked me to heaven and back again. His tongue did things to my clit that caused every muscle in my body to jerk like mad. My eyes rolled back in my head and I let his storm sweep me away, circling deeper into his passion, coming for this sexy, merciless bastard I'd just told the bitter truth.

Quaking, moaning, and sliding all over his mouth and stubble, I let sheer ecstasy carry me away.

When it ended, I was panting. He wasn't finished.

My lover reared up, wiping his mouth, the fearsome tattoos on his chest contorting with his awesome muscle. "This pussy tastes better than ever tonight. I'd eat it again if it weren't so wet it was begging for my dick."

He reached for my nipple, and rolled it until I moaned.

Eyes shut, I whimpered, letting my words match the plea in my body.

"Do it. I want you inside me."

Like he needed any encouragement. Firefly's weight shifted between my legs, the head of his thick cock rubbing through my folds.

"Damned good thing nobody knows where we are. I'd blow their brains out and still keep fucking you if we got interrupted now," he growled, kissing my throat, then digging his teeth into my tender skin. "Turn over. I want you on your knees, taking every inch of me that's about to go off like a hand grenade, darlin'."

He helped shuffle me onto my hands and knees. Then I felt him, pressed hard against my ass, tense and oh-so-ready to plunge deep.

"Fuckin' love your greedy, sweet little cunt. I'm gonna give it everything it wants, and then some," he said, pushing into me. His hand slapped my ass – the cheek that hadn't been stamped with his name earlier tonight. "Fuck. You were beautiful before, baby, but seeing my name on your ass? Hotter than all the fuckin' stars rolled into one."

He began thrusting, pumping, fucking me deep. I buried my face in the fancy pillows, all that was stopping me from screaming my lungs out.

It didn't take long before the first climax crashed over me. I was prone, open to his power, every single inch of me shaking when his hips collided with mine.

His fingers dug into both ass cheeks, the leverage he needed for fucking me harder. Mine went straight into the sheets. Holding, tangling, pulling them, desperate to ground myself to something before he fucked me right off the face of the earth.

Every piston of his cock into me fed the fireball building near my womb. I couldn't take it, the way he fucked me, filled me, owned me.

Then he took my hair in his fist, threatening to get me to make this place echo with my shrieks.

"Come on this cock, darling. Come 'til you soak the fuckin' sheets."

Oh, hell. Hellllllllllllllll!

I exploded. Saw stars. Convulsed on him as he went balls deep, grinding his length into me, making me feel every throbbing inch as he added his heat to mine.

His cock lit me on fire, searing every nerve. His seed would extinguish it, but only after we'd both been wracked with so much pleasure we were spent.

Completely, unquestionably exhausted.

"Love this beautiful fucking pussy. Love fucking it. Love owning it," he said, his voice a harsh whisper, growling through his pleasure. "Fuckin' love you."

That last part set me off all over again. My body milked a few last bursts of pleasure from his cock before I collapsed, wondering if we'd left scorched holes in the fancy silk sheets.

IX: Where There's Smoke (Firefly)

"You gotta be shittin' me. It's raining *again?*" I climbed out of bed, walking over to the huge French doors leading to the balcony. Took a couple seconds for my legs to limber up after fucking all night. "Day fuckin' ten. Where does the time go?"

"I'll give you three good guesses," Cora said, sauntering up behind me and placing her soft, sweet hands on my shoulders. Woman rubbed them like a masseuse, using my body to shield her from the chill air.

It had turned damned cold with the rain blowing in from the Smokies the past three days – or was it four?

Hell, we'd both lost track of time, being cooped up here for a solid week. Easy to ignore everything when I'd spent every damned day inside her.

"Gonna have to make a run to town for food soon. We've chewed our way through all the shit here that I know how to pronounce, much less make." I looked at her and smiled.

She hugged my waist, running her hands over my abs, teasing my cock hard again. "I'd like to come with," she whispered.

Turning around, I pulled her hands off me, and shot her the look that said *bodyguard,* not just lover. "No. Rules are rules, Cora. You're staying put, whatever the fuck I do. I really oughta call the prospects to look in on you if I ain't around, but the club's been so damned short handed…"

My brow furrowed. Couldn't even hide it. The constant danger hanging over us was beginning to sting my ass like a swarm of hornets.

At first, it was easy just to settle, to ignore the bullshit. Bringing her off like a goddamned bull in rut every night helped.

A man didn't have to worry when he had the best pussy of his life throttling his dick. All the hell wilted when I threw her legs over my shoulders and slid the fuck into her, making her feel every smack of my balls on her ass.

But every second I wasn't in Cora, wedged between her legs as she thrashed all over my cock, I couldn't stop thinking about the mission.

The Atlanta Torches were coming. Sooner or later, some rat from the Heel would tell them I'd married the chick they were looking for. They'd sweep into Tennessee anytime now.

Searching. Coming for my girl. Coming to raise hell and kick my club's balls off.

Blood? Guaranteed. Shit, mine boiled with the certainty.

"I'm calling Lion and Tin now," I said, pulling out my phone. "They'll keep an eye on shit here while I make a supply run. Gotta stop by the clubhouse too, make sure everything's still in line."

No sooner than I hit the button to dial, somebody began banging on the door.

We both almost hit the fucking roof.

"Get down!" I growled, pushing her gently to the floor. I swept my hand across our pile of clothes 'til I found my nine.

If somebody was coming in to fuck with us, they were gonna catch a bullet through the chest.

The double door looked fancy, but the hinges were complete trash. It busted a second later, and I held her down, crouching behind the bed with my gun aimed at the intruder.

My arm wilted in a heartbeat when I saw who it was. I blinked, did a double take like something outta a damned cartoon.

"Prez?! No fuckin' way."

"Way, asshole." He stepped in, heading toward me without stopping. Dust had a white band wrapped around his neck, hiding the damage he'd taken from Red Beard. "Took me all damned day to get it outta Joker. Only gonna ask you one time – what the *fuck* did I tell you, boy?"

He stopped in front of me, drew his blade, and looked at us. Cora whimpered on the ground. I grit my teeth, wondering why the hell we had the worst timing in the world.

"Fuck. You okay, darlin'?"

"Okay?" She sat up, pulling her gown tight, flushing bright red. "Okay?! Jesus, no. I thought he was somebody coming to kill us! Dust, can't you at least knock or yell through the damned door first?"

"Well…" Prez looked at me like she wasn't far from the truth.

She stood up, got in his face. Shit, this was bad. I hopped up too, ready to pull her back. Girl needed a reminder she shouldn't be getting in the middle of club biz like this.

"Leave him alone," she said harshly. "Firefly's doing everything you told him to do. He's protecting me. He's kept me company. Isn't that enough?"

Prez looked past her, giving me the stink eye. "Motherfucker. You put her up to this, didn't you?"

He blew toward me, put his hands around my throat, and backed us all the way to the wall. We crashed against it, fighting for the upper hand.

Fucking shit! Couldn't bring myself to throw a punch at the Cap'n – not when he'd saved my ass more times than I could count.

Wouldn't have done me a lick of good anyway, after he'd brandished his switchblade near my nose, telling me exactly what would happen if I didn't settle the fuck down.

"Firefly!" Cora split the room in two with her shrill cry. "No!"

"Didn't put her up to shit. She loves me. I love her," I croaked, fighting for every word through the choke hold the bastard had on my neck. For a man who'd lost a lot of blood, he'd gotten a tiger's strength back.

"You've been down too long, Prez. Know you said you'd take my dick. You do that shit, you'll be making a big fuckin' mistake. I already claimed her. Ain't just for show.

She's mine, dammit. I ain't letting go. Not even for you. Mine, mine, mine…"

Oxygen levels shat themselves. My ears hummed, the harder the pushed his fingers against the veins in my neck. Stars in my vision exploded into fireworks, warning me I'd be passing the fuck out in another minute or two.

"Don't make me fight you, Dust," Cora said behind him. "You couldn't stop daddy from killing himself! I *won't* let you take the only man who's meant anything since. Back off!"

Dust's cool gray eyes beamed pure death into mine. He shook his head, digging his fingers into my neck, growling like a fucking psychopath.

He didn't believe me. Didn't buy Cora backing me up.

Fuck. He thought I'd walked in when she was broken, warped her mind, taken her like a demon for nothing more than that tight, hot hole between her legs.

Asshole was flat out wrong. So fucking wrong I'd show him how bad he'd fucked up, assuming I managed to walk outta here alive.

"Fuck!" Snarling, the Prez released his grip, and his blade clattered to the floor.

I staggered sideways, clutching my knees, gasping for air. Holding out a hand, I reached for Cora, tried to stop her from rushing between us and picking up his blade.

Shit on a shingle, she'd lost her fuckin' mind!

Dust snorted as she picked it up and pointed it at him. "Already got my throat cut once this season, little girl. You can't scare me."

"Don't need to," she said. Her hand trembled as she pointed it at the Prez, but it forced him to keep his distance. "You'll get this back when you accept Firefly and me."

"Yeah? So I'm just supposed to believe you've suddenly fallen in love with this big, dirty sonofabitch who spent his free time fuckin' and drinkin'? Jimmy raised you better than that. What's he giving you to cook up these damned lies?"

"Better, yeah," she said, running a tense tongue along her lips. "He raised me well, all right. Then he killed himself. Daddy left me all alone. Firefly saved me. I don't care what you believe. I'm falling for him, and I'm never going back. I'm proud to be his old lady, and soon I'll be his wife."

Prez's lips twitched. He turned away from her, keeping the corner of his eye on her hand, steadying the blade.

"This true?" Dust looked at me as I finally got between them, still weak in the head from all the blood rushing to my brain.

"Yeah, Prez. Already told you. Everything between me and this girl, it's real. She ain't just another casual fuck. Believe me, brother, I can get that shit anywhere. You've seen me over the years. I've been a fuck and dump machine. I've been a bastard. I was waiting for the right one to come along. Didn't have a thing to care about except this patch 'til you threw her into my life."

Dust stroked his chin, rubbing his fingers across the gray slivers in his dark stubble. "Damn, brother. I want to believe you. I really do."

I held his gaze while I threw my arms around Cora,

dragged her tight into my chest. The blade dropped from her hands and hit the floor with a grating crinkle.

Thank fuck. Crisis averted.

"Believe it, Prez. Swear on all my colors, on my oath to this club. If I ever hurt this girl, don't worry about taking off my cock and balls. You can fuckin' gut me. I'll hand you the knife to do it, too."

I cupped her chin and kissed her. Made sure he was watching every little way I looked at her, feeling the heat in my lips when I crushed them down on hers.

Cora's eyes closed, her lids fluttering, swept up in the raw, wicked storm of the moment. We kissed for a small eternity before I heard him clear his throat.

"Here's what we're gonna do," he said, waiting 'til I broke the kiss and looked at him. "I'm gonna take you on your word, and hold you to it. You keep her safe, Firefly. Treat her right. You're damned right about this shit being as serious as the oath you swore to your patch. Consequences are just as dire too – you go rat on her, you die."

We locked eyes. He came closer, stopping a few paces away, serious as a snake eyeballing a rabbit.

"This wouldn't be such a big fucking deal if she were just any pussy. We know damned well she ain't. This girl, she deserves better, more than my buddy gave her before he blew his brains out. You're gonna give it to her, gonna make her smile, or I'll skin you alive from the dick on up."

Deal. I nodded, loosening my grip, walking over to him. "Hear you loud and clear, Prez. Cora's part of me, ever since

I made her my old lady. Gonna make her my wife. Just as soon as she's ready to wear that ring on her finger permanently."

"Baby, I already am," she whispered. "It's never coming off."

My damned head almost did a 360, I whipped it toward her so fast. "Yeah?"

"Yeah. I wasn't last week, but now...it's real. I know it is. When this all blows over, we're going to have a real wedding. We'll be together. Forever, Firefly."

"You hear that, Prez? I'm gonna be the happiest bastard in the world."

We kissed again. I could sense the Prez shaking his damned head the entire time. When I finally took my mouth off hers, he picked up his blade and looked at me.

"Get the prospects out here to watch her. Need you to come with me. Intel says the Torches are winding their way through Georgia right now, heading our way. We'll need everything lined up to blow their heads off when they get here. Wouldn't dream of doing it without my Enforcer on the job."

"Cap'n, you got it. Let's ride."

* * * *

Hurt like hell saying goodbye. It'd only be for twenty-four hours, maybe several days if Lady Luck decided to be a real bitch to me and the club. Tin and Lion would do great watching the house, yeah, but it should've been me protecting her.

Didn't like turning over control to them. No fuckin' way.

Too bad the Prez and I were the only boys with military combat experience behind us. He'd done his time in the merchant fleet, even fought pirates or some shit before he'd taken the club over when his old man passed the torch.

The Cap'n name stuck around for good reason. I rode behind him, taking the twists and turns through the Smokies in the rain.

Thunder clapped above us. The damned deluge soaked both of us, right through our cuts.

And I loved it. This was the shit I lived for before Cora, and it still got my blood pumping about half as hot as she did.

I'd ride these mountains wild 'til the day I died. Rain, sleet, or even snow. Out here, on the open road, a man was free. His heart strummed along with the engine hurling us through nature. His very life growled in his skin and didn't quit when his bike tore straight over God's green earth.

Speaking of which, everything was becoming a whole lot greener now. Spring was in full swing, making the forests so lush it was almost blinding. Soon, we'd be feeling the humid steam of summer.

Fuck, boy, you'll be a married man by then. Living your first summer as a biker, a bastard, and a husband.

I gripped my bike's handlebars harder as I followed Dust off the curvy exit leading toward Knoxville. Couldn't stop grinning like a goddamned fool, wondering why it had taken this many years to make the future look so bright.

* * * *

"Flash bangs!" I called out.

"Check."

"Fresh clips?"

"Check."

"Bayonets mounted on those fuckin' guns?"

"Yeah, Firefly, they're – aw, shit." Sixty spat at the ground and held his rifle up.

I yanked it outta his hands and saw it was missing the blade on the end. "This is why we drill," I growled, walking it over to the big storage lockers where we kept our gear.

If my years in Afghanistan taught me anything about war, it was that you could always beat the other bastards if you were better at killing shit than they were. And all too often *better* meant *organized*.

I reached for one of the big dagger shaped bayonets and clipped it to the gun. "Never know when you're gonna exhaust your ammo. If some prick gets the jump, you can tear his fuckin' head off before he does it to you first."

Sixty nodded as I shoved the rifle into his arms. "We're ready, Firefly. Nobody's getting an edge on this club."

"Correction, nobody's getting an edge on us if we've got one so big and sharp it'll cut their hands off at the fuckin' stumps."

Next to him, Crawl chuckled, cleaning his gun. I spun around, giving him the same look my old drill sergeant used to give me.

"Keep going, Chuckles. I'll have you cleaning and

polishing all this shit if you think this is a damned joke. Get serious."

Being Enforcer wasn't just about making sure the weapons were lined up and the bikes were tuned to carry us into battle in the blink of an eye. I also made sure these boys remembered what they were getting into it, reinforcing the chain of command.

This life wasn't all about riding, brotherhood, and partying. Every man who'd ever worn the one-percenter diamond on his cut knew we earned it down to the last drop of blood, sweat, and tears.

"Listen to the man," Skin piped up, laying out a group of fresh nines on a cart. "Numbers only go so far here, and he knows the math better than I do when we've got a rival club out for blood."

I walked over, inspecting the handguns, ready to slap him on the back. He'd been a better brother since I brought Cora into my life.

Shit, I finally understood everything Skinny boy had gone through with Meg. I respected the hell outta that.

Ready for a brotherly slap, my palm stopped in mid-air when I heard Bingo start barking out back. The big dog always let out a few yips when the Veep was around, but this time it sounded urgent, angry, grinding into a growl a second later.

"The fuck?" Skin started moving as quick as me, and soon the others were behind us.

I slammed the door going out back to our makeshift shooting range with both hands. Damned thing blew open, just in time to see Bingo tearing the shit out of some poor motherfucker's leg.

The stranger rolled on the ground, screaming bloody murder, something black and plastic squeezed in his fist. "Get off, off, off, for the love of fuck!"

Veep came rushing out from the opposite direction. I tackled him first, but Joker wasn't far behind, pulling on his dog's collar to ease him away.

"It's all good, boy. We'll take it from here," he growled, and then he was next to me, his blade drawn and poised against the bastard's throat.

"How'd you get in here? You with the Torches?" I pulled him by the flannel jacket he had on, shaking the sonofabitch with all my might before I smashed him into the ground again. "Answer me, you piece of shit!"

"What's going on out here?" Prez came walking up a second later, his fists tense at his sides. "Shit," he said, soon as he saw the shitshow in front of us.

"Don't know, Prez. Bingo caught him wandering in, sneaking around out back. He's got himself a present." I pried the object outta his hands while Joker put the knife near his wrist, scaring him so shitless he let it go without a fight.

"Christ. It's a fuckin' switch. This motherfucker was rigging up our clubhouse!" I lost my shit.

Coming after Cora, after my brothers, after the place that'd always be home...I pushed him into the dirt and punched his smug face 'til I saw blood smearing my knuckles.

Took the entire crew screaming to make me back off, just short of leaving the bones in his face a broken mess.

"Who. The. Fuck. Sent. You?!" I roared, throwing him into the ground like a goddamned ragdoll, over and over. Didn't stop 'til I heard the fucker trying to gurgle some words through the teeth I'd knocked out.

"Assholesss," he slurred like a snake. "You're done. All of you."

"Other way around, shit stain." Veep pushed his knife against the bastard's belly, and ripped it upward, slicing through the shirt he had on underneath the open jacket.

If he had a Torches tattoo, that shit would be coming off, inch by brutal inch. We'd take ourselves a fuckin' trophy before we put lead in his skull and buried him deep in Smoky Mountain soil.

His chest was clean, except for some shitty looking lantern with a skull inside it, like something a skater kid would wear. I pulled his shaggy blonde hair, jerking his head so hard I could hear his spine creak.

"Better start talking, asshole. Or else Joker here's gonna take your tongue first. You've gotta be a fuckin' prospect if you're not wearing their ink."

The bastard laughed. Prez just stood over us, watching, his eyes fixed on the asshole's chest. Then the Veep pushed his knife against his throat, ready to start peeling skin.

"He ain't gonna tell us shit unless we make him. I say we get serious, before we're wasting our fucking time. He already upset my dog!"

The knife flipped around in the Veep's hand. Crazy

brother was about to let it sink in, somewhere in the man's face, when Dust kicked it outta his hand.

"Hold it, Joker – no! Should've seen it fucking sooner. He's Irish. Muddy Bray Clan. Took me a minute to remember where the fuck I'd seen that shitty ink job before."

"So what?" I growled, my eyes searching the Prez's.

"So, we kill him, or fuck him up too bad, we'll have the Torches and all this asshole's hitman brothers after us. And you'd better believe they've got an easy road to Knoxville, straight through Charleston or Norfolk. These bastards got themselves a little monopoly going on all the shipyards east side. I remember that shit from my Navy days."

Fuck. Goddamn, I hated it when he talked sense.

Not as much as Joker, though, who still looked at the fuckhead like he wanted to skin him alive. Losing the knife didn't matter, he'd have done it with his bare hands if the Prez wasn't holding him back.

I moved outta the way reluctantly, watching as our leader put his boot down on the bastard's chest. "How much they paying you?" Dust asked, murder in his voice. "We'll double it."

Asshole started laughing again before he answered. "Your little piss trickle of a club? Come on, mate. Everybody across the Atlantic knows the Deadly Pistols have been broke for years – anyone who's heard of you, anyway."

"Skin – go to the vault and grab a stack," Prez ordered, grinding his boot deeper against the man's sternum while we waited.

Skinny boy moved fast. Came running back in a minute or less with at least ten big clutched in his hands, two fat, crumpled stacks of cold cash.

"We ain't broke no more," I said, taking the money from him and shoving it in the fucker's face while his big green eyes bugged out. "Start talking, or you're going home with nothing more than a few broken ribs and bruises to show for it."

"I'll need more than this, lad," the man said.

More?! Wrong fuckin' answer.

My fist went straight into his guts and kept going, reaching underneath his ribs, stopping just short of cracking a couple more. Punched so hard I bruised organs.

I stood up, watching him writhe. Dust nodded, suppressing a smug smile, and he took over the space I'd just vacated, leaning over the bastard with his frigid gray eyes.

"My old man did plenty of biz with the Irish back in the day. We can do it again, but not if we're gonna get ourselves off on the wrong foot. Be a sport and tell me about the Torches' plan."

"No more blows to the gut, mate. Promise me that," mafia man growled, his words a harsh rattle.

"Sorry, *mate.*" Dust growled the last word. "Don't make promises I can't keep. I'll make sure you're able to speak clearly for the next few minutes as a sign of good faith. Where's yours?"

"All right, you bloody fucking bastards," Irish said, staring at the money in my fists. I wanted to finish beating the fuck outta him with it, drown it in his blood. "They'll be here soon. Torches hired me to sneak in and rig up your place, then blow the charges when I got the call that they're coming into town. Maybe it would've killed a couple of you up front, who knows. Definitely would've sent your men scurrying like vermin, scared, straight into their trap."

Dust wasn't looking at him anymore. He crouched next to the mobster, looking bored, and slowly pulled out his pipe. He lit it, taking a good, long pull before he said anything else.

"Fuckin' amateurs," the Prez rumbled.

Sixty grinned. Joker and I shared the same dark glance.

"Tell you what, Irish, we'll keep your phone and send you on a ride back to your chaps in the Carolinas or Virginia or wherever the fuck. You'll get half of what my boy Firefly's holding. Take a few hundred to lick your wounds, and give the rest of your bosses. Tell 'em there's plenty more where that came from, long as you cut the Torches out of your deals tomorrow."

The bastard's eyes jumped from the Prez to me, and then to Joker. He licked his lips, like a fuckin' hawk eyeing a mouse creeping along near its burrow.

"The whole ten thousand. For my pain and suffering."

"Six and a half. That's my final offer. I'm already meeting you in the middle here. Also doing you a solid by keeping my men from fucking you up worse than you already are."

Irish snorted, spat blood, and swore, rolling so he could stagger to his feet. We'd already patted the fucker down, took his gun, so we knew he wasn't gonna draw shit on us.

"Bullocks! You lads don't have the piss to draw more blood, and we both know it."

Dust stood, lending him a hand. "Wish that was true. I run a tight ship, no doubt about it. But that boy over there, my Veep, his name's Joker. He's fuckin' crazy, and so's his dog."

Bingo chose the perfect time to wander up next to Joker on his leash, and the big wolfhound bared his teeth, letting out another ferocious growl. Joker stroked the dog's head with one hand, and put his switchblade between his own teeth with the other, running his tongue along the edge.

Just seeing my brother tongue-fucking the knife caused my guts to churn. It must've worked because the Irishman started going pale, and not just from the blows we'd given him.

"Look, friend, I'll do everything I can to keep my boy under control if you wanna try to walk past, but I can't make promises. Sometimes these Pistols got a mind of their own, Irish. You know how it is here in the States. Hell, forget the US of A. This is Dixie. Things are a little wilder out here. We've got a history of knowing when we need to take the law into our own hands."

"You...you wouldn't dare, Dusty. Don't bullshit me, now."

"No bullshit. Just fair warning."

Joker snapped his neck up, launching the blade high into the sky. The knife spun overhead, and I shielded my eyes while that fucker whirled like something in orbit, coming down a second later, aimed right at our psycho Veep's face.

Even the damned dog looked jealous when Joker caught it in his teeth again. Sixty burst out laughing. Prez and I gawked, and Irish – well, that fucker damned near shit himself.

"Okay! Fucking hell, you win," he hissed, stepping away from Dust, pawing at my hand for the cash. "Six and a half, like you said. I'll take your offer back to the round table, and we'll see what they say. No guarantees."

"Understood," Dust said, taking another long drag from his pipe. "Firefly, take this boy in and watch him while he gets cleaned up. We'll have the prospects haul his ass across the state line when they're done with your girl. Oh, and one more thing."

Prez walked up, reached into the Irishman's pocket, and pulled out his burner. "Gonna have to keep this. Easy way of knowing when the Torches get into town, plus we'll make sure you don't have a remote detonator wired into this shit some way. Wouldn't want any hard feelings to ruin the fine new friendship we've started here today."

Friendship, my fucking ass. Working with the pukes who'd just tried to blow our headquarters to kingdom come made me wanna choke.

But the Prez had an eye for strategy, I couldn't deny it.

Buying ourselves time, or maybe even a working relationship with the Irish mob, that was valuable when the time came to fuck the Torches hard. Shit, might be more useful down the road, when we had our next run in with the Deads.

"Follow me, and don't step the fuck outta my sight for

a single second," I warned him, taking the asshole by the wrist like an overgrown kid.

"Firefly!" Prez yelled after me, when we'd only taken a couple steps. "Drag him along the wall. We'll make damned sure all the charges are pulled before he's pulling his fuckin' pud in the shower."

Irish looked at me, moving at a hobble. That pain in his chest must've been settling in something furious.

"You heard the man," I growled, slamming him against the wall.

Made him tear off each of the three explosives he'd stuck to the clubhouse's perimeter. When the bastard was finally done, I led him inside, straight to the bathroom.

Thought about my girl the whole time while I stripped his ass down and shoved him into the showers, waiting for Laynie to show up and look him over. Hoped Lion and Tin were taking good care of her.

I watched him move like he was eighty, slowly running soap and water all over his skinny body. "Hurry up, asshole," I said, slapping the tile wall.

I meant it, too.

Soon, we'd be finishing this shit. Just had to wait 'til Irish's burner phone rang with a call from the Torches.

Once they got into town, they wouldn't be leaving our home turf alive.

We'd gut their asses and hang their fuckin' insides from the trees, deep in the dense mountain forests.

Then I'd give my woman and this club one fuck of a wedding bash like nothing they'd ever seen.

X: Thin Pink Line (Cora)

I woke up sick, throwing up, the second time since he'd left. It had been three days, and Firefly had only called me once in the mad rush to do...whatever the hell these men did when they ran off to play hero.

"Mercy," I whimpered to myself, huddled on the floor next to the toilet.

After the breakfast I'd just lost, I was ready to call out to Jesus, Buddha, and Zeus all the same. Anyone who'd make my poor stomach stop flinging my insides around like they were on a roller coaster would win my good graces forever.

I'd had my stomach bugs before, like any girl in her twenties, but this...this was different. When the room stopped spinning, I stood up, grasping the wall.

Cupping cold water in my hands, I splashed it across my face.

Horrid timing. I'd just taken a shower before the nausea hit, and now I looked like total crap again.

The strange tension and sickness wasn't just in my belly. It stabbed deeper, through my entire body,. A shaky, tingling sensation took hold and wouldn't let go, suggesting possibilities that turned my blood cold.

It couldn't be...

Oh, but it could.

I had to know. I had to get out of here.

Unfortunately, the prospects who'd replaced Firefly as my temporary bodyguards sniffed out every movement I made like bloodhounds. They watched me when I went down to the kitchen, checked on me every other hour, even when I tried to sleep.

Lion, the beefy young man with the scruffy beard going down to his collar, hiding his whole neck.

Tinman, roughly the same age. Tall, silent, and lean, like someone who'd seen too much. He only spoke when he had to.

They manned their posts like sentinels, protecting me from crashing into men who were supposedly much worse. But they felt like wardens, too, keeping me here when all I wanted to do was run to the nearest drug store and discover the terrifying truth...

I closed my eyes, fighting against another ache in my belly.

Think, Cora, think. There has to be a way. There always is.

It came to me when Lion knocked gently on the door, asking if I'd like him to bring something up for breakfast. I ordered a good old pimento sandwich with lemonade, hot tea, and brown sugar. I also asked him if there were any pickles.

They'd done some real damage to me when I was a kid.

Ever since daddy left me alone with a homemade jar of pickles and I'd eaten my fill until I threw them up, they'd never sat well with me.

If pickles, sugar, and a cheese sandwich didn't trigger my gag reflex, nothing would.

I was already feeling fifty-fifty by the time my food arrived. Downing the food quickly, I let the pain come, racing for the bathroom when it was time.

* * * *

"Cora? You all right?"

I answered him with another retch, one that tore at my stomach so hard I knocked the tray of food to the floor. No sooner than it crashed on the bathroom tile, Lion burst in, Tinman right behind him.

"Fuck." The prospects both swore the instant they saw the mess.

I'd barely made it to the toilet. It hurt like hell coming out. I dabbed at my face with a wet towel, hoping it would give my face an extra sickly sheen to go with my genuine sweat.

"Guys, I'm really sorry. I'm real sick. I need a doctor…"

"Fuck," Lion growled again, spinning around while Tinman helped me stand. "You're not supposed to leave the house. Firefly's orders. Maybe if we get Laynie to come out here…"

"No!" I snapped, feeling my temples throb like mad when I did. Yes, my own voice was much too loud. "I need a real doctor. And a friend. I have a gut disorder...something I haven't checked for a few years. I think it might be coming back."

The two men looked at each other. Lion shook his head, determined to do what he'd said, keep me under lock and key while they got the club's medic to look at me.

I had to make them do better than that.

"Can't let you outta here," he said, giving me a hard look.

"Dunno, Lion. Feels like she's burning the fuck up. Woman looks like hell." Surprisingly, Tinman cracked first. "Uh, meaning no offense, ma'am."

"No, of course not. It's true," I mumbled weakly, feeling my stomach rolling again. "Oh, God. Put me down fast. A little privacy, please."

They both stepped outside while I lost it. I strained to hear what they were saying outside while I went through my own private hell.

"It's our fucking asses on the line if anything bad happens to her. No, bro, it ain't the Torches. But if she gets fucked up just the same, by germs or some shit..."

"*Shhhit.* You're right. We'd better do what she says. Long as we're with her the whole time, keeping an eye on everything..."

"Think we should tell Firefly?"

"Fuck me stupid." Lion groaned. "Nah. He'll wonder when the fuck this started, and our dicks'll be nailed to the pavement twice as hard if something goes wrong. We got this. We can handle a sick woman, I think, or neither of us deserve a damned bottom rocker."

"Cora?" Tinman called softly, knocking at the door when I'd finally gone silent. "Let's get you some water. Soon as you're good to ride, we'll take you into town."

"Oh, bless you," I said, putting on my sweetest smile through the sickness as he stuck his head through the crack in the door. "I won't forget this, boys, just so you know. I'll put in a good word for both of you with Dust and Firefly once this is all over."

If I needed to seal the deal, that did it. They were both on me like my own private entourage, rubbing my shoulders and helping me wipe my face clean.

I didn't like the fact that I had to stretch the truth. Okay, fine, more than stretch. I outright lied.

Pickles aside, my health had always been solid. I'd never suffered from any serious stomach disorders.

No one had to know that just yet, of course. The need for my own truth trumped everything just now.

If something else was causing the cramps and morning sickness, then I had a lot more to worry about than being cooped up while we waited for a shootout with the Torches MC.

* * * *

As soon as we got to the Ruby Heel, I told them to sneak me into Meg's office. The door going backstage was locked, which upset me. Probably some new security measure that cropped since the club had gone into lockdown mode.

We slipped through a side entrance instead, away from the girls. Thank God for small favors. I didn't want them seeing me in this state, or disrupting the important job ahead.

"Wait here," I told them, batting my eyes as I slid Meg's door shut. "I've got some spare meds in the office."

They listened, and I headed straight for the little cabinet in the corner, where she kept a spare box of pregnancy tests for the girls.

I pulled one out, stuffed it in my pocket, and popped the door.

"The fuck? That was fast," Lion said, scratching his scruffy beard. "Everything okay in there?"

"Yeah, I was just looking for something to settle my stomach. Found it in the boss' medicine cabinet."

"Couldn't you have picked this shit up at the drugstore?" Tinman asked, his eyes focusing on me suspiciously.

"No, prescription only. This is my reserve supply. The rest was lost in the commotion lately. I'll find Meg as quick as I can and see about a checkup. That's what we're here for too. Oh, God…" I pursed my lips dramatically, grabbing my stomach. "Need to use the bathroom."

The men limped behind me as I ran for the lady's room backstage. This time, I slammed the door to the stall shut and pretended to throw up, careful to make sure my act didn't really make me do the real thing.

When I flushed, I sat down and did the test. My heart could've beat its way out of my chest.

Gripping the small, plastic stick in my hand, heaven and

hell flashed before my eyes like one of those intense opium dreams I used to read in poems as a little girl.

A straight, sharp line going from daddy and straight through me, through Firefly, to our unborn baby. Blood red.

Scary. Dark. Vibrant.

It tethered me to my badass lover in all his beautiful, rough glory. He'd go crazy protecting me when he found out. I'd either have a husband and the happy family life I'd always dreamed about since mom died, or else I'd lose everything, and end up alone.

As long as I had my baby.

God, was I really going to have *his* baby?

I pinched my eyes shut as I held up the test, counting down another sixty seconds. Sweat dripped off my skin, pulled out by the intoxicating fear, excitement, and adrenaline pummeling my heart.

Just look, damn you. Look!

Eyes open. It took me another second to adjust to the light, but when I did, I saw it.

The thin, neon pink line for positive hit me like a shot to the head. I lost my grip, and the plastic stick clattered to the floor, sliding out of the stall.

"Shit!" I swore, trying to stand and fix my clothes. I had to stop and prop myself up against the stall, the only thing that would stop the universe from spinning.

"Cora, you okay? What's happening in there?" Lion's voice growled, and I heard the door squeak halfway open.

Oh, Christ. I couldn't let him barge in here and see what

I'd lost on the floor!

"I'm fine!" I hollered back, banging on the tarnished metallic wall for emphasis. "Be out in just a second, okay?"

"Yeah, all right. You need anything, you yell."

The door banged shut. *Mercy.*

Pants up, I slumped back down on the toilet for a second, trying not to lose my mind. Through the tiny crack in the stall door where the metal met, I could see the little plastic test, laying where anybody could see.

I barely cared anymore. Being laughed at by one of the dancers or judged by the prospects was nothing, nothing, *nothing* compared to telling Firefly.

How the hell was I going to break the news?

Was he ready to be a father? He'd only talked about family a few times before. I only knew about his sister, the one I still hadn't met, face-to-face.

Honestly, worrying about *him* being ready was the least of my concerns. I knew that I wasn't.

But I wasn't giving it up either.

This baby, this piece of him and I...I had to protect it. I had to have it. I had to give it more – so much more – than everything I'd been given in this life gone off track, everything my own stupid father had handed away when he ended his life.

I stood up, shaking, wiping my brow. Somehow, I staggered out of the stall, picked up the test, and shoved it back into my pocket.

I had enough sense not to drop it in the trash can – if anyone else stumbled across it, I didn't want any of the girls to get in trouble, making Meg think they'd hidden a pregnancy.

No, this was worse than that. It was *me* doing the hiding, and I honestly didn't know how I'd ever show my face to Firefly again, without instantly spilling the truth.

I couldn't hide it from him. Much less myself.

This wonderful, unthinkable child was going to the only thing on my mind every time I drew breath. I just knew it, just like realizing how quickly those strange, maternal instincts I'd always heard about can take a girl over.

"Cora?" Someone banged the door as they pushed it open, this time a woman's voice calling.

Meg. *Shit.*

The prospects must've found her and filled her in.

I finished washing up and turned around, flashing her my biggest, brightest, fakest smile. "I was just looking for you."

"Holy shit. You look like…well…"

She caught herself. I just laughed, shaking my head.

"Go ahead and say it. I feel like it, too."

We both laughed. "God. Let me get you you get some fluids. I'll help you find a comfy spot to rest and give Laynie a call. She'll make sure it's nothing serious."

Then she threw her arm around me, leading me out of the bathroom, past the two burly prospects. Lion stepped in her path, his big arms folded.

"Sorry, ma'am. Can't let her go anywhere if it ain't in our sight. Orders from Firefly."

"Oh, jeez." Meg rolled her eyes and let out a sigh.

"Okay, okay. I've already been through several of these situations with you boys before. You can both tag along behind us if you'd like. Probably good you have something to do here besides hitting on my girls."

Lion nudged Tinman, who was already staring at Tawny and a couple other strippers, their legs propped up in the corner, rolling on their stockings and heels for tonight's acts. Honey-Bee was trying on her wings, smiling like a pixie in the mirror. She saw him, and winked.

Tinman grinned like a fool, until Lion elbowed him in the stomach. "Come the fuck on. We got work. There'll be pussy aplenty waiting to ride our cocks when we're full patch."

I stopped a snicker. It was good to have some comic relief, and I needed it in spades after I'd just had an a-bomb dropped on my brain.

We headed through the narrow backstage corridor leading to the bar so she could get me something to drink. Out in the club itself, it wasn't terribly busy. I was grateful for that – too much noise or too many glances from gross, horny men would've roiled my stomach even more.

"Come on. I think O'Brien keeps some good mineral water back here in the bar for drinks." Meg dipped into the small bar while I stood next to her, nervously scanning the crowd.

That feeling I used to get in the pit of my stomach, right before something dark and ugly hit me in the face, surged like a heavy wave.

I should've seen him coming.

Somehow, the asshole got past my bodyguards. He was on top of me before I knew what was happening, screaming in my face.

"You goddamned stupid fuckin' bitch! You see the shit you did to me? Take a nice, long look!" Tony Pearson's face roared, only inches from mine, big and red and loud as a fire alarm going full crash.

He stank like strong whiskey. The only smell I'd ever associate with him, except now there was another odor, something like antibiotic and medical tape that hadn't been changed for a few days.

I squinted through the darkness, staring at the huge band of white wrapped around his chest, underneath his cheap leather jacket. "Let me go. Do it now, before you really mess up."

I decided to be tough, the pregnancy test only minutes before giving me crazy courage. Too bad he wasn't having it.

The bastard slapped me. So hard my head spun, and I saw stars.

He grabbed me, nostrils flaring. "Where you been hiding yourself? Tri-Cities or some shit? I've been all over town trying to spot your ass, find out where you and that biker asshole disappeared to. Goddamned *knew* you'd show your whore face here if I waited long enough. I was fucking right!"

I clawed at his wrist, barely stopping another blow, digging my nails in until I drew blood.

"F-Fuck! Fucking bitch! Just you wait, Cora-Bora! You

know they took my Billy away after this goddamned bar fight? Cunt of an ex just up and grabbed him. My own fuckin' son – said I was an irresponsible piece of shit – and it's *your fault!* Fuck you!" he snarled, grabbing me by the throat.

"Been waiting for you, teacher-bitch-whore. Gonna turn your cunt over to get throttled day in, and day out. Gonna raze this fuckin' place to the goddamned ground for what you assholes did to me, make sure that fucker who stomped me gets his neck broke. Gonna hear you scream how sorry you are! But it'll be too late. It'll be too –"

"Oh my God!" Meg's scream froze him mid-sentence. She'd finally caught up to us. The thick glass of water she'd brought me slammed into Tony's skull.

"Fuck!" he swore, ripped his hands off me, and went for Meg.

Several drunkards near the front stage came stumbling back, ready to join the fight, or at least gawk at the new entertainment. Lion and Tinman finally woke up and raced ahead of the crowd, shoving several boozers out of the way.

I crouched on the floor, reaching for a shard of broken glass to protect myself.

Never again, I told myself. *I'll never let myself be ambushed and abused like this. I'm fighting for more than just myself now.*

Tony swung wildly at Meg, missing every time. I was ready to spring up and slam the glass into the back of his neck. One more second, and thankfully, it wasn't necessary.

The two big men hit Tony like a rocket, knocking him

to the floor. They whaled on him, using the bandages wrapped around him like a target. Kicking, punching, drawing blood.

"Idiots! Where were you?!" Meg screamed as two pot bellied bouncers came trotting up behind us. Then she gave the prospects a sharp look. "Let him go. We can't have a murder here, however much he deserves it. We're going to throw him out, and this time, he's on his own for finding a fucking ambulance. I want Tim and Roger to do it. Better that nobody outside sees Pistols colors doing the shit-kicking."

She looked at me, stepped forward, and threw her arms around my neck. "Jesus, Cora, I'm so fucking sorry. We should've done a better job keeping him from coming back."

"Not your fault," I said, letting the glass slip from my hand. It thudded on the floor. "Really."

"No, no, you wait right here at the bar. I'm going to have Lion and Tin stay with you, and you're going to get some water into your system, girl. I won't let you walk out of here sick *and* scared for your life."

Meg sat me down at one of the bar benches, moving with a speed that would've impressed a bartender. If only she knew it wasn't my life I worried about the most.

My hands moved tenderly across my belly. My son, my daughter, my baby quickened in me, the brightest light I'd seen yet in this long, dark tunnel I'd been forced to walk through.

I had to keep it safe. I'd get myself healthy, let Laynie give me a checkup, without letting her onto the pregnancy yet. Then we'd head back to Hannah's place so I could get some rest.

I'd ride out the rest of this nightmare in the big, comfy bed I already missed sharing with my man. The words to break the news to him would come, once I was in my right mind.

I had faith.

* * * *

The rest of my time at the Heel blurred by. Not surprisingly, Meg was pulled away by a couple officers who'd come to find out about the fight, whenever the paramedics picked up Tony for the second time.

I hoped to hell I'd never have to watch his drunken, worthless ass get kicked by anyone with a Deadly Pistols patch again. I'd settle for never seeing him.

I nursed my water through the whole exam with Laynie.

She asked me about symptoms. I gave her the usual run-through for a stomach bug. Sudden onset, cramps, fever, vomiting.

The older woman calmly told me to get some more fluids, preferably something with electrolytes, before I started in on re-introducing simple foods. I nodded, thanked her, and stood up, hopeful I wouldn't have to use the club's bathroom again before we left.

I was too sick to ride with them on their bikes, so Lion drove the truck, while Tinman rode on ahead of us. Kind of a relief.

Only one man's bike made me feel whole. I didn't want to ride with anyone else, long as I lived. When the wind was in our faces and I was snug against him, my hands wrapped around his hard, magnificent abs, I was alive.

I missed it. I missed him. We were halfway out of Knoxville, heading along the winding shortcut to Hannah's place, when I turned to Lion and asked.

"So, is there any news?"

"That's club business," he growled, giving me a knowing glance. "I can tell you your old man calls every day to check up. Two, maybe three times. Makes damned sure you're safe and sound. You've got nothing to worry about, little mama."

"Little mama?" My eyebrows shot up, way more annoyed at the nickname than I should have been.

Oh, God. Could he possibly know?

Lion coughed. "Uh, sorry. Habit. You look like some chick I used to know."

Without saying anything more, he pulled out a cigarette. I panicked, started coughing before he'd lit it, and exaggerated slumping against my window.

"Oh, crap, I'm really sorry. My stomach still hurts. I don't think I can take the smell right now."

He scratched his beard, gave me an understanding smile, and stuffed the fresh stick into his pocket. Thank God. With this baby in me, I wasn't taking any chances.

"Gotcha. Tell you what, I'll keep all that shit outta your hair when we're back at the house. Tin and I take shifts anyway. You won't get a single whiff of anything but fucking potpourri."

I laughed. He was a good man, or else just crazy desperate to earn his bottom rocker. Hearing a big, rough biker talking about potpourri seemed so out of place.

Almost as much as the big blockade we nearly crashed through a second later. My hands darted out and hit the dash as he slammed on the breaks.

It came up so fast for Tinman that he slid, turning his bike to the side.

"Fuck. Sorry," he said, rolling down his window to call to his brother. "What the fuck's going on out there? I see the whole damned road's closed off, but I'm not seeing any fuckers directing traffic."

"No fuckin' detour signs neither!" Tin yelled back.

The hand cupped over his mouth to amplify shifted to his brow, and he stared into the woods off to the side, sensing something. Lion had his seat belt off, reaching for his gun, when the first evil looking bastard stepped out of the brush.

"Fucking prospects," a big man with a long jaw snorted, his colors different, somehow dirtier than the Deadly Pistols. "Don't you assholes know you don't shoot when you're completely surrounded?"

"Fuck you!" Tinman shouted, ready to fire.

Another man rammed a shotgun into his back before he could pull the trigger.

I covered my mouth, trying not to scream. I was fully expecting to see the poor prospect get sliced in two by gunfire. By some miracle, nobody let their bullets go – yet.

I held my breath. A big, mean bastard with a ginger

beard and a scarred face came stepping out next to the first man, wearing a similar cut.

"Good man, Sharp. Get their fucking weapons. All of 'em. We ain't taking no chances with these crazy motherfuckers after Dusty slashed his fucking throat on my knife."

Another man came to my door, ripped it open, and began pulling me out. He was big, bald, and mean. He made sure to dig his hand into my breast when he got hold. He spun me around, and I finally saw the back of the leader, a flaming black torch with crossbones underneath it sewn on his back.

TORCHES MC, GEORGIA, it said.

I wanted to scream.

Before I could, the bastard holding me clapped his hand over my mouth. He carried me out to the small group forming in the middle of the road.

"This the bitch, Prez? Hot little thing. Gonna fetch us a pretty penny to recoup her daddy's losses, and then some!"

This can't be happening. Somebody help me!

I looked at the prospects in horror. Tinman was down on his knees, shaking with rage while the Torches bound his hands.

Lion cracked first. He pushed the two snakes holding him, wheeled around before they could take his gun, and fired.

One of the bastards took a shot right through the shoulder. The man screamed, using his last energy to ram Lion in the stomach, before he crumpled to the ground.

"Sharp!" Red Beard screamed.

"On it, Prez." All of them surrounded Lion, and their fists began to fall.

I squirmed away, trying to hide the horror, watching as they beat him to death. Thirty seconds in, he was a gasping, shaking mess on the ground.

The demon holding me grabbed my face and twisted it to face the carnage, chuckling as he did. "You like that, bitch? Believe me, you're a little more valuable than that turd, but we got no problem breaking your bones if you get outta line. This is your one chance to learn."

"Rawdog – enough." The big man with the ginger beard barked, pacing in front of Tinman, who'd finally lost his nerve.

"Goddamn. Shit. Fuck," the brother whispered, looking up at the man with pure hatred in his eyes.

"You tell your pisser friends that we got what we came for. I'm a reasonable man, even though knocking the shit outta your brother says otherwise. This is all about Jimmy fuckin' Chase's debt. Nothing else. Don't need no more blood between clubs." He paused, spat tobacco juice on the ground, dangerously close to Tinman."

"Fuck you, asshole," Tin growled. "Dust's gonna kill you when he catches up to your crew. You're talking about blood, blood, blood, but you already drew it, you stupid sonofabitch. That's if Firefly doesn't get to you first, fuckin' with his girl like this…"

"Yeah, yeah," the Torches' leader said, eerily calm.

"Tinman!" I screamed, yelling through the greasy fingers

over my mouth one second before ginger beard pulled his gun.

It happened so fast. My eyes pinched shut as I heard the shot, echoing through the mountains. Tinman screamed.

"Look at him, bitch. Look at what's gonna happen if you don't follow everything we say to a fuckin' T."

I did. He was still breathing, thank God, crumpled to the ground, writhing. They'd shot him through the shoulder – roughly the same spot where Lion's bullet had ripped through the Torches biker, now over the nearby the tree, nursing his wound.

"Gag him, Sharp. Get the bitch in the truck downstream, and let's hit the fucking road. We're done here."

"Red, you think we can blow the state before the Pistols catch up? Sources says they haven't left their home turf. Fuckers are close. Too bad the Irish have gone quiet on us the last couple days."

I blinked, and then looked at the big man's name tag. Jesus Christ. His name was actually Red Beard?

For a thousand different reasons, I was going to be sick.

"Fuck off, Veep. Those crazy sons of bitches can barely fight their own asses outta a paper fuckin' bag. They can't even defend their shit in their territory. Broke ass, sorry motherfuckers. We'll be back in Atlanta before they realize this bitch is gone. And when they do, they'll know she ain't worth raiding over. They're not gonna face down the Deads and us for one bitch."

An engine growled behind us. A car came roaring up the

road, toward the barricade. My heart swelled hopefully. I prayed it was the MC, sending backup, or at least some bystander who'd see us and call the cops over the phony barricade.

"Shit!" Red Beard swore, raising his gun. His men followed suit.

The two guys holding me pushed me forward, toward the forest, dragging me behind the trees before anyone could see me up close.

"Get the fuck outta here, you little idiot! Get out, get out, get out!" Red Beard waved his gun at the party crasher, before he raised it in the air and fired a hail of bullets. Then he snatched another one from Sharp, and emptied its clip just as quickly.

The horror just didn't stop. I caught a flash of a gray haired old man inside the car, his eyes wide and scared, clumsily revving his car in reverse. He almost drove off into the gorge below in his race to get away.

No! Goddamnit! I thought. *Go, and pick up your phone. Pick it up. Pick it —*

"We go. Right now, dammit. Too many assholes coming around to watch us jack ourselves off. We've already wasted enough time."

The bastards holding me chuckled softly. I knew it then, as they marched me deeper into the woods. Help wouldn't be coming.

I'd be their prisoner, totally at their mercy. They'd do whatever they wanted to me.

It took all my strength not to vomit. Everything inside

me tightened up, blurred together, a killing anguish fused with physical exhaustion. Numbness seeped through me like my entire body trying to flush out some poison – except it was all on the outside, sinking in, going deeper.

I couldn't get rid of it fast enough. Not before I passed out.

"Prez, she's dragging," Rawdog said, slapping me across the face. I couldn't feel it when the blackness welled up, swallowing me under.

I'm sorry, little one. Firefly, forgive me.
There's no more fight left. I tried.
I can't. I just can't anymore.
We're going to pay daddy's debt now. All of us.
Jesus Christ, forgive me.

XI: Gone (Firefly)

I was riding with Joker, Skin, and Sixty on the edge of town when I got the call. Crawl was on the line. Soon as I picked up, he said the words that stopped my fucking heart.

"Prospects haven't checked in. Can't get a hold of Lion or Tin. Lion's phone's completely fucking dead, Firefly. Got a bad feeling about this. Real fuckin' bad."

Fuck, fuck, fuck. FUCK.

"Tell the Prez, goddamn it!"

"Already did."

I gripped my bike, flooring it so damned hard the roar nearly drowned his ass out. "Then you watch the clubhouse the hangarounds. Tell Dust to get the fuck out here. Just take the road to my sis' place. That's where we're going 'til we find 'em."

I never should've left her with those fuckin' clowns. *Never!*

Yeah, I was being harsh, but just then I didn't give a shit.

Lion and Tin would've done their best, whatever the fuck happened. Damned shame their best wasn't good enough – not when every man who'd earned his full patch had years of experience on those boys.

Something vile and dark tugged at the pit of my stomach. My guts were on fire, feeding pure hatred into veins.

I'd been ready to kill since lockdown started, anything to get this bullshit over and done, so I could bring my woman home.

Killing didn't cut it anymore.

A lot of motherfuckers wearing the black flame on their cuts were still gonna die. That much was certain. Their whole fuckin' club was about to go extinct.

But now they'd hurt *bad* before they drew their last breaths. A bullet to the head or a knife to the throat wouldn't do. That was letting the fucks off free and easy.

A thousand tortures came charging through my skull like a damned cattle herd.

Fire. Kerosene. A bed of broken glass. Their heads stuffed on a pike like a fucking kabob, gagged with their own filthy balls.

I'd do it all. I'd turn into a mad dog killing machine 'til I got my Cora home, and anybody who tried to stop me was gonna pay with blood.

I started dialing the brothers riding with me. Joker heard me breathing raw hell into my phone.

He grunted. Didn't ask what the fuck was wrong, or what the hell had happened. Just cleared his throat and growled into the line.

"Drive on ahead of me, brother. Lead us wherever you think'll kill them quickest."

Amen.

* * * *

Half an hour later, we tore down the loneliest stretch of highway, the shortcut between Knoxville and Tri-Cities that I always took to Hannah's place.

Found a mess of cones and barriers along the mountain road, something that looked like it'd been ripped apart lightning quick. I slowed my bike and parked along the curb, raising my hand for the rest of the boys to do the same.

Then I saw Lion's dirty blue truck, one of the doors popped open, and my heart began to beat the fuck outta my chest.

Shit. Fuck. Goddamn!

Heard the groan as soon as I got off my bike. Sixty swore, ran to the opposite side of the road, and started looking in the ditch.

Shit was full of weeds, half-flooded with mud. Took about two minutes just to see the dark, dirty metal sticking up in the muck.

"Fuck! That's our boy's bike." Sixty got on his hands and knees, sliding down into the crap.

Heard it again, a man grinding his teeth, or trying to scream through several layers who fuck knew what.

Where the hell was it coming from? I slid down behind my brother, looking up at Joker, who gave me a nod. Drew my nine as Sixty and me waded through thick, stagnant pond scum, heading for a sewer drain.

Couldn't stop thinking about the worst every step we took. Might find anything lurking in the slime, even what was left of my girl.

A man groaned again, this time in the darkness. I stopped by the edge, motioned to Sixty, and gripped my gun.

He nodded. *Ready, Firefly.*

I had to go in. Had to find out who the fuck was in there. If it was one of the Torches, bleeding out like a stuck fucking animal, I'd put a bullet right through his head.

"Put your fuckin' hands up!" I roared, whipping around and peering into the shadowy blackness.

More groaning. Shrill, but muffled. Fuck.

I dove in. Sixty was right behind me as soon as he heard it. Found Tin up against a wall with a dirty rag in his mouth, his wrists cut from working off some shitty plastic handcuffs. We dragged them both out, Tinman with his bleeding shoulder, and the poor, beaten brother he'd been protecting.

Both our boys were in bad shape, but Lion was worse. Tin's hands were too fucked up to get a good pull on the gag in his mouth. I ripped it out for him.

"Oh, fuck! Firefly. Shit, you've gotta help him!" Tinman tried to bolt outta my arms when he saw Lion moving his head. "That's the first he's moved since those fuckers beat the shit out of him. He's hurt real bad, boss. Been struggling to breathe for like ten or twenty minutes."

Stooping to Sixty, I carefully picked up Lion. Carried the brother over to Joker, who'd come down into the muck with us. Veep helped me haul him up, trying to do our damnedest not to rattle him much more.

I'd seen guys torn to pieces in Uncle Sam's service, and with the club. Lion was one of the worst I'd ever seen. He moved in and out of consciousness every second, groaning and swearing, too many bones feeling like rocks rolling around in a sack underneath his skin.

Those sick, sadistic motherfuckers were paying for what they'd done to him ten times over. And shit, I still hadn't even asked about Cora.

So damned desperate to get this boy loaded to the nearest fuckin' hospital I hadn't had the chance. *Fuck!*

Dust roared up just as we got him in the back of the truck. "What the hell's going on here?" Prez shouted, staring at us all covered in grime.

"Torches fucked up both our prospects," Sixty said, his fingers trembling slightly as he pulled out a smoke. "Don't know if Lion's gonna make it. Boy's been ripped to hell and back."

Joker lost his nerve first. He didn't say shit, just slammed his fist into the side of the truck so hard he left a dent.

"Easy, boys, easy. Save that shit for the Torches," Dust growled, coming toward me. Probably because I was the only one with the ruthless calm. "Where's Cora?"

"Tin!" I called his name, leading the Prez around to the passenger side, where we found the prospect blowing into his hands and rubbing 'em together, desperate to warm up. "Debrief us. Quick as you can. Gotta get you and Lion into checkup real fuckin' quick."

"Fuckers ambushed us, brothers. It all happened so fast, they were moving like devils, Firefly, we couldn't fight 'em off." He looked at the Dust. "Prez, we fucked up bad. We should've both went down dying, but they would've hurt the girl. Red Beard, the fuckin' snake, left me in one piece to tell you he says you're even. They got what they came for. They're gonna keep her. No more fighting, if we let her go."

"Fuck, no," I growled, before the Prez could speak. "You're letting the bruises those bastards left on your brain do the talking if you think we're quitting. We have to go to Atlanta. Kill them. Wipe out the fuckin' Torches for good. Deads, miles, and blood be damned."

I looked at Dust. He squinted, his cold gray eyes more like a wolf's than ever before. There was nothing there, nothing fucking human. Just the same silent, cold glint I saw reflected back in my own eyes.

Slowly, he pulled out a smoke and nodded, before he finally turned to Sixty. "Land these boys a doctor. Drop them off. Tell Crawl to leave the clubhouse and watch over 'em. Then get your asses back up here, pronto."

"Yeah? I'm on it, Prez. Where we goin'?"

Dust waited for me to say it. When I did, it hissed out through my teeth like hellfire in a rusty furnace.

"Atlanta."

* * * *

We rode hard, all through the night, feeling the cool Georgia rain pouring down our backs.

I saw demons everywhere. On the road, old men riding

who looked like Deads at first, ready to catch my bullets, before I saw they were harmless.

Old farts out for joy rides. Nothing more.

The fucks were everywhere, though, ghosts of the bastard MC we should've been fighting with the Torches – but they'd pissed away our alliance forever.

I only saw traps and thieves everywhere, horseshit obstacles stopping me from bringing her home. They had to go.

Every last one of 'em.

Granny always said I had a gift growing up, just like her, when she hallucinated shit before it really happened. Didn't know about that, but I did see a hundred bloody visions unfurling on the road ahead, steaming and savage.

I saw my girl in some shitty clubhouse in Atlanta, being held down, a pitch black hood over her head. I saw them doing terrible, soul-killing things to her.

I vowed I'd hold one blood-soaked Torches' cut every time they did.

But that promise didn't mean a fuckin' thing. All that mattered was bringing her home, safe and sound.

Having her at my side again, in my bed, on the back of this bike beneath the warm, sunny Smokies.

Anything beat riding in the cold, cruel rain. And even ice rolling down my back beat the fuck outta living without my woman.

I saw us tangled together again. Cora's hot lips on mine. I'd kiss her twice as hard, pull her hips into mine, flatten her against our bed, grinding 'til I fucked every ounce of pain outta her, and then some.

I'd already had her pussy, her heart, and a piece of her soul. I'd given her all mine in spades, shit I swore I'd never give up to any chick, long as I walked this earth a free man.

That was before her, sweet Cora, and there was no goddamned fuckin' way I'd *ever* go back to that soulless, empty void.

Dust and Joker rolled on ahead of me like machines, with Sixty and Skin behind me, a slow moving anaconda of bikers prowling into the night. We were out to murder, to un-fuck ourselves after the vicious humiliation of having our two youngest brothers beat to hell and home again on our own turf.

Every brother had a thousand reasons to send the Torches hurling down to the blackest pit of hell where they belonged.

I had a thousand and one.

Didn't fuckin' care how hard the rest of the boys fought. I'd fight harder.

I gripped my handlebars 'til my wrists went numb, all I could do to keep myself sane through the long, hard ride south.

Cora, I'm coming for you, darlin'. Coming 'til I bring you home.

Atlanta loomed large in the distance by the middle of the night, its lights twinkling in the rain. We'd never been to the Torches' clubhouse, but we had a map straight up their assholes.

Just then, I hated those fuck outta those city lights. They

were a prison, holding my girl hostage, beacons for the vipers we'd been sent to destroy.

I wanted to slink through the night like a goddamned villain and punch out every single one of 'em with my bare hands. No time for that shit.

Sending the Torches to the underworld would have to do.

They'd die for me to bring her home. And I would, I promised, crossing my fuckin' heart as we rolled off the exit leading to the outskirts of town. I'd never been a church going man 'til now, but I'd have sworn my loyalty to anything that brought the Torches down, and put Cora back into my arms.

Faith in myself and the club would have to do. I had plenty of that to go around.

Faith meant courage. We'd ram down their fuckin' doors and kill them all, or I'd die twelve times.

They'd already sliced my fuckin' heart out for failing to protect her. If it wasn't too late, I'd make amends.

I'd feel her safe again, snug in our apartment, moaning underneath me all over again. And then I'd put her under lock and key for the rest of my life, keep her away from every last pile of this deadly, monstrous shit between outlaws.

My engine rumbled like a lion as we flew down the main stretch, approaching the run down shithole by the abandoned warehouses that the Torches called home. Something wet my face, too warm to be rain.

Reached up and wiped a single, hot tear working its way outta my eye before the other boys could see, riding beneath the pale, orange streetlamps.

She wasn't leaving. Cora wasn't fuckin' leaving me!

I wouldn't let her.

Nobody – motherfucking nobody! – was ever taking her away from me. Not when I'd spent thirty fuckin' years searching for this kind of woman, taming her, branding her hot little lips on my skin 'til I drew my last breath.

Cora was coming home. I'd never been so sure of anything else in my life. My brain felt fire every single second, even when Dust motioned for us to pull over, lock our shit up, and walk the last few blocks to their seedy fuckin' clubhouse.

Hang on, Cora, I thought, grabbing extra ammo outta my saddlebag.

Just a little while longer, baby. Firefly's coming.

He's fucking coming.

And he's bringing you home.

XII: Debt To Pay (Cora)

"Stop fucking squirming, slut." Red Beard had a vile, soft edge to his voice as he tore off the black hood covering my face.

My eyes hurt, suddenly flooded with blinding light from the hot, unshielded lamp swinging overhead. It had been a long, painful ride in the back of a truck to what I guessed was Atlanta.

Then they'd dragged me through their dirty clubhouse, men laughing, the stink of beer and tobacco so thick all around me I could smell it through the hood. Event he air itself was different between clubs.

The Pistols' headquarters smelled like the forest compared to this dank, dirty sewer. None of the bastards left me much time to dwell on it, though. They just dragged me down the halls, down a cramped staircase, and threw me straight into my cell.

I couldn't shake the prison cell comparison in this dingy room. It looked like an old storm shelter with concrete walls and a mottled cement floor. Heavy iron bars covered the narrow slits for windows, completing the illusion.

It took me five or ten minutes just to gather my breath, and stop my eyes from hurting. There was nothing left to do except the only sane thing anybody would try.

Bargain.

"Let me go," I said, my voice a low, dry whisper. "Please. You used to be on the same side as the Deadly Pistols, right? It's not too late."

Red Beard tipped his head back and laughed. Next to him, Sharp beamed, his bald head gleaming underneath the light. The metal teeth in his long jaw matched the same industrial-looking tattoos lining his forehead.

"Fuckin' bitch doesn't have a clue, does she, Prez?"

"Nah." Red Beard smiled at his VP, and then looked at me. "You're flat-out wrong, girlie-girl. We don't deal with liars who stick their fangs in our backs. It was too fuckin' late for them the second they decided not to dump you off on our doorstep. Dusty put personal ties over the pact he made with us like a goddamned fool."

"You're not going to use me to pay my father's debt," I said. "He's already dead. Gone. You never should've loaned him the money. You knew he was wracking up losses he could never repay!"

Too much. Red Beard's hand shot out and slapped me on the cheek, so hard my head spun. I slumped in the uncomfortable wooden chair, wondering how long it would take my ears to stop ringing.

"Fucking bitch! Not your place to talk back, and it damned sure ain't your place to talk to me about my own fucking business! Your daddy really raised a stupid cunt."

"Stupid, but good looking," Sharp said, smiling and rubbing his chin. "We gonna start in on her, or what? We oughta find out how much cock this whore can take, and how hard, before we figure out whether we're selling or keeping her."

A feeble groan slipped out of my mouth. I looked up, too numb from the weakness in my body to seriously comprehend the savage threats being discussed right in front of me.

"You won't," I muttered.

"Yeah, whore, we will," Red Beard growled, stepping up behind me, jerking my hair.

He stuck out his tongue. I knew he was running it slowly up my cheek like a starving dog, but I couldn't even feel it beneath the burn.

Thank God for small favors, right?

"Cold piece of ass. Doesn't even flinch," he grunted, stepping away. His hand stayed on my shoulder, wandering down, down…oh, God.

I closed my eyes and thought about Firefly as he grabbed my breast. My man wouldn't want me to fight. He'd want me to stay safe, to buy time, anything to stop this living nightmare.

No! I couldn't do it.

My hands shot out, grabbed Red Beard's arm, and I bit him, as hard as I could. The bastard screamed, and his filthy blood filled my mouth.

Sharp was on me in half a heartbeat, shoving me so hard I hit the floor.

Oh, shit. Shit! *The baby!*

I rolled, threw my hands out, crouching in the most protective position I could. The two big men stood over me.

I braced for their fists, their kicks, whatever they were going to do.

"Get her fucking clothes off," Red Beard snarled. "Gonna take her ass first. Pound the fuckin' shit out of this bitch 'til she's crying for that dead cocksucker who took our shit to the grave."

"Wait a minute, Prez?" Sharp looked up, something small and plastic in his hand.

"What?" Red Beard snapped his hand around, one hand on my shoulder, ready to tear my shirt off.

I gasped when I realized what he had, covering my mouth. The pregnancy test I'd stuffed in my pocket at the club.

"Fucking shit. Looks like this slut's already been taking cock a-plenty." Sharp held it out so Red Beard could see the sign on it.

The big, ugly bastard looked like he was about to explode. And he did a second later, turning to face the wall, screaming as he kicked and punched the concrete.

"Fuck. You! Fuck. You! Fuck. You!" When he peeled himself away from the wall, his knuckles were scraped off, dripping blood.

Jesus. I can't give up if he comes a step closer. I have to fight...

I crouched on my heels, ready to slam into him with all my might, the only Hail Mary I had that might keep his dirty hands off me for a few more seconds.

"Bitch!" he screamed, wagging a finger at me. "Why the fuck didn't you say anything? Why, why, why?"

"Prez, what the fuck does it matter? Don't change a damned thing –"

"Like hell it doesn't!" Red Beard screamed, turning away from Sharp. "She's gonna shit out somebody's fuckin' kid! Probably that asshole calling her his old lady, his fucking wife."

"That's right," I said softly, standing up, trying to choke down the fear. "He's coming to kill you if you lay a single hand on me. Better back off, before you wind up with my husband's knife in your throat."

Husband. That word stabbed at me worse than any blade, knowing I'd missed the chance to truly marry Firefly. I might never get another one.

And speaking of blades, Sharp pulled his out, shooting me a dirty look as his knife popped out. "You're even stupider than I thought if you think you can stand here and threaten us, slut. Fuck, Prez, just say the word and I'll gut her and her goddamned kid!"

"No!" Red Beard's big arm went out in front of his chest. "You lost your fuckin' mind, brother? We do a lotta shit out here, fighting tooth and nail with the Deads and half the fuckin' gangs in Atlanta. But we don't kill kids – including the ones that ain't born yet."

"Goddammit, Red, don't tell me this is about that Margie chick again?"

Red Beard slowly looked at him. Suddenly, all the hatred

he'd been aiming at me swelled, and I watched the big man's fist plow into Sharp's gut, doubling him over. His blade fell, clattering on the concrete floor.

"Say her name again, and I'll knock your fucking teeth out." Baring his teeth, he looked up, pain and rage swarming in his dark eyes. "Stay put, slut. We're gonna sort this shit out, one way or another. I've got some shit to chew on."

I didn't say anything as he grabbed the back of Sharp's cut and pulled him forward, heading for the door.

"Come on, asshole!" he barked, and then they were gone, slamming the door behind them.

The lock snapping shut echoed through the dingy room like a tomb. I was alone. Again.

I could've curled up and started to cry, but it wouldn't have done me a bit of good. I brought the chair to the furthest corner and sat down. Was this how prisoners felt on death row, waiting for the end?

I let my hand reach out to the concrete wall and rested it there, just feeling the coolness, letting it become warm for a slow, hazy minute.

Don't leave me here, Firefly. I know you'll come, if I can just stall them long enough.

My heart didn't know what to believe anymore. But for now, I'd *make* myself hold out hope. I had to believe, I had to keep the faith, and I had to remember his rough, wonderful lips against mine.

My old man's kiss was all I had to keep me warm in this cold, evil place at the end of the world.

* * * *

Hours passed. Or was it only minutes?

The first thing that goes when you're really a prisoner is your sense of time. I was drifting off in the chair, thoroughly exhausted, when the door swung open.

Red Beard stepped inside. This time, he was alone. His black eyes were a hideous compliment to the gnarled beard hiding half his pock marked face. He looked almost like he'd been burned at some point, but I couldn't be sure.

He had something in his hands. A bottle of water, and what looked like a couple cheap sausages from a gas station, wrapped in plastic.

"Eat it, bitch. Fucking eat, and then we'll talk." He shoved them into my lap.

I drank, but I barely took a bite off the snacks, too queasy after everything I'd been through the past twenty-four hours. I couldn't get sick again, not here, or I'd never walk out alive.

"Your daddy fucked up bad," he growled, pacing in front of me. "Fucker owed us more than a hundred big. Money he promised us a return on investment with. Money we could've used to kill the fuckin' Deads and then come for your loser old man and his brothers in the Pistols MC. You're the *only* fucking thing we've got left to pay his shit!"

Red Beard spun, slamming his fist into the wall above me. I ducked, feeling the air distort, ruffling my hair.

"He's dead!" I shouted, feeling the lead in my heart as I said the words. "Why do I have to pay for his mistakes? Tell me!"

Red Beard drew in a long, harsh breath, his huge chest rippling underneath his dirty cut. "Because when a man's got no money, he takes a pound of flesh instead. That's you, Cora. You were gonna be my personal fuck-toy for me to use *hard,* before I sold you off to the dirtiest, richest motherfucker I could find. This club's run outta money to spare for owning this city, and everything's on the table. Everything."

He looked at me darkly. I started into his sick brown eyes, refusing to look away.

I missed Firefly's glacier blue irises so bad. What I would've given just then to feel his hand on my chin, tipping my head up, staring into my man's face before he crushed his lips on mine...

"Trouble is," Red Beard said, beginning to pace again like a caged tiger, "you threw a huge fucking wrench into my goddamned plans. I needed a bitch – not a fuckin' bitch with a baby!"

"Why would you let that stop you?" I said, turning up my nose. "You and your men, you're animals. You've already hit me, taken me prisoner. I can't believe there's a code, some line you can't cross."

"You don't know shit," he said, stopping and folding his arms. "I'm not having another bitch get fucked and bleed out in this clubhouse, however fucking much you deserve it, after all that money we pissed away on your dead daddy."

"What happened to you?" I asked, fighting with everything I had to dial down my defiance, lower my voice to a whisper.

Maybe, if I could get underneath his skin, find out what made him tick, I'd gain the wisdom I needed to get through this…

"None of your fucking business," he snarled.

"No, I think it is. If you aren't going to let me go…at least tell me why I'm here. Why you seem so hurt."

His dark eyes drilled into mine for a long, angry second. Then he tore himself away, heading for the door. He stopped, slamming his hands into it. His wrists creaked painfully, and he swore.

Whatever was eating at him, it was so bad he wanted to hurt himself to forget.

A wicked smile tugged at my lips. The bastard had a weakness.

Something awful had happened to him, some kind of trauma.

What had his VP said? Something about losing a baby, a girl?

I could play him. Get him to open up to me, earning his trust. More importantly, I'd buy myself some extra time. And right now, that was gold while I waited to hear the roar of Pistols' bikes outside the clubhouse.

"You don't have to be like this," I said, slowly standing up, coming toward him. "If you're going to keep me, maybe you can use me a different way, Red. Tell me what you've suffered, what's screwing you up like this, day and night."

"No!" he spun around, and I stumbled backwards, tripping over my own feet. I swore he was about to hit me again, but he caught himself at the last second, slowly tugging his hand back with new rage shining in his eyes.

"Bitch ass slut! Look what you almost made me do! I'm not safe, goddammit. You're not getting in my head. I ain't letting you go, either. I can't, can't, I fuckin' can't!"

I was dealing with a volcano, ready to blow any second. But I was in too deep to stop, watching him crack, losing his senses the more I pushed.

I had to keep pushing. Harder.

"What happened?" I echoed again, this time gingerly reaching out, laying a soft hand on his back. "Something terrible, wasn't it? It's like poison, holding it all in. You shouldn't. It'll destroy you."

"Already fuckin' did, woman. I'm tainted meat," he growled, pushing my hand off. He spun around, looked at me, and I saw – *Oh, Christ.*

Tears. So out of place in a monster's eyes.

"It's too goddamned late for me. I fucking killed my own wife and kid. Got 'em caught in a shootout with the Deads a couple years ago…"

"I'm sorry," I said softly, oozing false compassion. "It wasn't your fault."

He wiped his hot, raging tears on his arm and laughed, pulling on his thick ginger beard. "Fuck if it wasn't. I was driving when the bullets ripped right through my truck. Killed Margie on the spot when she was three months in, too fuckin' soon to save the kid. I lost her. Lost everything. Gave it all up to the Deads, karma for this life of sinning, fucking, killing I've been living since my nuts dropped."

"It's not too late. You've done some terrible things, I get

that. This world swallows you up. But maybe you can negotiate, send me home as a show of good faith. I'll even do everything I can to talk the Pistols down from –"

I hesitated. *Murdering you and all your men,* I wanted to say.

Hell, I wanted to happen, too, whatever tiny shred of compassion I might feel for this evil, broken man. My baby was the only thing holding him back from doing worse.

Would he have me on the floor by now if he didn't know? Tearing my clothes off, forcing his way inside me, holding a gun to my head while he had his way?

"You're fucking clueless," he snarled. "Shit don't work like that in this world, whore. Not even close. This is the real fuckin' deal – so damned real you don't get second chances. You fuck up, you die. You go too deep down the trenches, fighting and killing and fucking other bastards harder than they fucked you, you're buried. Too deep to ever climb back out. You're there, bitch, and that's where you belong. Forever."

I sucked my bottom lip, wondering how long I could keep this up. *Think, Cora.*

He's going to kill you if you don't. You've got to keep feeding the tiger, before he sinks his teeth into you.

"So change it," I said. "You're the leader here. Your men will do what you say. Not so long ago, you were on good terms with the Pistols. I've met Dust, he's a reasonable man. I'm in love with Firefly. He'll hear me. I can make them listen, change their minds about what they're planning to –"

"Shut the fuck up!" His fists flew down by his sides like

rocks and slapped his thighs. "Close your fuckin' lips before you make me do it for you. You ain't talking me outta shit. I'm in too goddamned deep, and so are you, girl. You're staying. I'm not a fucking fool, and I'm not turning into one by letting you sweet talk your ass outta this. It's too motherfuckin' late. Even if we turned you over, the Pistols ain't shaking our hands when we almost killed two of their damned prospects."

This time, he came at me, serious as a lion smelling meat. I backed up against the wall. His hands jerked my wrists and pulled me into him, into his face.

"You wanna help me, you can make up for what I fucking lost. Pay your daddy's debt in full. I'll make you my old lady, wait 'til you shit out asshole's kid…" He pushed his face to my cheek, snarling his growl into my ear. "Then I'll give you mine."

I shuddered, sick to death at the thought of ever having a baby with anyone except Firefly. Eyes pinched shut, I swallowed the bitter lump in my throat and nodded.

I had to keep lying. Anything to buy time, time, precious time.

"Yes, Red. I told you, it's not too late. You can still have all the things you want. With me."

Jesus, no. I wanted to cut out my own tongue.

The words tasted like ash.

Harsh, biting, poisonous.

But they worked. He jerked away from me, covering his face. When he looked up, his brutal eyes were shining with tears, just as deranged as the rest of him.

"You're a fucking godsend, woman. Fuckin' knew we'd get something sweet after getting fucked over by your daddy." He stepped closer, brushing his arms against mine more gently this time, a wicked smile pulling at his lips. "You do everything I say, love, and we'll be cool. We'll have it all. I'll make you the best goddamned old lady in the whole world, happier than that fuckass you wed could ever make you..."

His mouthed moved toward mine. I locked lips with the filthiest animal I'd ever kiss, and then I couldn't stop the tears. They ripped out of me, flooding, pulled out by Firefly raging in my head.

No, no, no. I can't do this. There has to be a weakness here...

Something. Anything!

Running my hand over his belt and up his cut, I felt it. His knife was loose. He was distracted.

I kissed him harder while I fingered what he had, pulled it out, and let my tears flow.

When Red Beard pulled away, he saw the rivulets running down my cheeks, and his voice rumbled an octave lower. "The fuck? What's wrong? Don't you like it, babe?"

I'd kissed him just long enough to fish around his side. He'd been so overwhelmed with emotion, *shaking* when his lips touched mine, that he'd let his guard down.

I'd never opened a switchblade before, much less jabbed it into human flesh. But I'd seen Firefly and the other guys do it several times over, whether they were fighting or just sharpening them.

"I'm sorry, Red," I moaned, tilting my face up so I could look into his vicious eyes one more time. "You're beyond my help. And you taste fucking disgusting!"

The metal glowed hot in my hand as the blade popped out, and I drove it straight into his back with all my might. It went in easier than I expected, thank God, so sharp and dangerous it surprised me.

The bastard let out a ferocious scream. I kneed him in the balls, before he could come after me.

He hit the floor, snarling and rolling like a beast caught in a trap. I backed into the corner, grabbed the chair, and began smashing it across his head. I had to shut him up, I had to kill him, before the other men came running.

Too late. The door busted open, and I heard the gunshots exploding in the hallway. Then Sharp stepped in, his bald head shining like a demon, and he pulled his gun.

"What the fuck?" He lifted it, aiming it right between my eyes. Down on the floor, Red Beard moaned, grabbing at my leg while he bled.

"Don't fucking shoot. We murder her nice and fucking slow for this, goddamnit. I die, this bitch's blood is gonna paint this clubhouse." The wounded leader's hand clawed at my leg, tight and angry, his fingers pinching into my calf so hard it hurt.

His eyes stared up at me, half-glazed, angrier and crazier than ever before. *Fucking bitch. I will watch you die before I do.*

I could hear his threat in my mind. But when Sharp rushed forward, pushing his gun to my temple, I couldn't

259

hear anything except the roar of my own frantic heartbeat throbbing in my ears.

"Step the fuck away from him, cunt, or I'll blow your fuckin' brains out!"

His words were so small. So far away. And Jesus, what were all those gunshots outside?

The whole world shrank away from me. I expected my lift to start flashing before my eyes any second.

If Firefly and his men were here, they'd shown up about five minutes too late.

I'd fought, and lost. I closed my eyes, letting the hot tears come, mouthing the words the savage men at my throat and at my knees wouldn't understand.

I'm sorry, Firefly. I love you. Forever.

XIII: Inferno Rising (Firefly)

Ten Minutes Earlier

Skinny boy saw the first lazy prospect milling around just past the gate to their clubhouse, a smoke hanging outta his mouth. He was staring at his phone, texting some bitch, judging by the smug look on his face.

Fucker died happier than he deserved.

"Now!" I whispered, standing next to Skin in the alley, motioning with my hand.

His high powered rifle barked.

Perfect shot. The asshole's head exploded in a cherry mist, and then Sixty revved the truck up. We just saw our brother's mouth hanging open, his goatee twitching, and heard him let out a rebel yell that would've made Stonewall smile in his grave as the truck smashed down the Torches' gate.

"Go, go, go!" Dust roared.

We moved fast, pouring in behind it.

For a second, with all the thick dust swirling around and men running in like infantry behind a tank, I swore I was back in Afghanistan, ready to mow down some terrorist shits before they murdered villagers.

Same adrenaline rush. No, fuck no, it was worse this time.

My girl was on the line. Cora, the most valuable thing of all, everything I'd sworn my own fucking life to protect.

Torches came flying outta the clubhouse like angry hornets, about five seconds after they heard the commotion. That was five second too long. Sixty ducked down in his driver's seat, and we fired our guns, hiding around the rear of his truck.

Bullets went everywhere. Men dropped. Joker jumped out, rolled on the ground, and threw a flash grenade through the smoke, rolling toward their entrance.

Fucking thing exploded in a clap of lightning, blinding all the bastards in front of us. They all swore bloody murder as their retinas temporarily got wiped.

"Let's fucking move," I said to Skin. He nodded, following my lead, laying down more suppressing fire as I worked my way through the thick of it, killing one of the nasty looking bastards clawing at his eyes on the ground.

Skinny and me were almost punching our way through the main door when their garage opened up. Several big, mean motherfuckers hurled hellfire at us, crouched on the ground. A bullet cracked past my ear, clipping the very edge of my lobe, sending a hot blood trail trickling down my neck.

Fuck, fuck. No goddamned time for this shit!

The other boys were on it by the time I hopped up and

fired. Got a better angle, sent lead through another fuck's head, and watched the rest of my crew off a few more of them.

"It's all clear!" Skin roared, poking his head inside their clubhouse.

I shuffled in, moving past him, deep into the snake pit. Soon as we got to their bar, a big train of screams came rushing toward us. We held our guns up.

My finger eased off the trigger when we saw the women coming.

"Hold it!" I growled, throwing myself in front of Skin's rifle.

At least five beat up, dirty looking bitches in nothing but bras and panties went running. They howled all the way out the fire exit, dashing for their lives. Who the fuck could blame 'em?

Kept my eyes fixed on their slim, bruised bodies the whole way out, making sure Cora wasn't mixed in. No, there wasn't sign of her.

Didn't know if that shit made me sick with relief or worry. Right now, my guts did another flip, churning foul at the thought that we'd been working with these sick motherfuckers.

"Come on." I walked forward with Skin, creeping toward the hall leading to their rooms. We'd have to clear this shit one at a time.

We each took a side, kicking in the doors, most of 'em unlocked. Didn't find a damned soul inside, just a whole lotta filth, all over the fucking place.

Panties and burned out cigarettes. Busted bottles and dildos. Even a couple syringes crunched under our boots, and so did the crinkled snack bags and fuck only knows what else they'd been piling into a garbage heap.

The Torches and their whores had both checked out. Some dying, and others just fleeing this madhouse for their fucking lives. Brutal satisfaction hummed in my veins, knowing today was the day we'd smother the black flame forever.

But it didn't count for shit unless I brought my girl home safe. Where the fuck was she?

I was in the meeting room when I got a hand on my shoulder. I spun around, and saw Skin looking at me, accidentally digging my gun into his chest. Lowered it as soon as he spoke.

"Back room, brother. Their shit's laid out a lot like ours. There's a bunch of ammo, some guns, old bike parts, and what looks like a door leading down."

"Let's move."

Fuck. Going down a spider's hole was just about the last thing we needed.

Too fuckin' bad. I'd smash my way through hell itself to get to Cora, feel her in my arms, get her hot little mouth underneath my lips again.

Skin stood back, aiming his gun down the hole, as I jerked the doors open. We crouched and headed down the small, winding staircase, careful to listen to any assholes who might be ready to pop out near the bottom.

Basement was bigger than it looked like. Damned thing

was dark, shadowy, and had two doors at the end of a hall. One of them was open, and we both heard the noise inside.

A harsh, low voice. Recognized that shit as Red Beard's Veep, the same bald, horse-faced asshole who I'd almost fucking killed the day they showed up at our garages.

"Step the fuck away from him, cunt, or I'll blow your fuckin' brains out!" The bastard growled. Cora whimpered.

"Firefly," Skin hissed, trying to hold me back, but it was too fucking late.

I kicked the half-cracked door open and saw the asshole with his gun on her head. I'd never aimed so carefully in my life. My nine went up with a supernatural calm and the fucker, Sharp, barely had a split second to look at me.

I fired. Cora screamed, ducked, and caught his filthy blood as his brains went out his skull. Bastard toppled to the floor a second later, right next to where the other asshole was twitching, Red Beard himself.

He'd caught a knife in his back. She finally looked up as we stepped inside, and I saw those beautiful light blue eyes. This time, I swore I'd keep 'em shining forever.

"You do this?" I asked, coming over to her.

Asshole Prez twitched on the ground, trying to climb over his fallen brother's dead body, reaching for her like something out of a fuckin' horror movie. Cora moved back, threw herself into me, clutching my arm.

"Yeah," she said, gathering her breath. "Finish him, Firefly. Please."

"Fuck!" Red Beard screamed when Skin put his boot down on his grotesque body, and pressed down hard. "You fucks are gonna die for this shit. Gonna kill every last one of you, skin that fucking tease alive."

I looked at my brother, and Skin nodded. Taking Cora's hand, I led her over to him, stepping past the trash cringing on the floor. Bastard didn't know we'd probably killed his whole fucking crew by now, but he would in just a few more seconds.

"Babe, wait with Skin outside. This'll only take a minute or two." I leaned in, gave her a quick, hard kiss, and then pushed her gently into my brother's arms. He led her out, looking back over his shoulder.

"Make it quick. Gotta make sure everything's locked down upstairs so we can all get the hell outta here."

Boy was right. I saw Cora looking at me one more time, a thin, tortured smile on her face as I closed the half-busted door as best as I could.

I had about ten seconds to think up the most gruesome torture I could to flay this fucking demon alive. Good thing I had a lot of experience underneath my belt.

"You're dead, asshole, fucker, king shit," Red Beard snarled, wide eyed and staring up at me, the wicked energy leaving his body a little more by the second.

"Whatever." I crouched next to him, ripped the knife out of his back, and looked at it for a second while I held my own blade in my other hand.

Bastard managed one more scream while I rubbed the blades together, sharpening them real good, and then laid into him.

* * * *

When it was all over, I had blood all over me. I stepped outside and took Cora from Skin, pulled her tight, and kissed her with all my might.

Finally, all the bullshit was over. We were both a mess. Tired, sick, and exhausted as hell from the adrenaline burn still raging in our veins.

Fuck if it stopped me from pushing my tongue against hers, reminding my girl who owned every inch of her. Fuck if anything would ever stop me from showing her, every single day, 'til we were both ashes and dust.

Skin's burner phone sputtered. Heard him talking to one of the boys upstairs while we kissed. I didn't move a damned muscle 'til he walked up, pushed himself between us, and slung his rifle over his shoulder.

"Gotta move. Dust says the place is cleaned up, and he wants us to get the fuck outta here before half the Atlanta PD surrounds this shithole."

No argument. I picked up Cora, slung her arms over my neck, and carried her upstairs, pressing her face tight into my chest so she wouldn't have to look at this graveyard a second time.

"You know how much I love you, right?" she whimpered, looking at me with those half-closed lids that made me want to shove her against the nearest wall and fuck her brains out.

Even in this fucked up war zone, the woman was beautiful. Perfection. So glorious my dick throbbed harder than my trigger finger, smelling smoke and blood.

"Yeah," I growled back, pushing my forehead against hers as we made our way to the street, where the rest of the boys were gathered. "Love you too, baby girl. Love you 'til the day I die, and that ain't today. We've got a long fuckin' way to go before they ever put me to rest. You're coming along for the whole ride. No ifs, ands, or bullshit allowed."

* * * *

It was a long, hard journey home to Atlanta. The crew was drained, quietly grateful nobody had been killed or seriously fucked over in the battle.

The Torches were good, and they fought tooth and nail to their deaths. We were better.

I drove on with Cora draped around me, careful going around every bend. Knew her strength wasn't up to peak, and there was no fucking way I'd risk losing her on my bike.

Atlanta disappeared quickly in a dash of smoke and sirens. Darkness and a few shortcuts Joker remembered from old trips through the city saved us from running smack into the cops.

Wouldn't be long before the big brawl in the dead industrial district hit the news. With any luck, no smartass detective would ever know the Pistols had put those fuckers down.

We'd scattered old, torn cuts and guns we'd pulled off the Deads in previous battles across the ruined clubhouse. Framed our enemies with our other enemies. We also had to keep our eyes peeled for those assholes all the way through Georgia, knowing this was their territory. They'd probably already heard about the Torches being smoked out, and they'd be moving in to pick up the pieces.

Someday, we'd be back to settle the score with their sick club, but we had a long ass road to ruling more of Dixie than the cool Tennessee mountains.

Drive on. Get her home, you bastard. Club biz almost ate your ass alive today.

For once, I shut up and listened to that shit rolling around in my skull. In just a few more hours, I'd have her at Hannah's place. And when we got the all clear, we'd finally be rolling back to our apartment, this time for good.

* * * *

Dust and the boys waved as we broke away on the highway. Prez or Joker would be busting my balls to show up early for debriefing tomorrow, but the rest of night was ours.

Twenty minutes later, we rolled up the long driveway to my sis' place, and I parked my shit in the back, taking the door.

My girl was barely holding on, fighting sleep with everything she had by the time I pulled her off. She hung limp in my arms, soft and warm. Cradled her against my chest as I worked the lock, brought her inside, and carried her upstairs.

She didn't say shit 'til I walked into the giant guestroom, refusing to put her down on the bed. Just carried her sweet ass straight into the huge bathroom, sat her near the tub, and started pulling her clothes off.

"Firefly, no. I'm tired. I'm going to go nuts if you don't put me down and tuck me in!"

"Patience, babe. You've been through a fuck of a lot. You're not going anywhere, much less to sleep, 'til I've got you cleaned up and put some water in your system. Get the fuck in the tub."

Groaning, she finished tugging off her clothes and obeyed, while I reached into the cabinet near the sink and pulled out some bottled water.

Seeing her naked and dirty did something mad to these bones. I wanted to take her, push between her legs, rule every sweet fucking inch of her I'd been denied for a couple days.

Everything I thought I'd lost for good.

"Drink, babe," I ordered, watching her curl up as I ran the water.

She took the bottle and sipped like a damned bird, taking it a little faster as I ran my fingers through her hair. "Fuck, there's nothing on this planet that'll ever stop my dick from twitching every time I look at you."

I reached for a washcloth and rubbed it across her back, soaping her up, trying my damnedest not to jump into the tub after everything she'd been through. The girl needed rest – even if that was the last thing on my earth my cock wanted to give her just then.

"I can think of a few things," she said, smiling and craning her body into my hands. I let the rag slip into the water and rubbed her with my bare hands, loving every damned inch of her.

"Yeah, and we beat 'em all, babe. Knocked 'em into the fucking ground. It's just you and me. No more bullshit. We've got a bright future ahead."

She gave me a long, tense look, like she had something heavy on her mind. "We do."

My hands moved lower, cleaning her good, stopping for just a second to rub between her legs. She was hot. Wet. And it wasn't just the damned bath.

My fingers found her clit and pinched around it. She closed her eyes and moaned, her whole body shuddering.

Fuck, I wanted her. We'd both been through the wringer.

I couldn't fuck her yet, not unless she opened those pearly blues and gave me that look.

Next thing I knew, it happened. She pursed her lips, suppressing a wider smile than the one creeping across her face. "Come join me in here," she purred.

"You're tired, babe. You gotta rest. My dick's a greedy motherfucker, but I've got him on a tight leash tonight. Seriously."

"I didn't ask." She winked. "You know what I need."

Yeah, I did. *Fuck, yeah.*

Never dropped my pants and ripped off the rest of my clothes so fast in my life. I slid into the water, pushing between her legs. She started moaning the second I pushed into her.

We fucked hot. Messy. Hard.

I took her like a storm, not even giving a damn about the droplets flying all around us. My hips drove into hers, crashing into her, taking everything I cared about.

"You're wearing my ring next, woman," I told her, pulling her face into mine for a kiss. "Say you'll fucking marry me, Cora. Say it. I need to hear that shit from your own lips before I shoot my come inside you."

My hips rolled harder. I fucked her 'til she was speechless, her lips open, her eyes rolling back. Reached down between her legs, flicking the hell out of her clit, before I slowed my strokes down to a mad tease.

"Oh, God!" she groaned.

"Say it, girl," I growled, echoing the only thing on my mind except for the fire, roaring in my balls.

Just. Fucking. Say. It.

"Yes!" she whimpered, right before I took her mouth with mine, digging my teeth into her bottom lip. "Yes, yes, yes, Firefly!"

Those words tasted sweeter than whiskey on my tongue.

They were all I needed to hear before my hips went into overdrive. I fucked her so fast, so hard, so furious I thought we'd crack the damned tub.

Water churned around us, and her legs wrapped around mine. Her whole fucking body begged for sweet mercy before I lost it, and she took it in spades.

She tensed up, broke the kiss, and screamed, convulsing on my dick. I shot my load deep, harder than I'd ever come in my life, growling the entire time.

* * * *

We got into bed and slept off our hellacious hangover. Prez rang my burner phone half a dozen times while I drifted in and out, laying on the huge bed, holding her tighter than any man oughta be able to keep a woman close in his sleep.

Ignored that shit every time. I'd already done my part for the club. The brothers could wait 'til after I slept off the ruthless fuckery of the last few days, right next to my girl, my wife, where I belonged.

Sometime around noon, I opened my eyes without feeling like the sunlight trickling in would set my fucking eyes on fire.

The little minx had slipped outta bed at some point during the morning. Cora sat in the chair by the window, tea and toast in her hand, blonde locks and blue eyes shining.

Great fuckin' sight first thing in the morning. Only one I wanted to see for the rest of my days. My dick ached like it was gonna fuck its way straight off my body to get to her.

I rolled outta bed, stood up, and watched her smile.

"Hey, old man," she purred, waving at the little tray on the stand.

I walked over and took the chair next to her, grabbing for the coffee thermos and the cup she'd brought up for me. "Helluva morning, ain't it, babe?"

"Yeah," she said, reaching over to squeeze my arm as I took my first slug of coffee. "It's great, now that you're here, and we're safe."

I leaned up, shoving the curtains aside. We both watched the sun piercing through the thick clouds hanging over the mountains. The Smokies towered around us, green and alive as ever, like God himself had reached down and painted the landscape something beautiful.

It was gonna be summer soon. Already felt like it. I took another long pull of my coffee, twining her fingers with mine, giving her hand a possessive squeeze.

"Gotta make a run to the clubhouse today. The boys'll keep busting my balls if I don't. You come with, and then maybe we'll drop by the Heel to figure out when Meg wants you back at work."

"I've been thinking about that," she said, still wearing the same tense, loving smile.

Goddamn, I wanted to bite those lips. Even when she looked at me like no woman ever had, the looks that went straight through my chest, I still wanted to rule her like a fuckin' Neanderthal.

"Yeah? Thinking about what, darlin'?"

"The future. I'll stay on with the Heel until we get a little more established, bring in some extra dough…but I'm not sure about doing it forever."

My hand cut through the air. "Bullshit. Club's really building up it's business. You wanna go off and do something else, you just say the word."

"No. I need experience, Huck," she said, clinking her cup down on the tray. Hearing my real name got my attention, temporarily numbing the need to fuck her senseless. "I want to make my own way. Up until now, there's always been something in the way. Daddy's demands, the club, everything we just went through…God!"

She pinched her eyes shut, remembering all the bullshit. That look on her face made me wanna bring the Torches back to life just to kill their asses dead again.

"Babe, no, it's gonna be okay. You said it yourself – we're all about the future now," I growled, standing up. I reached down, jerked her out of her chair, and then took her back to my seat, plopping my woman in my lap where she belonged. "Listen to me. We've got money. I'll never be as rich as my fucking sis here, but I'm not into this fancy horseshit anyway. I've got plenty to help you do whatever the hell you want. Plenty for *us* to start a life as man and wife."

She smiled, blinking back fresh tears. I pushed my lips down on hers before that shit fell, making her burn. She wasn't crying anymore if I had anything to say about it.

"You're a good man. I'm sorry it took me so long to see it."

"No, I ain't, Cora." I looked at her, cupping her chin in my fingers, tilting her face to mine. "I'm an outlaw. I'm a bastard. I'm good to you and my brothers. That's the only world where I'm ever gonna fit, the only one I'll ever fuckin' need. Sky's the limit for you, for us. That's where I'm all in. Everybody else, everything else – it can all get fucked."

"I want to teach again someday," she said. "Maybe figure out something I can do in business education. I know we've got money, Firefly, but I need experience. I need to learn more from Meg, about how to manage a company, so one day I won't screw it up when I've got my own."

"Fuck yeah, you'll own it," I said, running my fingers through her soft, golden locks. Had to fight the urge to tangle it around my fingers and fist it like I did when we fucked. "You stick with me, babe, and you can have the damned moon. Shit, maybe Mars and Jupiter, too. I'm gonna make you the happiest woman alive who ever wore another man's ink and took his ring."

"You don't understand," she said softly, grabbing my hand with both her little ones. "You already have. Even without the wedding, or anything else."

"What're you saying?" The look in her eyes was heavy, but it was happy, too, and I didn't know what the fuck to make of that.

"All the time we've been spending together lately, before the Torches took me." She swallowed, and new tears glowed in her eyes. "There's no easy way to say this. I'm *pregnant,* Firefly. We're going to have a baby!"

Right. Between. The. Eyes.

The whole damned world shrank down like some bastard had shoved it through a tunnel, narrowing on her and I, wiping away everything else.

No, not just the two of us. Me, Cora, and the kid.

My kid. *Holy mother of fuck.*

"What? What is it? You're not scared, are you?" she said nervously.

I jumped up, still holding her in my arms, and let out the happiest fucking war cry of my life. Must've shaken a few shingles off my sis' fancy roof as I swung her around, before pulling her in gently, remembering I had to protect the fuck out of this girl from now on.

"Oh, God, you're happy!" she chirped, the realization dawning on her before she burst into soft, sweet laughter.

"Babe, you don't got a clue. Think you just made me the happiest SOB in the entire fucking universe!"

I kissed her like a maniac. So hard and long my tongue owned her little mouth, lips moving all over hers, taking what was mine, mine.

Mine down to flesh and blood and bone.

Knowing I'd knocked her up caused my dick to sizzle. About ten more seconds, and I'd fuck her up against the window. The brothers could wait a few more minutes, and so could everything else – all except one thing.

"We're getting hitched today. No more waiting. Can't fuckin' stand it, Cora."

Thought she'd resist. Hell, the girl deserved something special, a full on palace coronation for becoming my wife, but there'd be years to renew our vows a thousand times over.

I gazed into her eyes, diving deep into the blue, knowing just one thing. I needed my ring on her finger. Now.

Not tomorrow. *Today, goddammit.*

"Today, darlin'. Don't force me to make you scream yes again..." Growling, I grabbed her thigh, and squeezed.

"Yes! Let's do it!" she whimpered, about one second before she threw her hands across my neck.

We kissed. Christ, I could've kept myself glued to those lips all day.

Next thing I knew, I had her back in bed, tearing off her robe.

One more animal fuck, and we'd get down to business.

Just two or three dozen kisses from now, she'd be mine forever. My wife.

* * * *

"Hurry the fuck up, Prez. We've got a wedding to get to." I sat down at Dust's side at the big meeting table, watching the brothers grin.

"You're goddamned lucky it's your wedding day, boy. I'd be thinking about taking your balls again for coming in so late if it weren't."

I smiled, looked at Skin, and he gave me a wink. "Fuck, you're gonna need those, brother. Can't get hard without 'em, and these chicks are insatiable once they're wearing your brand."

"I'll take the insatiable part," Joker said, his knife out, slowly tapping the blade between his fingers on wood he'd scratched to hell about a hundred meetings ago.

"Joker!" Dust slammed his gavel down. "Put that shit down and let's talk biz."

When the room fell silent, Prez pulled something out of his lap. It was a small, dark gun case, and I knew he had an antique on hand before he opened it.

"You boys know what this is?" he growled, pulling out an old Colt revolver that probably hadn't seen action since the Civil War.

I shrugged. "Some shit your old man left behind?"

"This gun belonged to my great, great grandfather, plus all the other men sharing my blood in between. This tough old motherfucker's one more reason we got our club name, calling ourselves the Pistols, and not the fuckin' Rifles or some shit. This is our namesake. This is everything."

"Shit, Prez, didn't know we were here for a history lesson." Sixty said, scratching his goatee and pulling out a smoke. "We gonna debrief about the Torches, or what?"

"No need," Prez said slowly, staring at the old revolver in his hands. "We were all there. They're all dead. No signs the cops figured out it was us, instead of the Deads."

I stared at him as he looked up, turning his gray eyes to me. "It's over, boys. Torches have been snuffed the fuck out. And we've got a long way to go before we catch the Deads."

"We really planning to? Go on the offense?" Skin asked, looking around at Crawl and Sixty, then at me.

"We gotta," Joker growled. "We fuck them first, or they'll fuck us harder."

"He's right, of course," Dust said, turning the gun over in his hands. "We're damned lucky they haven't been back for more since we bailed out your old lady, Skin. Lady fuckin' Luck gave us all a blowjob here, keeping them off our backs so we could hit the Torches and bring Cora home."

A couple brothers snickered, Sixty and Crawl. Dust's cold, dead eyes shut them right up.

"We can't wait for the bastards to nail us again. Gotta

hit them fucking harder, hit them first, and knock their asses out. Get ready, boys. These pistols have only been firing to protect ourselves too much lately. It's high time we start shooting first."

"It's risky," I said, imaging all the shit we'd have to do to hit 'em in Georgia, the Carolinas, wherever the fuck the Prez thought we had an in. "They're gonna be busy moving into Atlanta proper, now that the Torches are outta their way. You really think it's worth it?"

"Think harder, Firefly," Dust said, staring at his own reflection in the gun's cold steel. "We did the evil fucks a favor taking out the Torches because we had to. They're gonna have a fuckin' field day in the big city, even if they've gotta fight off a few more street gangs to truly claim it. But they'll get their peckers up sooner or later, own their chunk of that city. Who you think they're coming after then?"

Every brother in the room felt his blood ran cold. Mine dropped to sub-zero, before it turned lightning hot.

That shit couldn't happen. No fucking way.

I'd never let any bastards get the jump on my club again, here on our own turf. This was my home, and I'd keep their paws off setting it on fire. Much less my girl, my wife, my kid!

My fist hit the table so hard half the guys jumped. "I'm sold. You name the time and place, Prez. I'll be the first on my bike, ready to ride to war."

"I've got a few ideas. A few more gun shipments to collect, and a couple more maps to study. All you boys gotta know for now is, it's happening. Get ready. Get your shit right with your women, those of you who got 'em. Rest of you, get right with yourselves. Might be your last fuckin' chance before catching a bullet."

"Got it, Prez. We all know this club doesn't have a choice. We can't do shit with these fucking wolves breathing down our necks," Crawl said, dragging tense fingers through his dark hair.

"You're wrong about that, brother," I growled. "We can do plenty. Before we go to war, we can live. We can ride. We can laugh or fuck or booze, however the hell we please. That's the privilege wearing this patch gives us. As for me, I'm gonna marry my wife and take her home, put her where she belongs. Outside this club, that's the only thing that matters."

"It'll pay off in time," Dust said, moving the old revolver from hand to hand, looking at each of us. "I promise. All the good things Firefly mentioned, that's what anybody wearing a Pistols patch deserves. I'll die to make it happen. Fuck, I'm gonna make us rich. Gonna beat our way to the goddamned sea and make Blackjack or Throttle come *begging* us for a deal!"

"Yeah! Fucking make 'em!" Sixty shouted, moving his mouth so fast he lost his cig, and had to pat it out before it torched his jeans.

Several pairs of hands slapped the table. Prez wasn't shy about his dreams of building the MC into something big, something worthy of standing shoulder to shoulder with the powerful Grizzlies and Devils out West, or the Phantoms in the East.

Me? I didn't give a shit about any of that. I just wanted us to be safe, build a damned wall around Tennessee so I could live with my brothers, my girl, and my family in peace.

The commotion hit its sweet spot when Dust stood up, aimed the old Colt at the ceiling, and fired. Half the brothers cheered, happier than I thought I'd ever see guys get over a hole being blown in our own clubhouse.

"Don't cheer the damned roof off yet, boys," he said, turning to me. "Firefly, what's happening with our boys? We need all our numbers again."

"Checked with the hospital this morning. Tin's back at home, resting his bum shoulder and bruisers. Lion's gonna need another week or two. Lots of casts to heel those bones after the beating those shitheads gave him, but he'll live. He'll ride again. Full patch, I hope."

Prez nodded solemnly, along with all the brothers in the room. "We'll take a vote as soon as he's out. Far as I'm concerned, these boys have earned their bottom rockers, and then some."

"I'm wondering about something else," I said, leaning forward. "What about that other loose end? Tony What-the-fucks-his-face? The asshole who roughed up my girl at the Heel and ratted her out to the Torches?"

Joker dragged his knife across the edge of the table, making a sound like screws on chalkboard. Everybody swore.

"Already done, brother." He flashed me a crazy ass smile. "Paid the asshole a visit last night on the way home. Crawl, too. Bastard bit it quick and dirty in his sleep. Now he's rotting in the forest, close to the usual spot."

I nodded. Knew from everything Cora told me that the prick had been the worst kinda family man. Neglected his kid, beat up his woman before she left his evil ass, never paid his child support. Thank fuck the little boy had gotten a better home the first time we'd fucked him up at the Heel.

His family would be better off without him. That went double for the whole damned world. Easily a better place today with one less miserable stain on it named Tony fuckin' Pearson.

"Thank you, brother," I said, reaching across the table to fist-bump the wild-eyed Veep.

Between us, Prez's lips twitched, and he slowly pulled out his pipe.

"Now, we're done," Dust said. "Ya'll know what's coming, and what's behind us. Get the fuck out there and make hay before the storm."

Joker looked at me, his face as stern and mysterious as ever. "We got a wedding to get to, don't we?"

I grinned. Hearing it from the Veep meant something. Standing, I walked around the table, slapping him on the back.

"Yeah, brothers, we do. This is the day I start living the rest of my life like the man I was always meant to be."

Everyone growled their approval. A second before Dust's gavel smacked the table, dismissing church, I was heading for the door, ready to scoop up my girl and drag her to the makeshift altar.

XIV: This Side of Destiny (Cora)

I sat at the bar while the men streamed out of their meeting, talking to Dust's mom, Laynie. She'd heard all about the big wedding plans. No sooner than I told her, the older woman flew into a storm, calling up a preacher and trying to find me a dress.

I told her I didn't need one. I just needed Firefly, a ring, and someone official who could make us tie the knot.

She wasn't having it. Her eyes twinkled as she grabbed me by the shoulders, nearly knocking the water of my hands.

"You wait! Don't let any of the guys start a damned thing 'til you're all dolled up. I'll put in the word with Dusty myself!" She winked, and trotted off to find her son.

Hard to believe Laynie once raised the MC's fearsome leader. Hell, I'd have to think about raising my own son or daughter soon. I hoped I'd still have a fraction of her energy when I hit my sixties.

"Let's get moving, darlin'. I'm eager as fuck to get down to it." Firefly pulled me off the stool and wrapped his arms around me, grabbing my hips.

"Hold up. Laynie wants to help me find a dress," I whispered, tilting my face to kiss him from the side.

Yeah, forget getting old. I wasn't thinking about what I'd be like at Laynie's age anymore.

Today was a day like I'd never imagined. I leaned into him, just savoring the moment. More grateful than ever before that we both had a long, bright future ahead.

And today – sweet, sweet today – was just the beginning.

"Babe, fuck, you look hot no matter what you're wearing." Smiling, Firefly grabbed my ass, pulling my hips to his. "No more delays. Let's get Laynie's guy here and do it."

"Come on, Huck. I'll look so hot in lily white you might have to spank me for the tease."

"Shit." His eyes went wide, giving me a perfect view of those big, blue eyes I loved. "Fuck…you're gonna get your ass slapped here before the ceremony if you say much more."

I stuck my tongue out at him. It was all the taunting he needed before his lips clamped down on mine, hot and electric.

"All right, whatever," he growled, reluctantly pulling away. "You get your shit together with the Prez's mama. I'll make sure the brothers are all ready. Gotta get my sister out here too."

"Oh? I finally get to meet Hannah?"

It was strange that we'd stayed at her huge, luxurious house through all this without ever meeting her. Still, there was nowhere I'd rather be than back in our apartment, a perfectly cozy start to something amazing.

"'Course you do, darlin'. You're family now."

I smiled like a fool for the dozenth time that day. Listening to him dial, I heard him start talking while I sipped the last of my water, laying a gentle hand across my womb.

Family. That was a word I'd be hearing a lot in the near future. I thought I'd lost it forever when daddy selfishly took his life.

Sure, I had a lot to learn, but it warmed me like nothing else to know I had one. It hadn't been taken away. I'd taken it back.

And knowing how Firefly did everything big and bold – especially between the sheets – this first baby wouldn't be our last.

* * * *

A couple hours later, I stood in his old room at the clubhouse, helping Laynie shape everything in the mirror. The neat white dress she'd picked out looked a little old fashioned, with one noticeable difference.

The short white skirt attached was made for a woman to tighten up and ride off after tying the knot. Something she'd had custom made years ago when she'd gotten married to Dust's father, Early.

"See? It's like you were meant to wear it!" she said, her wrinkled face smiling as she clasped her hands together. "Turn around."

I gave myself a little whirl, and we both laughed. "Backside okay?"

"Okay? Girl, you look gorgeous! You're really going to turn his crank tonight."

Laughing more, we hugged, and then I heard music starting outside. Men laughed, chairs slid across the big bar section of the clubhouse, rearranging everything into a makeshift space for our wedding.

Oh, God. It's really happening, isn't it?

"Go ahead, Cora," Laynie said, as if she could read my mind, a thousand memories flashing in her eyes. "Go get married."

* * * *

The same wiry preacher man who'd almost hitched us before stood behind the podium, looking like a turtle. He read the script I'd heard a hundred times in movies and songs.

Do you take this man...in sickness and in health... 'til death do you part?

It all washed over me. I looked at Firefly for a long, hot second, the most intense of my life. Behind us, a couple brothers shifted in their seats.

Somewhere, Bingo whined. I heard Joker reach down, scratching the giant wolfhound's muzzle.

"No." As soon as I said it, the room was alive with gasps, sounds of men and women choking. Preacher man's jaw dropped. He looked ready to sink into his shell of a suit.

I made sure to shout the next part.

"I say it because just telling him 'I do' isn't nearly good enough. You, Firefly, saved my life. You saved me from the past. Hell, you saved me from myself. I would've said yes to being your wife just to repay you, but you're luckier than that. We both are. I do, Firefly…Huck…because I really, truly love you."

Grabbing his hand, I brought it to my lips. The look of awesome shock on his strong, handsome face evaporated into a mischievous smirk.

Preacher man waited for the chatter to die down, and then he continued, this time putting my man on the spot with the same fateful question.

Do you take this woman…your lawfully wedded wife…for better, for worse, 'til death do you part?

"Fuck no."

My heart almost stopped. Once again, more gasps, more shocks, more manic energy rippling through the crowd of bikers, plus the few women along for the ride. It got so loud Bingo let out a yip, and Joker had to grab his collar just to calm him down.

"Babe, just taking you ain't half good enough." Firefly looked at the crowd, and then at me, waiting for the madness to settle down. "You stepped into a world of shit, the one I'd been in for God knows how long. You came out on the other side better, stronger, and you made me love. Every damned second. Love you, Cora. Own you. Gonna keep you mine forever."

Preacher man smiled, staring at us while several more

rowdy brothers let out loud hollers. At last, he said the words we'd been waiting for since we'd stepped up to the strangest altar I'd ever seen. The only one I'd *ever* stand in front of, promising the rest of my life to this man.

"By the power vested in me by the great state of Tennessee, I now pronounce you man and wife. You may now —"

"Just fuckin' kiss her!" Sixty shouted, laughing as he was dragged back violently into his seat by several wild bikers.

And he did. Good God, Firefly kissed me!

So deep, so hot, so blinding I could barely feel my fingers and toes.

For one wondrous second, there was nothing but him, this kiss, and our baby inside me.

He owned me, just like he'd said, but he didn't realize what that fully meant.

Thankfully for us, I had a few good decades to show him, every single day of our crazy lives.

* * * *

Brothers roared, slapped each other on their backs, and exchanged so many rowdy jokes a troop of Marines would've blushed. We sat at the head of the table, feasting on good barbecue and the best apple pie a la mode I'd ever had.

The badasses around us banged their bottles constantly, urging us to kiss. Bingo howled through the commotion, adding to the joyful chaos. I was used to the fork and glass thing at normal weddings, but this…well, nothing about it was traditional.

And that's why I loved it. A couple hours in, after we were full and happy, surrounded by friends and family, I couldn't keep my lips off him anymore.

Something about the flashpoint wedding, dressed in this old lily white skirt and matching heels, just made me feel like a virgin again.

One who was ready to give *everything* up to him tonight.

We'd just gotten through having our first real conversation as man and wife with Huck's sister. Hannah sounded more rough and tumble than I'd expected, a country girl at heart, despite her wild success in business.

I smiled the whole way through and laughed at her jokes – surprisingly dirty. She elbowed Firefly in the side, whispering not-so-quietly in his face.

"Go get her, bro. I'm glad it won't be at my place this time. Poor Mika had *a ton* of cleaning after you moved out. Those sheets took several cycles to rinse, you know."

"Aw, fuck me, sis," he growled, playfully shielding himself as she punched his arm. "You're gonna be on the receiving end one day. You can only fuck around with gazillionaires for so long before one of 'em wants more than a hot new deal for making coin."

She stuck her tongue out, and we all laughed. I sipped my sparkling cider – non-alcoholic, of course – enjoying the sweet, sugary fizz along my tongue. Dust appeared over Hannah's shoulder.

"What the fuck you two still doing here?" he said, his

NEVER LOVE AN OUTLAW

cold gray eyes shining. "Hit the road and get this gal out on her honeymoon, boy. That's an order. Besides, I'm fixing to borrow your sis for a minute. Got something business-like to discuss in the backroom."

Hannah and Dust shared a hungry look. My chest tightened, and I pawed at Firefly's hand, hoping nothing insane would happen.

Firefly just looked at both of them, standing a little taller. "Club business, or personal?"

"You wouldn't understand how to mix business and pleasure, Huck," Hannah chirped, slowly sizing up the huge, handsome MC President with her eyes. Judging by the way she flipped her hair over her shoulder, she liked what she saw.

And what girl wouldn't? There wasn't an ugly man in the entire club. Lucky for me, I'd bagged the handsomest one of all.

"Whatever. I'm too damned happy today to give a damn," Firefly said, turning to me and squeezing my hand. "Come on, darlin'. Let's blow this fuckin' bash."

We turned to go, and we were halfway to the garages when Dust caught up to us. He grabbed me by the shoulder, and I stopped in my tracks, staring anxiously at the look of tension on his face.

"Had to come out here and say it, Cora. I think Jimmy would be proud. You've got your reasons for hating your old man, yeah, nobody's gonna blame you. You found yourself a good man," he said, looking at Firefly, too. "My old buddy would've shit bricks if he'd found out you were

291

marrying a biker. Hell, I nearly did myself, 'til I realized my boy here really meant this fuckin' crush. But he'd be happy, knowing you're with a good man. Hope it's helped him find peace, wherever he is. Oughta do the same for you, too."

"That means a lot, Dust. Thank you." I smiled, trying not to let the sadness of losing daddy so suddenly creep back into my heart.

"You enjoy yourselves. This glorious lovin' only happens once in a man and woman's life." We both nodded solemnly, letting his words sink in, and Dust walked back to Hannah, leaving us to finish our short walk to Firefly's bike.

His words turned over in my mind on the way out the door. I'd thought about daddy a lot lately, somewhere in the space between getting tortured by monsters and falling in love.

He'd been a selfish, stupid prick for getting himself killed, for taking his own life. But he was also family, and that was beginning to mean the world to me with the baby on the way.

Firefly helped me put on my helmet and then took the seat in front of me, driving us to the gate. It was finally hot outside, the first sweet, sticky day of many, starting a typical Smoky Mountain summer.

We were planning to ride free, wherever the roads took us for the next week or more. We'd probably wind up somewhere around Gatlinburg and take in the touristy attractions for a few days, before we found ourselves a cozy cabin deep in the forests.

The sun shined bright and hot, but the air was crisp. My man was even hotter.

He was hard, and wonderfully ready for me, rippling underneath my fingertips as I held onto him. We took the winding roads leading deeper into the mountains with a smile on our faces, both knowing we had at least a solid week ahead with nothing but fun, love, and excitement.

I hadn't been this happy since the day I'd lost my father. Hell, maybe not even before then.

Life went on. The wedding proved it, and so did the fact that we were about to start a family.

Why should I hold onto the hate, the anger, the bitterness weighing down my heart? I had to set it free.

When we took a tight turn and I knew Firefly couldn't hear me over the growl of the engine, I mouthed the words, just a soft whisper disappearing in biker thunder.

I forgive you, daddy. I'll love you, always.

You were only human, and so am I.

I won't make your mistakes. But I won't hold them against you any longer.

I'll do better. I'll miss you.

Mark my words, your grandkids will grow up with the happiest smiles on their faces anyone's ever seen.

* * * *

We passed the exit to Gatlinburg a short while later. I squeezed his shoulders, pushing my face close to his ear, fighting to keep my lips off him.

"What's with the detour?"

"Gonna take you somewhere special," he said. "By the time we get into town, half the shit'll be deserted and the fucks will move slow as molasses to get us checked in anyway. Can't wait that long, Cora. Can't fucking *wait*."

He reached up and squeezed my hand, slowing as we turned onto an unpaved forest road. Little pebbles bounced all around us, jumping away from the bike. Thankfully, he'd slowed us down, taking us deeper, through the narrow veil of trees hanging overhead.

When he stopped near a couple large rocks and cut the engine, I heard it. A soft, peaceful stream burbled nearby, lending a natural white noise to this whole stretch of forest.

Overhead, the moonlight poured in through breaks in the trees and the kudzu vines, blanketing us in a soft, almost otherworldly glow. Firefly looked at me, his cold blue eyes big, bright, and finally, warm.

"It's beautiful out here. How do you find these places?"

He smiled, stepping toward me, pulling me into his arms. "Babe, I've got a whole damned map burned into my brain marking all the places I'm gonna fuck you someday. This one's a good start for our honeymoon."

His hand slid slow, moving down my back, before he stopped on my ass and cupped it. I let out a moan for a split second, before his hungry lips covered mine.

We kissed. We twined tongues. We wedged our bodies together closer than the rocks lining the stream. Gradually, he led me toward it, into the clearing where more lovely moonlight filled the night.

"Fuck," Firefly snarled, pulling me down to the ground with him. He tore at my clothes, nearly shredding poor Laynie's skirt.

I had to fight him to take it off without any damage, keeping my promise to return it to her in one piece. Once my sleek, bare legs were wrapped around him, there was no stopping him.

He tore at my top, threw off his own clothes, and hauled me up on his knees. The man looked so good out here in nature, so rough and primal, that I almost came the second he took my nipple in his mouth.

His teeth locked around it, all while his hand aggressively mauled my other breast.

Hungry. Possessive. *Fucking hot.*

My fingers reached across his shoulders, touching his back. I dragged my nails across his skin, careful not to rip him up, but wanting to just the same.

We'd shared too much blood, sweat, and tears. Tonight, we'd share bodies yet again.

I wondered why it always felt like it was new, exciting, and forbidden. He reminded me when his face sunk lower, kissing and nipping down my belly, before he started working on my thighs.

Growling, Firefly held my legs apart, the perfect view for watching the huge, dark stripes inked along his back ripple.

"Oh, Jesus. You're going to ruin me tonight," I whispered, losing my words when his teeth pushed into the soft, sizzling skin around my inner thigh.

"Ruin you?" he echoed, forcing me to feel the heat of his

breath in every word, dangerously close to my soft, aching pussy. "Baby girl, I'm owning you tonight, and every night after. Wrecking you for my dick's just the best part."

Shit, shit! His tongue slid into me, pushing up in a slow, torturous lick. I practically self-combusted on the spot.

My hips rolled, dying to have his face wedged there good and proper. I craved his lips, his tongue, his everything without hesitation. They shot me straight to the beautiful stars and moon lighting up the night, all the places I wanted to frolic, alone with my man.

Sweet energy pulsed through me the instant he grabbed my legs, pulling them apart. All the better to take me with his tongue. Firefly licked straight through my folds.

He licked *deep*. Forced me to feel every scratchy prick of his stubble, one more thing that reminded me I'd married a real man, a big, beautiful bastard so hard and serious no one would ever question our love.

My body tensed up as his tongue lashes quickened. He found my clit, drew it into his mouth, and sank his teeth down just right, delicately holding the little bud taut while his tongue flicked over, and over, and over.

Holy hell! My fingers and toes instantly curled.

I needed something to grab onto, but there were no sheets out here. My legs folded completely around his body. My hands pushed through the scratchy earth, knocking the pebbles underneath us around while the stream sang to my pleasure.

Come, come, fucking come for me, darlin'!

I could feel him saying it, and nature urging him on.

Hot, naked, and sweating underneath the moonlight, it hit me. I'd never done something this taboo!

Anyone could be watching out here. Anything, too.

And somehow, I didn't even care. Nothing else mattered except knowing that I had a man who wasn't afraid to strip me naked and fuck me stupid.

Anytime, any place, any way he pleased.

"Firefly, Firefly, don't stop!" I pleaded, scratching his short, dark hair when his tongue slowed.

He always teased me near the end. The bastard knew how to tie my body in knots and then cut them loose at once, sending me spinning off to pleasures I was just starting to comprehend.

But there wasn't any fathoming the ecstasy that swept in, picked me up, and slammed me down again.

I came – hard enough to make the stars quadruple in the sky.

Blood turned to fire, raging in my veins. The stream's gentle hum became a roar, pounding harsh and staccato in my head.

My hips bucked wild on his face, riding his tongue. His fingers dug deep into my thighs as he held me down, lashing me with strokes again and again.

Soon the stars were swallowed up in blinding white as every muscle in my body oozed sweetness. Tingling, burning, shooting up my spine, I writhed on his face, barely conscious of calling his name like a mantra.

"Firefly…"

My lover, my husband, my old man.

"Firefly."

My love, my life, the outlaw I'd given my soul to.

"Oh, fuck, fuck, Firefly!" I screamed it, my entire body shaking as his wicked mouth sent a few final pleasure bursts streaking through my skin.

I'd love him forever. And the fact that he was so damned amazing at owning my body was just Reason One Thousand and One on the list.

"Hot fucking start," he growled, pushing his cock teasingly against my entrance as I shook off my pleasure coma. "But we can do better than that. Everything we just did, that's good for a warm up, darlin'. You're gonna *scream* before this night's over. You'll come harder for me, Cora, and we'll both fuckin' love it."

Harder? Oh, hell!

I reached up, brushed his Adonis abs with my fingertips, slowly dragging them down to the huge, throbbing perfection about to push inside me. Reaching for his shaft, I wrapped my fingers around it, and squeezed.

"Fuck, yeah!" he rumbled, closing his eyes as I stroked him slowly, up and down. "Just like that, baby. Make me hard as nails, ready to charge the fuck into you."

It must've been well into the high seventies, and humid too, but goosebumps peppered my skin. I couldn't hold them back, knowing what was coming. I stroked his thick cock several more times, feeling it twitch in my hand, drooling pre-come just above my pussy.

Before, I was wet. Now, I ached worse, soaked like he hadn't just brought me off with the best oral pleasure I'd ever had in my short, sweet sex life.

"I need you in me now," I whispered, trying not to bite through my lip. "Please!"

"No, darlin'," he said, grasping my hand and pushing it away.

He couldn't be serious?! I followed his eyes, turned toward something to side, before they locked onto mine.

"Let's go." With those two words, he picked me up, and carried me back to his bike.

For a split second, I thought the absolute madman was going to throw me down and ride off, both of us still buck naked.

He set me down instead. I pushed my toes into the soft Tennessee soil as he got behind me, took my hands, and bent me across the seat of his bike.

"Get a good hold, and keep it, woman. I'm gonna fuck you so hard that bike might flip," he growled, kissing at my neck. His fingers pushed through my hair, wound it tight, and pulled, exposing even more of my neck to him. "We're making the only run that really counts, Cora. Not fuckin' stopping 'til the trees are shaking with your moans."

Just like that, he pushed inside me. My eyes went wide and my fingers hugged the leather seat.

Oh, fuck. Holy hell!

Here. We. Go.

His cock drove deep, straight up to my womb, and then stopped for a second. His hands moved across my body while he held himself there, feeling me, listening to our breath coming heavier by the second.

"You love this shit, don't you?" His first thrust glided through me, stoking the fire in my veins.

"Yes!" It was hard to even speak with raw pleasure overwhelming my nerves.

His hand pulled my hair. The other wrapped around my front side, went low, and pushed between my legs. He pinched and flicked my clit while we fucked, hurling me out of my mind.

"Firefly…"

I whispered his name in between the strokes, saying it a little faster and harder each time he drove into me. The bike's wheels squeaked softly in the soil, supporting our weight, the only leverage I had to weather this storm of a man leaving me soaked and tingling to the core.

He tore me up each time his hips rolled, wrecking what little remained of the walls I'd put up since day one.

Firefly shredded me. Every thrust pierced deeper into my body, my heart, my soul.

Fucking wasn't supposed to be like this. It was supposed to be vicious, carnal, and crude.

But he did so much more than that. Sex with him was a trifecta.

Love. Devotion. Family.

Every rampant flick of his fingers between my legs struck like lightning. I held onto the bike like the edge of a cliff.

Anything to keep myself from collapsing in the earthquake that was Huck Davis, my Firefly.

He jerked my hair tighter, bending my face to his until my ear laid against his lips. "Fucking come for me, baby girl!

Come just like you're begging me to. Your pussy's clenching like a goddamned wildcat, drowning my dick in your juice. Let it all run wild."

I bent my head a little more, moving into his grip, and kissed him. He plunged his tongue into my mouth, quickening his violent, ass slapping thrusts.

Another second, and I was gone.

Just lost it. Right on the spot.

My body went numb, joining my fingers. They'd lost their feeling about thirty seconds ago, digging into the bike's seat so hard I almost broke my hands.

He jerked my head, forced my mouth off his, and I screamed into the night. Oh, God, I shrieked like crazy, straight to the heavens, spilling all the nasty things he did to me.

About ten seconds in, I heard him make the feral grunt he always did right before he was about to explode. Our bodies crashed together even harder, and he pinned me to the motorcycle, slamming his cock into me so hard his thighs clapped against my ass like I was getting spanked.

That sound razed me all over again. I came harder, feeling him balloon against my womb, right before his cock jerked fierce.

He flooded me. Groaning, twitching, smashing his body into mine. We hugged and fucked and came together, grunting out our pleasure, breathless by the end of it.

My pussy took every molten drop of him. Even though he'd given me a baby, it still wasn't enough.

I *craved* him, needed his seed inside me on some

desperate primal level I couldn't understand.

My body was made to be a vessel, and I'd finally found the only man I ever wanted – the only man I needed – to fill the empty void forever.

Our lips pulsed together again as we came down from the high. Then he grabbed my hand, pulling it off the bike, shadowing me against him as he pulled out.

"Fuck me blind. Never thought I'd see anything hotter than having my brand on your skin, babe."

"Yeah?"

"Yeah. That ring…" He held my hand up to his mouth, staring at the golden loop before he kissed it. "Hotter than the fuckin' desert sun. I want to see that thing sparkling every time you reach down and blow me."

I turned around in his arms, facing him, unable to hide the smile twisting my lips. His words were filthy, but I loved them anyway. Every single one.

"I'm ready for town when you are," I said, feeling my tongue sweeping across my lips.

I already wanted to taste him. Imagining those hard muscles twitching while I sucked him, rolled him against my tongue, and caused him to explode in my mouth…

He saw the glint in my eye and took my chin, turning my face into his kiss.

I'd become insatiable.

I loved Firefly. I wanted to remind him how much it all meant to me every waking second.

"Bullshit," he growled, when he could finally take his lips off mine. "We're not leaving 'til I'm ready to crash in a warm bed. Let's clean ourselves up."

He took my hand and led us into the nearby stream. Before I knew what was happening, clear mountain water rushed around us, barely up to our waists. Cold, but cleansing.

"Feels damned good rushing around you, don't it?" he asked, playfully splashing water further up my back. "Nothing in this world like cooling off proper after a nice fuck."

He tossed more water up my back, massaging me in between. I smiled, cupping a small puddle in both hands, and slowly turned to face him.

"Nah. I can think of one thing…"

I shivered, letting my body acclimate to it, before I spun around and threw it in his eyes.

Firefly stopped. For a second, we both stood there, my toes anxiously grasping at the soft, round pebbles under the water.

"Did you really just splash me right in the fuckin' face?" he growled, his voice turning stone cold killer.

Uh, oh. I folded my arms and looked at him, never losing the defiant smile tugging at my lips.

"If you really wanted a spanking before I'm in you again, babe, next time just ask." I could tell he was trying hard not to laugh as he grabbed me, bent me over, and pulled me from the water, ass up.

Yeah, I thought, *but where's the fun in that?*

Who the hell knew? He showed me a different kind of fun a second later, rubbing my right cheek before his palm moved backward, winding up.

He spanked me hard as I clung to the edge of the dry rocks. My body twitched, shaking and overheating, knowing what would be making me shiver next, after his hands had their fill.

"Love you, babe," he said, pushing inside me. I didn't think a man could get this hard again so fast. "Love you so damned much I can't even think straight."

"Better work it out, then. We've got a lot of planning to do for the baby after this honeymoon."

I tried to tease him. Nothing compared to the slow, tense push of his hips on mine, a thrust to remind me who was really in control.

I moaned. His teeth dug gently into my shoulder, and he slammed himself into me a few more times, pushing my throat into the cradle of his hand. Perfect for holding me in place, right where he wanted.

"Oh, darlin', we're gonna work it out like the end of the earth depends on it this week. If I'm holding your waist and you ain't naked, I'm not happy."

Smiling, I let myself slip into the pleasure all over again. He sealed his vow with another sharp thrust of his hips, carrying us all the way home.

XV: Forgiven (Firefly)

Two Years Later

We'd only seen this spot once since our honeymoon. This was the second time, and the whole damned world had changed, getting bigger and wilder like the stream in front of us.

Wished I could've ridden us in on my bike like the first time. But I had Lucy to tote around now on these family outings, plus kid on the way. The truck would have to do, muddy and reliable, for hauling all our asses to the right spot.

Soon as we were out, I took Cora's hand, watching as she pulled our daughter outta the kiddie seat.

"Come to mama, baby girl!" she cooed.

That shit never failed to light up my face. She was as good a ma as she was my wife, my old lady, and hearing her say it reminded me I had two baby girls to look after now.

"I've got the canister," I said, pulling out the box in the small compartment behind Lucy's seat. "Let's go."

I held onto Cora's free hand as we walked down by the

water. She put on a brave face, holding a smile, despite the hell up ahead.

My eyes crawled to the boulder just a few paces away from the stream. I stopped and remembered the start of our awesome fuckin' honeymoon, the first time I ever bent her over my ride, fucking the ever-living shit outta both of us.

I'd done that about a thousand times since. Real miracle was, it never got old.

Never. Ever. My grip tightened on her hand.

We shared a look while little Lucy laughed, locked in a memory that'd never be rated anything except X.

"This spot good?" I asked, as soon as we touched the edge of the earth.

"Yeah," Cora said, leaning down to plant a kiss on Lucy's forehead. She giggled, and that got my girl to laugh a little too.

Thank fuck. We all needed to lighten up today.

Music to my ears, hearing both of 'em happy. The kid was too young to understand what was happening. A blessing, really. Cora was the one who needed all the bright sunny shit she could get just now.

The high summer sun gave us a little bit of that. Me, I'd give her the rest.

I reached into my pocket, pulled out my switchblade, and sliced through the tape holding the box together. The silver urn inside was smaller than I thought. Hard to believe a whole man fit inside it, scorched down to nothing but dust.

Ashes to ashes. I looked at my girl, holding out my arms.

306

She traded me the kid for the can.

Lucy reached up and stroked the short beard I'd been sprouting since I added dad to my resume. "What you doing, girlie? You're gonna pull my face off one of these days. Girl's got her old man's strength."

"Da-da-da!" Lucy purred, playfully tugging on my whiskers.

That stuff shouldn't make a man happier than a pig in shit, but it did. Hell, it made me a thousand times happier than all the Jack and whore ass I used to pound, a million years ago before Cora Chase.

I looked up as my wife let out a small laugh, all she could manage with her old man's remains in her hands. Pushing my chin lower into Lucy's small hands, I watched her screw off the cap, and crouch next to the water.

She looked at it for a second, unsure. The stream ran harder today, quicker and angrier than I remembered that night I fucked her in the water.

I looked through the trees, studying the path. "It's good here. That force'll be sure to carry it all down, spread him up equally. Whenever you're ready, babe."

Suddenly, she straightened up, staring at the open urn in her hands. "I finally am. You know, I forgave him a couple years ago, the night we got married. Dust's advice helped."

"Prez is always good at that," I said, walking up next to her, holding Lucy tighter as I gazed into the water.

"Nobody helped like you, love," she said, smiling and reaching for my hand.

I took it, squeezing her fingers in between her, me, and our little girl. "Whenever you're ready, babe. Let the man fly home."

Nothing in the world could've stopped her from tearing up when she tipped the urn upside down. The three of us went quiet and watched while she emptied it, the dead man who'd brought her into my life disappearing in a slim smoke trail going downstream.

The water swallowed him up fast. She rinsed the urn in the cool water and stood up, gently shaking a few last drops into the roaring stream.

"I can't believe it took me two years," she said softly, walking with me along the trees lining the water. "So much has happened to us, Huck."

"Babe, we're only getting started," I said, smiling as Lucy cooed in my arms. The kid couldn't decide if she wanted to take a nap or go for my whiskers some more. "We've got our whole lives ahead. It's been a helluva thing, these last two years, and the next two are gonna be wilder. Count on it."

I grabbed her, pulled her into us, holding the babe in the middle. She was smiling through the tears shining in her eyes. Behind us, the stream shuffled faster, or maybe we just opened our ears to the steady roar.

"I love you, Firefly. I couldn't be standing here, doing this, without you." She paused, looked at the kid, and then at me. "Not without our family by my side."

"Gonna have a whole lot more of us next time we're here to pay our dues. Baby number two's coming up in seven months. Keep being beautiful, darlin'. You're giving me at least three more."

Laughing, she punched me in the arm, sticking that soft little tongue out between her teeth. Fuck if my cock didn't twitch, deep in my jeans. Never stopped wanting her. When the sun caught her just right or she moved the right way – and she always did – it was like flipping a damned switch.

Even during the most somber bullshit, I couldn't turn it off.

Well, fuck the sad and black. I wasn't letting the heavy weight of the past drag us down. Not today, when we were saying goodbye to old cancers.

"Let's go, Cora. Back to the truck. We've got a long ride through the Smokies coming up. Lucy's gonna see every spot along the road worth seeing before she's five, and then we're gonna do the same with her brothers and sisters."

"Only if you save room for me," she said, leaning into me for a hot, long kiss.

Goddamned, those lips. Those sweet, fiery, suckable lips.

They'd never get old. Not even when our hair turned gray and I'd be lucky to get it up for a third round without a goddamned blue pill.

Fuck that shit. Fuck it all!

This woman, this kid, this life we were building one day at a time meant the world to me, with my brothers coming in a close second behind it.

"Baby girl," I whispered, sliding Lucy into her arms, and opening the door to the truck. "There's all the room in the world for you, wherever the hell I go. You're my wife. You know damned well where you belong."

Smiling, she tucked our little girl into the kiddie seat. For a second, we stood there, watching Lucy doze in the open truck, my woman wrapped up in my arms.

"I've gotten to the point where I can say I don't regret anything. For real, Firefly. How about you?" she asked, a mischievous sparkle in her baby blues.

"Cora, you ask me silly fuckin' questions again, and I'm gonna remind you that when I lay my claim, there's no going back. No doubt. No regrets. Never-fucking-ever."

One hand slipped down her belly, rounding her backside. I caught her ass and squeezed, growling as I pulled her into me.

She'd get it all later, 'til we were spent and flushed all over, just like we'd been hundreds of times before. For now, I'd savor her slow.

Fingers tangled in her hair, I buried her in another merciless kiss.

Thanks!

Want more Nicole Snow? Sign up for my newsletter to hear about new releases, subscriber only goodies, and other fun stuff!

JOIN THE NICOLE SNOW NEWSLETTER! - http://eepurl.com/HwFW1

Thank you so much for buying this book. I hope my romances will brighten your mornings and darken your evenings with total pleasure. Sensuality makes everything more vivid, doesn't it?

If you liked this book, please consider leaving a review and checking out my other erotic romance tales.

Got a comment on my work? Email me at nicolesnowerotica@gmail.com. I love hearing from my fans!

Kisses,
Nicole Snow

More Erotic Romance
by Nicole Snow

FIGHT FOR HER HEART

BIG BAD DARE: TATTOOS AND SUBMISSION

MERCILESS LOVE: A DARK ROMANCE

LOVE SCARS: BAD BOY'S BRIDE

RECKLESSLY HIS: A BAD BOY MAFIA
ROMANCE

STEPBROTHER CHARMING: A BILLIONAIRE
BAD BOY ROMANCE

STEPBROTHER UNSEALED: A BAD BOY
MILITARY ROMANCE

Outlaw Love/Prairie Devils MC Books

OUTLAW KIND OF LOVE

NOMAD KIND OF LOVE

SAVAGE KIND OF LOVE

WICKED KIND OF LOVE

BITTER KIND OF LOVE

Grizzlies MC Books

OUTLAW'S KISS

OUTLAW'S OBSESSION

OUTLAW'S BRIDE

OUTLAW'S VOW

Deadly Pistols MC Books

NEVER LOVE AN OUTLAW

NEVER KISS AN OUTLAW

SEXY SAMPLES: NEVER LOVE AN OUTLAW

I: Smothered in Shadows (Megan)

I couldn't remember my own name sometimes.

When you're so shocked, so broken, so completely sick at heart, the ego dies in every breath, and mine died fast.

My pimp kept me chained up like a dog when I wasn't being used. *Fresh,* he called me, the only name I responded to because Megan was so far away.

Megan was my name in another life. Megan was what they called me when I smiled and laughed, before I spent every waking minute in a nightmare.

"Fresh, baby, wake the fuck up." Ricky grabbed me by the hair and pulled me off my cot, breaking a beautiful sleep where I almost believed I wasn't trapped in this hellhole. "You've got business."

He grinned, showing his dirty teeth. Maybe I couldn't settle on a name or identity anymore, but I knew his.

Ricky the bastard was my judge, jury, and executioner for every day I managed to stay alive in this place.

"Okay, Ricky. Just give me a minute."

He nodded, satisfied, and then pulled the tarnished key out of his jeans. His coarse hands grazed my throat as he unlocked my collar. It was always too tight. I reached up and rubbed the tender, raw impression left by that damned collar like I always did.

Another day. Another John. Another chapter as Fresh, rather than Megan.

"The crew coming in means business for you and Bell," he growled, shoving a small plastic bin of soap, shampoo, and a towel in my face. "Get cleaned up. We're a little light today. Cherry Anne says she's sick, and I'm looking for you and Bell to pick up the slack. These guys aren't our regular big rig cocks. They're tough, mean, and they like to fuck *hard*. You'd better be ready to work for every red cent."

"Always, Ricky. Always."

I flashed him that soft, dead look that always seemed to make him shut up. I learned a long time ago not to negotiate, not to even speak to this man in anything resembling complete sentences. Saying more than I needed to got me into trouble, and sometimes planted nasty ideas in his brain, too.

He'd used me before, and it was always worse than the other Johns. The faceless men who came and went, paying for sex, rarely put any emotion into it. But when Ricky pushed my mouth over his cock, the pimp reminded me who held all the power here, and that I'd be his slave until the day he decided to sell me off to someone else.

Holding my breath, I squeezed the towel, almost ready to turn and head for the small bathroom attached to my room. I winced when I felt his fingers on my skin.

The pimp chuckled, running a fat hand all the way down my back, stopping in my inner thigh. He liked to pinch, and this time, he did it hard. I closed my eyes and let out a whimper.

"Fucking whore. You're the best one here, and you know it, don't you?" His dark eyes beamed down on mine, proud, sick, and demanding. "You're goddamned lucky I only let these boys have one hole. You'd think I was giving them the moon when they throw money at me for your hot little mouth. I can't wait to see what the rest of you earns someday soon. We're close to a buyer, baby. I just know it. I've got a couple bites."

His hand slid around my legs. Cupping my mound through my panties, he squeezed. My fingers twitched. I hadn't had to fight the urge to slap him, bite him, gouge his fucking eyes out for a long time.

But I did just then, praying he'd be done soon. I suppressed a shudder, holding in everything until he finally pulled his hand away.

"Go shower now, girl. These guys aren't the real patient type. I'll be watching today, keeping you safe, so no worries. You never know what these biker assholes can do."

Keeping me safe? It was so sick I wanted to laugh.

Bikers? Ugh. I remembered the last time I had to service them, the hard, vicious men from the Deadhands MC.

Their VP, Big Vic, was the only man who managed to scare me besides Ricky. The bastard grinned the entire time as he slammed my face into his crotch, hard enough to leave me sore for a couple days. Once, he leaned down and cursed in my ear between his ragged breaths, told me how much he'd like to shoot Ricky in the head and take me away forever.

I feared the day he'd actually come back and do it. The pimp was bad, but there were bigger bastards than him in this world, and that included everyone with a Deadhands' patch on their leather cut.

Ricky hit me with his dead-eyed *what-the-fuck-are-you-waiting-for?* stare.

I gave him another fake little smile, a nod, and then retreated into the bathroom. I heard my cot creek outside as he settled into it, humming lullabies to himself while he flipped his gun in his hands.

Those tunes made me think he had a soul once. The first few times I'd heard them, I thought maybe I could convince him to let me go once he was done with me. Maybe this was just business to him, money, and he didn't really want to hurt me unless he needed to.

Of course, the real Ricky wasn't like that at all. It was the ultimate wishful thinking. I had too many bruises and scars to prove it, too many nightmares that broke the only peace I got from hard labor in this miserable trucker whorehouse.

How many months has it been? I wondered, leaning into the shower to clean myself, loving the way the hissing shower head temporarily drowned out the horror of my life.

I couldn't figure out how much time had passed since my first day here, and I doubted I ever would. It had to be months, maybe years.

My reflection told the full story. The beautiful, confident, playful girl who used to stare back at me in the mirror turned into a dead-eyed whore with sunken cheeks, one I hated to even acknowledge.

Megan the socialite, the flirt, the dreamer, was dead. Long live the whore.

"Hey, Fresh! Hurry your sweet ass up! Don't bother with the fucking fishnets." He yelled it so loud I could practically feel the tremor in the tile underneath my feet.

Wincing, I dried myself quickly, and then slipped into a fresh change of clothes he'd laid out the day before. Calling it an outfit would be generous.

The purple lace bra was too damned tight. The Johns who managed to break them open always did me a favor, lending some relief to my poor boobs. Not that it mattered.

He had a near endless supply of the same cheap, suffocating lingerie for all the girls, including me.

"Yo, lady, hurry the fuck up!" This time, he slapped the wall. "I wanna get this show on the road. We don't got no time to dilly-dally, bitch, you hear me?"

"One more minute, Ricky. Almost ready. I promise."

The nervous bite in his voice made me smile. It never took much to upset him, really, and nothing did more than dealing with the Deadhands MC.

I couldn't completely blame the bastard for being worried. Hell, I wondered if this would be the day they decided to burn this place down and take the girls for themselves, including me. My heart pumped terror every time I remembered Big Vic's big, ugly grin, the nose ring in the middle of his fat face twitching every time he roared some new humiliation.

Bitch! Cunt! Whore!

Ricky called me all the same names as the biker, but he didn't have a tenth of the wicked outlaw's hateful energy when he said them.

Shimmying my panties up one more time, I slid into my heels, and stepped outside. Ricky leaned on the frame leading into the hall, making hushed words with some man I couldn't see.

"Look, buddy, you can have her tongue any way you want. Grab her hair and fuck her 'til she gags. If you haven't heard our Fresh is the best little cocksucker this side of the mountains, then you've been living under a rock. But I need to be there for security."

"Security." A low, dark voice repeated the word, dripping sarcasm. "What the fuck do I look like, pimp? Some chump who's going to stand there getting sucked off while you watch?"

"It's not like that, mister. I'm just hanging out to protect my property. Hell, I'll put my eyes on the ground. You pay up, and you can do anything you want to her –"

"And I'm telling you I want some goddamned privacy. Don't make us turn this place upside down more than we already are, asshole." My jaw dropped as I watched two huge tattooed arms shove Ricky against the wall. "You're a clueless little shit, aren't you, pimp? There's a lot you don't get if you're not following what's going down here today. I fuck the way I want and take whatever I need, and so does every other man in this club. Yeah, yeah, I know you've got Deadhands' protection. Your first mistake was thinking any of us gave a shit the minute we walked in here."

They scuffled again, spilling their noise into the hallway.

"Hey!" Ricky let out a yelp and desperately grabbed for the man. The biker ripped his gun out of his hands first.

I backed into a corner, my mouth still hanging open, watching as the stranger's hands flung Ricky's handgun around like a toy.

"Play nice. Go mop the toilets or some shit like a good little boy, and maybe you can have this back. Give all the brothers some peace and quiet, stay the fuck outta our way, and you'll walk outta here today without a hole in your head."

"Skin, you're making a big mistake. I didn't know this was a fucking shakedown. I thought you guys were just here for the regional fees or some shit. We can work this out. Just let me talk to your chief and explain –"

The sickening slap of metal on thin skin cut him off. I pinched my eyes shut, wondering if this was just another bad dream.

No, of course not, I'd never been so lucky. Not since this became my life. Ricky whimpered, staggering in the narrow hallway in a circle, the same way he sometimes did when he got really drunk. Except this time there was pain glowing in his eyes, hurt and terror, something I'd never seen before on his nasty face.

Why does that look make me feel so excited and scared simultaneously?

"Get the fuck outside, Ricky," the stranger growled. "Stop crying and listen. I don't waste my time saying the same thing twice. Next time you give me any bullshit, pretending you've got everything under control and we're just here for a tea party, I'll break your fucking jaw. You'll lose teeth. Now, outta my damned way."

Ricky hit the wall again with a loud thud. Other sinister sounding male voices filled the hallway, just as a huge shadow stepped into the doorway.

My heart came to a total stop when I stared at him. It was dark and dingy, the only dull light coming through the blinds, turning my world into a canvass of shadows.

Tall, dark, and handsome didn't begin to describe the giant about to enter my world, and probably my body too.

Shit, *tall* didn't do him a bit of justice.

He was so big he had to duck when he finally stepped through the frame, into my room. Instinct forced me to walk backwards, pressed me against the wall. I froze, running my eyes across his leather vest for telltale signs of the demon red lettering and severed hand symbols the MC always wore.

But he didn't have that at all. His cut looked...cleaner, somehow. I didn't recognize the symbols either. Smoking guns, skulls, and neon yellow one-percent signs plastered his chest, flanking the patch with his name.

I looked and looked, and I couldn't believe what I was seeing. This was another club, another man, another dangerous predator ready to rip me to shreds.

The fear and shock broke my protective wall. We locked eyes, and I trembled, saying his name.

"Skin? Seriously?" I instantly regretted the words.

I lost my smart mouth the first few times Ricky slapped

me across the face. I couldn't comprehend why it suddenly came back the second I was staring at a man ten times as dark and powerful as my brutal pimp.

He stopped less than a foot away from me, painfully close. His smile distorted the long scar across his cheek. All I could think about while I watched it was how it complimented his warrior look, like he'd just walked into the real world from the Norse legends I read about in college.

His huge, tattooed arm rose up to his chest, and he tapped the name patch with two fingers. "That's what they all call me, babe. Don't wear it out before I fuck you ragged."

Oh, God. My brain shut down. I couldn't understand why he was here anymore. Skin was too vicious, too strange, too devilishly good-looking to be in a whorehouse like this one.

I knew I'd just met my ruin.

* * * *

Six Months Ago

Becky laughed in the driver's seat, taking the mountain curves way too fast. I was too drunk to care that we might go careening off into the nearest ravine, right through the flimsy guard rails.

Tonight was ours. We were out to conquer a new set of boys like we always did and drink ourselves stupid.

NICOLE SNOW

If only those damned heels would've stopped digging into my ankles…

"You fighting with your shoes again, girl?" my best friend said with a laugh. "You try way too hard when you flirt!"

"Whatever, it's not like they'll be staying on for long anyway," I said. "Crawford's been texting me all week. Pretty funny, really. I thought the son of the biggest real estate mogul in Knoxville would be knee-deep in pussy…he seems kinda desperate."

"Oh, please, they're all like that. Awkward rich boys." Becky spun the wheel in her hands. My stomach lurched as we took the next hard turn.

"Hey, at least he's cute. If he isn't a total dud tonight, maybe we'll be onto something."

"*Pssht.* We're too young to go hubby hunting, and you know it! This party's going to be packed with hot guys, Meg. Don't get in too deep having the hots for Craw-daddy. He wants in your panties and he's a heart breaker."

I rolled my eyes. She'd always been the perfect foil for all my wild intentions, and sometimes a bigger party slut than me.

Too bad. Becky wouldn't put the brakes on my fun tonight, and I wasn't buying her carefree attitude for once.

Lately, I'd been thinking a lot about growing up. Something about being twenty-two without a man, maybe, or else the fact that Daddy was getting more frustrated with me by the day, having me around the house.

I barely went to the Wilder Corp offices, even though I

had an internship there through his strings. What did it matter? I had the same sweet trust fund that had gotten me through college. My salary rolled in like clockwork, whether I went in and answered a few phones each week, or slept off my latest hangover.

I'd plowed through college last spring and walked out with my Communications degree. Good for setting me up as the public face of Daddy's company after he decided to retire. And honestly, as long as I had my fun and landed a good husband, I didn't really care.

I was born a Wilder, and that meant living life on easy mode. I had the money and the name to be whoever I wanted.

It wasn't a sin to be figuring that out in my early twenties, right?

Sure, the future mattered, but I didn't have to think too hard. I didn't have to settle tonight. I just wanted to *explore,* have some fun with Crawford, and see if he was more than fuck buddy material.

I'd drink with Becky and the guys. Then we'd have the best skinny dip of our young lives, cooling off in the private mountain pools, the perfect way to end a long, muggy September day.

The next mountain bend twisted my ankle as I dug my heel into the car's floor for support. *Fuck.*

Hiccuping, I reached down, fixing my strap. Becky laughed harder, snickering the whole time.

"You know, Meg, you could use some of that big family fortune to go to Nashville and have some fancy-schmacy designer there make you heels worth walking on. Last summer, when I went, I found this awesome little place where…"

Blah, blah, blah. I zoned out, too drunk and eager for fun to care about Becky lecturing me on fashion. My core tingled, excited for the night to come.

I lived for the chase, the first time with someone new. I'd never found anything better than taking on a new man, feeling his face and his hands all over my pussy. Despite my wild streak, I'd stayed a good girl.

I wouldn't give any man my cherry until he put a ring on my finger. I'd fuck him every other way, and feel his tongue all over me, but I wouldn't give *that* up.

Time was on my side, after all. I didn't care if I needed to suck off half of Eastern Tennessee before I found a man worthy of claiming me as his wife.

Becky was still blathering on about some fashion crap while I nodded and purred agreement. The car pulled onto Crawford family land, and we spied about a dozen other vehicles lined up on the side of the mountain.

For a second, I worried Becky was too trashed to parallel park without plowing into someone, but she managed. She always did.

As soon as the emergency brake was on, I popped my door, and staggered out, straightening my white summer dress. The slope leading up to the little party hut next to the mountain pools was hell on my legs, but I appreciated the warm-up.

I'd need it for all the fun I knew we'd have tonight.

There'd be flirting, necking, and maybe finding a little love.

It was just another carefree Smoky Mountain night, the kind I lived for. What could possibly go wrong?

* * * *

"Crawford, I don't know…"

"Aw, come on, baby. We've got this side of the waterfall all to ourselves. You're a lovely lady tonight, and I'm a hot blooded man, both of us rich as Midas. Stop fighting this thing we're both feeling. Let me be the first man to give it to you like nobody else ever will."

His hard cock moved against my leg. I laughed as he dove for my neck again.

Crawford was nice, lean, and strong, but he was either the clumsiest kisser I'd ever been with, or I was more drunk than I thought.

"Wait, wait. Let's not get carried away. I want to take this slow, Craw." I pushed against his chest until he rocked back.

His eyebrows furrowed. "You? Slow? Shit, that's not the Meg Willow Wilder everybody knows. They all said you'd have your lips wrapped around me by now…"

I froze up, staring at him like he'd just punched me in the face. Hot, drunken anger burned my cheeks, so sultry they'd rage like furnaces if I reached up and touched them.

Okay, sure, I knew I had a reputation. But he was calling me a slut to my face, and expecting me to act like one. Consider me blindsided.

"You've been talking to other guys about me?"

Crawford's turn to blush. "Meg, come on, it's not like that. I just mean I thought you'd want to have some fun tonight, that's all. I didn't know you'd become a good girl overnight. Baby, who do I look like?"

Smiling, he inched towards me, throwing an arm around my shoulder. "You don't have to use your mouth with me for anything but a warm-up. Your friends talk a lot. I know you're still a virgin in one way, Meg. I know I'm good enough to fuck you. Why are you fighting this so hard, baby? Give me what I want tonight, and I'll give you all kinds of things that'll make you scream."

This couldn't be happening. Was he seriously bribing me? Trying to buy me off with some sick quid pro quo? Hell, with the way he'd been talking, he probably just wanted to bang me and brag about it to his friends.

My eyes bugged out as I fought him off, pushing through the cool mountain pool, covering my boobs with one arm.

I'd heard enough. I turned my back to him, swam several strokes to the rocky wall lining the pool, and clambered out. Crawford yelled something after me, but I barely heard him over the burbling waterfall next to us.

"Meg, wait! We can talk this out. I'm sorry, I got carried away. Come back!"

I couldn't believe it. Just when I wanted to get my life together, this asshole rubbed my reputation in my face, acting like he expected me to suck him off just because I'd been a total slut in the past.

Well, those days were over. I found my dress and towel laying on the nearby cooler where I'd placed them. I quickly dried myself off and dressed.

I didn't want him to follow. If he had another chance to talk to me later, it'd only be after I cooled off.

Maybe I'd whored myself to too many men. That was my mistake. But *nobody* treated me like they were entitled to my body or my family name, and I wasn't going to let Crawford be the first.

I didn't care if his family was a little richer than mine. Being a Wilder gave me all the wealth I'd ever need. It also meant I wasn't backing down for anyone who came after my ego, whether or not they had some truth behind it.

I stomped into the forest, heading onto a half-overgrown path. The clear night stars shone overhead, complemented by a huge summer moon. A walk would clear my head, take the edge off his stupid comments. I'd return in an hour or two and go from there, depending on how I felt.

I knew Becky would be screwing around with Tim Yates for a few more hours. I expected to stumble across her in some corner of the forest, rolling in the dirt with her latest dirty talking pump and dump crush.

They never lasted long. I could say the same, and the old Meg would've just shut up and went along with Crawford for the night, if only he were a better kisser.

I hated getting older. Thinking about my career, my family, finding my future husband just brought more anxiety. But nothing made me more anxious than thinking about the party lifestyle forever.

I couldn't creep toward thirty still acting like I was twenty-one. No fucking way.

When I came into a cool, dark clearing, I stopped to admire the view. The moonlight came down through the break in the trees. I walked over to the smoothest mountain boulder and sat, feeling the dew veil against my legs.

God, what a beautiful night. So, why was it becoming so ugly?

Soft, transparent mist swirled low on the ground. They didn't call them the Smoky Mountains for nothing.

I was busy focusing on the beauty when I heard something snap nearby. I spun and saw a figure coming through the darkness. Figuring it was Crawford, I bolted up, folding my arms, ready to hear his pathetic apologies.

"Look, before you start, I'm not in the mood for excuses."

"Excuses? My, my, girl. I'd say you're right out of a dream, standing here in the dark up in these mountains, but you're too angry to be a fantasy." His voice was older, too arrogant and gravely to be Craw's.

I whipped around and faced a tall, rugged looking man with a cap pulled tight over his eyes. He wore tight jeans and an open shirt. He looked like he'd just wandered out of a lumber mill or something.

Great. Running into weirdos up here in the boonies was exactly what I needed.

"Sorry. I…I thought you were somebody else." I looked him up and down, sizing him up. "What're you doing out here?"

He smiled, raising an eyebrow. "I could ask you the same thing. Seems you've gone a long way from the party happening down by the springs."

Crap. How did he know? We must've been really noisy, or else he just knew his turf that well.

Better than me, if I had to run.

Shuffling my feet uncomfortably, I tried not to think about how fucked I really was. I didn't know this man, nor his intentions.

Nobody except Crawford knew I'd run off — and knowing how much of a bitter wimp he was, he wouldn't be coming to my rescue. I could only hold my ground, and hope to God this was just some eccentric mountain man wanting to make friendly conversation.

"Too noisy for me," I lied. "I wanted to get away and enjoy the forest beauty while I'm up here. I don't get out to the Smokies as often as I'd like."

His thin smile widened, and he took a step closer. I was about to bolt when he flopped down on the boulder next to me, spreading his arms wide, staring up at the sky.

"It's a gorgeous fucking night, ain't it? My name's Richard, by the way." He tilted his head up and shot me a wink. He reached into his pocket.

I couldn't help but smile and feel a little more ease creep in when he drew out a small silver flask.

"Care for a swig? It's our very own moonshine. My grandpa's recipe."

I shook my head. Okay, maybe he wasn't the danger I'd feared at first.

Just a big, drunken mountain goof. I hoped. I'd seen his type before out hiking, and they never did any harm.

Friendly or not, there was no way I'd share a flask with a stranger.

"Suit yourself, princess." He popped the cap and took a long pull, then emptied the rest on the ground. "I was bullshitting you about the moonshine. It's just plain ol' Jack."

"Decent choice. Do you come here often, or maybe live nearby?" I decided to make small talk, taking my place several rocks away, fixing my eyes on the same distant stares filling his eyes.

"I'm a hiker. Nothing builds a man up like a bull better than taking these mountains one step at a time. It's always an adventure up here. You ever see the abandoned ghost towns tucked back in these mountains? People worked and lived and died in these parts for generations before they flew the coop, leaving their homes and a few old tractors behind. There's something charming about that. It takes you back, away from all this shit in our lives, you know? Simpler times. I like 'em."

I nodded glumly. Redneck or not, he was nice, and eerily in touch with my own feelings tonight.

Just then, I'd have given anything to get away from all my frustrations. Sure, I could hop a flight to Europe or the Caribbean next week, like I'd done on my summers off from college, but those getaways never lasted forever.

"Tell me more about your adventures again. Sometimes I think I could use some of that."

He tucked the flask back in his pocket, then sat up and smiled. "I do a lot of trucking when I'm away from home. It's hell half the time, honestly, driving down the Florida panhandle or all the way out to Cali-fucking-fornia with some boss riding my ass. But there's always a new experience every route, and that's what keeps me working more than just the money. New faces, new things, new thrills. You haven't been living 'til you've been through Wyoming in the winter and almost felt the wind blow your rig over."

"Sounds scary," I said, warming up more than I really should. A lot of it was the alcohol, a delayed buzz in my veins, but his tone sounded so honest, authentic in a way all the rich boys and girls I always hung around with couldn't be.

"You'd better believe it. The shitty parts of LA will make you feel alive too, when some gangbanger decides to take potshots at your truck just for sport. It's funny how being on the open road and putting up with so much shit makes a man appreciate the quiet more."

He stood up and walked out into the clearing, stretching toward the sky. I believed him.

"You said you don't come out here often? Well, hell, neither do I. And that's what makes me love it when I do. When you're busy dealing with crowded cities and traffic jams half the time like I am, these mountains are a slice of heaven. I wouldn't trade my adventures for nothing, even the shitty parts, because they make home what it is." He turned, his eyes narrowed. "Don't tell me this is as wild as you get? Skipping out on your friends and looking like you're about to freak the second some stranger says 'hello?'"

Christ, was it really that obvious? I smiled uneasily, shaking my head.

"Sorry. I'm a little on edge tonight. Like I said, I don't come up here often. You never know what a strange man might want out in the boonies."

"What if he just wants to give you a good time?" He paused, just long enough to feel my heart sink, while tension roiled my belly. "I'm not talking about fucking, girl."

That caught me off guard. I twisted my head, stood up, creeping closer as he extended a hand.

"You're too pretty for me anyway. Let's be friends for the night. I'll take you out for a burger and a malt." His smile grew, and I watched him reach into his pocket, this time taking out a pack of cigarettes.

I didn't know what the hell to think. He was offering me a chance to leave my comfort zone behind. I had a weird feeling he could give me something authentic too, if only for an evening. He wasn't really my type – even for a fling – but if he really didn't care about that...

"No, Richard, I really shouldn't. I don't know you. My friends are waiting."

"Aw, come on. What's your name?"

"Megan."

His hand shot out, taking mine in his after I'd turned him down before, giving my fingers a tight, over-friendly squeeze.

"There. Now that we know each other, what do you say?

You're a local, aren't you? We'll go get some grub and keep this conversation going. Then I'll drop you off before midnight. I know you want to get outta here, I can see it in your face. What've you got to lose?"

His soft, whimsical tone held a challenge. I hated being taunted, and he wasn't even doing it openly.

He shrugged impatiently. "Go tell your girlfriends if you need to. Let 'em know you're going out with Richard for a bite. That's all this is, babe, I promise. What do you think's gonna happen? You'll wind up on some late night murder mystery show with your eyes blacked out and duct tape on your mouth?"

Laughter belted out his gut, echoing through the shadowy forest. His laugh was high, sharp, and so unexpected I couldn't stop myself from giggling too.

"Okay, you win. You don't look like a killer or a rapist."

He began walking me down the path, the one leading further and further into the Smokies, away from Crawford's private property.

One more wink was all I needed to let him lead me along like a stupid schoolgirl.

If only I'd done something then. I could've run, yelled, screamed bloody murder, or at least re-awakened my old instinct to sober up and ask myself why the *hell* I decided to walk through the eerie mountains to a total stranger's pickup truck.

But he never made a move, not even when I was securely in his passenger seat, and we headed down the lonesome highway. He had to lure me deeper first.

* * * *

I flipped the greasy burger over in my hands. I was hungry, yeah, but the deserted diner offered up some serious crap. I couldn't finish it.

The conversation wasn't going much better. Richard kept talking about his ex, some woman who walked out on him when he was my age, which must've been over a decade ago just looking at him.

I wasn't in the mood for lonely, stupid men tonight, however nice they might be. Whatever, at least it was better than hanging around, waiting for Crawford's awkward apologies. I reached into my purse for my phone at one point, only to realize I'd stupidly left it somewhere near the pool.

"Fuck," I sputtered, choking down a sickeningly sweet sip of strawberry milkshake.

"Yeah, I thought so too, baby doll. They always love you and leave you real fast, the bitches. If she'd stuck around, I'm sure my life would've been a lot more exciting by now. I wouldn't have to work my ass off every day and take these mountain hikes. Hell, I'd probably have a family, maybe a house, instead of renting a studio apartment above that goddamned forsaken place."

I blinked, barely even paying attention to his long, rambling life story anymore. "Hang on. I need to hit the restroom."

I headed in and splashed cool water over my face, looking for a pay phone on the way out. There had been one – I could see the faint gray outline where it used to attach to the wall, now ripped out, leaving a shadow like a relic from another time.

A cab ride home sounded awfully good right now. Unfortunately, short of asking the restaurant to make a call on their business phone, it wasn't looking like an option.

Richard was weird and needy, but he'd kept me company, and he didn't seem like a total creeper. Besides, I was getting more tired by the second, and what harm would there be in one more ride home?

If he was really going to ambush me, he'd have done it in the mountains.

I'd let him drop me off in my neighborhood so I could stumble home. He didn't need to see my parents' huge house and get his hopes up about doing favors for a woman who was richer and prettier than he'd ever be.

Total bitch? Yeah, sure. And also a *very* tired one.

Jesus, I was drained. It must've been the mountain walk. By the time I got back to the table, I could barely make my knees work, and I covered a brutal yawn with my hand.

I wanted to go to sleep right there. Luckily, he settled our bill with a waitress who was probably bored out of her skull. She didn't even stop to laugh at his wise cracks.

Closing my eyes for a second took what felt like five minutes. When I opened them again, Richard stood over me, pushing his hand into mine.

"Damn, girl. You're crashing on me, ain't you? We'd better get you home. Come on."

"I can stand," I moaned weakly.

No, no, I couldn't.

The instant I tried, my knees buckled, and I slumped into his arms. He scooped me up like a sleepy kitten and carried me outside, pushing me into the passenger seat, complete with a ratty old pillow he'd fished out of the back.

"Hold up, I need to give you my address," I said, struggling to remember the numbers in my own head as another jaw-popping yawn conquered me. "It's…uh…it's…"

"Don't think too hard, baby," he growled, starting up his truck. "I already know where you live. Just go to sleep. You'll need that energy for tomorrow."

What the fuck was this man talking about? Tomorrow? How did he know anything about me?

"Tomorrow? Huh?"

It felt like an entire hour slipped by before he answered me.

"That's the day you find out you fucked up bad tonight. I haven't picked up a new girl since Loretta left me when I was still a sad, broken little man, trying to make an honest living. That shit I told you at the diner tonight was true, but you didn't care. Nobody ever gives a fucking shit about some asshole hauling loads across the country. Whatever, baby, it's not your fault. You're a stuck up, rich little cunt, and I'm gonna give you something to care about."

I tried to jerk up, tried to scream, but I couldn't seem to move anything except my eyes. What happened to me? I hadn't been alone with him in the diner at all, except when I used the bathroom twice.

Twice. Goddamn it.

The first time, I'd come back, and our food was waiting for us. That had to be when he did it, slipped something into my food or drink, springing the trap he'd set from the very beginning.

The one I'd been too stupid and drunk to see.

"You…you lied."

His high, shrill laughter split the night, and everything in my head started spinning. "What? Were you expecting hugs and kisses and free meals from strange men in the woods? I don't know what kind of stupid bitch you are, but you're *mine* now. Sleep tight, little girl. And by the way, the name's Ricky. It fits me now. You ever heard of a pimp named Richard?"

Ricky. The last coherent thought before the blackness swallowed me up was knowing that I'd probably hate that name forever.

* * * *

Oh, how right I'd been. I knew it the next day, when he splashed ice cold water in my face, and I realized I was completely naked.

He had my driver's license in his hand, twirling it around like a wild card in some poker game he'd just won.

"Jeeesus H. Christ, woman! I think you've just made me the happiest man in the world."

I glared at him, saying nothing. If it wasn't for the fear constantly churning in my stomach, I would've spit in his face. I hated his arrogance, his treachery, and my own stupidity, but I hated his cruel joy more than anything else.

"Let me go, Richard. It's not too late to pull back. You can drop me off with the cops, my family, I don't care. I just want to go home. I won't even press charges."

Yeah, right. He saw right through my hollow promises. Next thing I knew, his palm slapped me across the face, so sharp and sudden my whole head spun.

"It's Ricky, bitch. Get used to it. I'll let you off light because you're something else." He paused and sniffed, staring excitedly at my license again. "You know, I really thought I'd hit the jackpot when I got myself a pretty mountain girl, all doped up and goddamned beautiful. But shit, you should've told me you were a Wilder girl sooner. Your pussy might make me retire early!"

Bastard. I swallowed the hard, hateful lump in my throat and forced myself to look at him, ignoring the fiery sting on my cheek.

"You're going to ransom me, then? Let me talk to Daddy. I can get you the money faster than if you do it alone, I swear, he'll –"

Ricky cut me off with his nasty, shrill laughter again. "Oh, please. You really think I'd give you up for a few bags of cash, only to have a SWAT team storm in here and tear this place apart? I've got better plans for you, little princess. You're gonna make some rich, twisted motherfucker *very* fucking happy. I just gotta spread the news through the grapevine and find myself a buyer."

My heart started pounding. I stood up, only to feel him

throw me back down against the shitty bed, the flimsy mattress snapping against my spine.

"Don't do this, asshole! You have no idea who you're dealing with. You *will* pay, one way or another. My family won't let me go. My friends know where I disappeared. We can't be that far from town, somebody'll come looking and then you'll regret the night you saw me in that forest."

He rolled his eyes. "Yeah, yeah, you're not the first bitch to say that, trust me. You're just the richest little cunt I've ever had in here."

The richest? For the first time I lifted my head up and took a good look around.

The door to the small room was cracked. Ricky sensed my hesitation, and he marched over, flinging it open. Across the hall, there was another room, also with its door wide open.

A dead-eyed, gray-faced woman sat on a bed, wearing nothing but cheap heels and torn stockings. She took a long look at me, pushing her long greasy hair behind one ear, and then turned back to her arm as if seeing a beautiful young woman with hot tears running down her face was completely normal here.

That passive, defeated look told me everything about the hellhole I'd fallen into. So did the rubber band around her arm. And so did the syringe she stabbed into her vein a second later, pushing it deep, until the junk hit her system and she let out a loud, heavenly moan.

"You starting to understand? A girl like you must have a fancy education. You're not stupid. Take a good, long look, bitch. That's your future. Only I ain't letting you have none of that junk. Gotta keep you happy and healthy for top dollar."

I lost it. I couldn't bear to take another look at the miserable woman, holed up just like me, and I couldn't stand for the pimp to see me cry either. I buried my face in my hands, letting the hot tears come, until he pinched my shoulder so hard I looked up.

"Stop crying, beautiful. I won't let you get hooked on shit. You're too valuable to me. Shit, I'm gonna make every boy who comes in here use rubbers too. I'm not letting anybody fuck you up with damage, drugs, or disease while you're working off your rent. You'll be treated like a queen compared to these other junkie whores."

I shook my head again. His cruel words blurred together, becoming incomprehensible. What the *fuck* was he getting at?

"What is this place?" My heart dropped another inch as I said it.

Deep down, I already knew.

Ricky stepped forward, wearing the same serpent smile I'd come to know too well, the one that strangled me, poisoned me, killed the woman named Megan.

"You kidding? Haven't you ever seen our billboards? Or are you one of those bitches who pays more attention to texting on her phone than the damned road when she's going down the highway?"

He reached into his pocket and pulled out a crumpled piece of paper. He slammed it against the wall, smoothing it out before he pressed it into my shaking hands.

It took everything not to retch when I saw the outrageous, neon letters and overdone whore with her lips pursed on the cover.

LONG HAUL? COME UNWIND AT THE BIGGEST, BADDEST, HOTTEST TRUCKER SPA IN EAST TENNESSEE!

A trucker spa. A dirty, ditzy fucking whorehouse. And now that I was on the inside, it was even more miserable and soul crushing than I'd ever imagined.

"Jesus…help me." It was the last thing I whispered before I took off running, flying into the cramped little bathroom attached to the beat up room.

Ricky held me like he actually cared while I spat out my guts. He reached over me when I was finished, flushing the bile down, a loud, harsh sound like the end of my life.

"There, there, baby girl. Be good for me. Get it all out of your system. Your first clients are coming this afternoon. I need those pretty lips clean and healthy for their dicks. I'll bet you suck a mean cock."

I wanted to vomit again, but there was nothing left in my system. "Don't do this. *Please.* I'm a virgin."

That got his attention. Ricky's eyes flickered, and the nasty smile he wore disappeared. He crouched next to me on one knee, grabbed my head, and pulled me close, until I was only inches from his evil face.

"You gotta be shitting me. A rich party cunt like you?"

I nodded, feeling my whole body shake. I didn't know if I was making another huge mistake, or telling him the

343

only thing that might save me, but I was way past caring.

I had to get out of this. I didn't belong here. Megan Willow Wilder wasn't ever supposed to be reduced to sucking off strangers in a creepy fucking trucker's spa.

If only I could delay him, trigger some mercy deep inside him…

But when I opened my eyes again and looked at him, his eyes were small and black. Cold, cruel, lifeless as coal.

"If I find out you're lying to me, bitch, I'll fuck you myself. I swear it." He reached for my chin, digging his fingers in so hard I could feel him on bone. "Last chance. You telling me the truth, or are you just fucking around?"

"It's true," I muttered, my voice cracking as more hot tears came.

"Fuck. I never believed in miracles before, but I'm starting to think somebody up there loves me." His sick smile reappeared, and he looked right through the ceiling, before turning back to me with the same vacant expression as before.

"Okay, Meg, here's what we're gonna do – you'll put those lips to work like a good little girl and earn me some money to keep you fed, clothed, and sheltered. In the meantime, I'll do my damnedest to land you a permanent home. It's out of my control the day I've got a buyer, but as long as you're here, I promise it'll be sane, sweet, and easy."

Sane, sweet, and easy. It wouldn't be the first time he used that phrase.

I'd hear it over and over again, almost every fucking day, whenever I was washing my mouth out with baking soda and water, trying to forget the foul taste of latex and cherry flavored lube.

"Take a couple minutes to yourself, baby. I'll bring you some breakfast, leave you alone to get your head straight. You haven't figured out why you're here yet, and that's okay. Give it a few more weeks, a month or two, and you'll understand." His rough palm patted my cheek, and I slumped down, holding myself in a fetal position until I heard the door close behind him.

Alone. Defeated. Confused.

I didn't believe him then. It didn't seem like it was possible for me to ever understand anything again.

* * * *

Six months showed me how wrong I was. They showed me I didn't even know who or what I was. I'd been stripped down, rebuilt, recreated in sorrow and shame and dozens of anonymous cocks.

My ego, my self, my mind disappeared in a haze of sweat and smoke. My pimp gave me food, shelter, and weed. I'd never been much of a pot head before, but I smoked up without hesitation.

I used the stuff to take the edge off, to take me away from this hell for a few blissful hours. I took the only escape he offered.

Ricky kept his word. Greed held the bastard to his promises, the only thing that saved me from the wretched existence of the other girls I shared a brothel with.

He carefully controlled the men who used me, and he even went so far to test me each week, steering the roughest, dirtiest truckers and thugs to his other girls – all of them except the Deadhands he feared. I became the golden girl again, the same thing I'd always been, but this time there was no glamor or pride.

I was still a whore, a prisoner, and completely broken.

Every day I stumbled awake and rubbed my sore eyes, I wondered if I was dreaming this demented fairy tale. Ricky wasn't the only demon here.

The bigger ones showed up just a few weeks in, the first time the bikers came to the whorehouse. I learned not to stick my head out of my room and stare at the men from the Deadhands MC too long. Whenever I did, they started to ask Ricky uncomfortable questions about his 'hot, new piece of ass.'

The first time Big Vic came after me, the brute shoved his gun in Ricky's face, told him he wouldn't hesitate to kill everybody here if he tried to get in the way. The pimp caved, pleading for his life, and begging them not to ruin his pet project – me.

I realized I wasn't the only one here forced into prostitution. Ricky groveled to the bikers. He feared them.

One day, he warned me point-blank, told me that if they ever wanted more, he couldn't protect me anymore. They'd take my virginity and whatever else they wanted, and he'd let them, since the alternative was ending up in a shallow grave.

These were the monsters in my story, my life, an endless

parade of them. Some days, they were all I saw. I wondered about the yin to my yang, all the joy bled from my life.

It wasn't fair. There wasn't any balance.

Where was my prince? Where was my happy ending?

There had to be more to my life than working for this grubby, cruel man who smiled like a crocodile and never paid me a single cent for my slavery. There had to be another way out besides ending up with a sicker, richer, more brutal stranger, right?

I hoped and prayed. The months wore on, long and cold and brutal. The police didn't find me.

Life in the whorehouse became such business as usual that I wondered if I'd ever known anything else, or if my life in the big ranch on the hill had been a dream. Only the faded white summer dress hanging in my closet told me the truth.

Some nights, I held it close, trying not to stain it with more tears, my only reminder that another world was possible. I'd had it once, and had it stolen away.

"Don't forget," I'd whisper to myself. "There's a whole, wide world beyond this place."

Yes, there was. I'd known it once. Mountains, grand family picnics, and beer fueled laughter with friends and soft, playful men. Times with girlfriends and lovers who laughed at the gaudy billboards along the highways, who'd never dream of stepping foot into a trucker's spa with the sticky floors and hallow-eyed women.

I thought about Becky, Crawford, and my parents the most. Too bad they weren't as easy to hold onto as my dress, the last thing I'd worn as a free woman.

Lately, I couldn't even cry about them anymore, and I wondered why they felt so empty. My memories were fading with my mind, perhaps. He'd already taken away my name, depersonalized me the second week, when he started calling me Fresh.

Fresh, as in Fresh Meat. At first, I despised it, but little by little, it wore me down, until I forgot what it even felt like to be called by anything that wasn't fit for a low budget whore.

I accepted my name. It fit this hell, and most anything else I could imagine.

Sooner or later, I had to stop waiting, wondering, hoping. I had to accept my fate.

There were no heroes in this story, and there wouldn't be a happy ending. I was going to be Ricky's until the bitter end.

And if I wanted to stay alive, I had to be dead inside to the man who took me next. Strangers used my lips, my tongue every single day, and giving up more of my body didn't bother me anymore.

But I wouldn't give them any joy, any spark, any life. I had none left to give.

Meg died. Fresh lived.

I swore I'd go to my grave with that name, and if any filthy bastard who touched me ever called me anything else, he'd have to strangle me to make me stop tearing pieces out of his flesh.

The pimp killed Meg without a fight. Fresh wouldn't go down so easy.

She wouldn't wait for her knight or her happy ending. She'd pick up the shattered pieces of herself and wield them like broken glass…

**Look for *Never Love an Outlaw*
at your favorite retailer!**

Made in the USA
Middletown, DE
01 April 2016